ALSO BY EDITH SCHEFFER

The Janie Chronicles

Saving Janie

Janie a Broad

Janie on Board

Janie vs. The Big Apple

* * *

Fallen Gracefully

* * *

Winged

JANIE vs. THE BIG APPLE
The Janie Chronicles, Book 4
ISBN 978-1-954174-07-8

Edited by Louise Zanotto

THE JANIE CHRONICLES

EDITH SCHEFFER

1

THE TERMINAL: TAKE TWO

"Run dammit!" I yelled when Fitz turned to come help me off the floor. "Hold the damn plane!" I yelled again as she turned away and headed for our boarding gate.

Picking up my lightning-bolt shaped rune, that had become a part of my everyday wardrobe, I wondered if its defection from my pocket was the *stone* trying to give me a sign; don't go back to New York!

"I got this!" Fitz yelled back to me as she ran.

I knew this would happen, I thought to myself as I stood and grabbed my carry-on. Limping, I soldiered on.

Historically, airports haven't been a great place for me. In fact, several months ago, I had been dumped at LAX. Not just dumped, I reminded myself; but dumped in public right before our flight to Hawaii, while his mistress stood waiting for my ticket so she could go and bask on the beach in my place with my boyfriend of almost two years. My luggage, sensing it was actually going nowhere, had gone on a trip without me. Actually, my luggage has seen more of the world than I have.

I began to hobble my way forward, somewhat Quasimdo-ish, as I threw my bag over my shoulder and limped onward.

Approaching my terminal, I heard Fitz say, "There she is, she's here!"

The desk attendant, 40-ish, ample in every way, with the biggest over-bleached hair helmet I had ever seen, turned her eyes to me, "That's not an eighty-year-old-woman on life support!"

"Did I say eighty?" Fitz asked with innocently rounded eyes. "I meant *crazy woman* who needs *mental support*." Fitz blamed her Irish accent, "A lot of people find me hard to understand."

I noticed she really Irish'd it up for effect.

The attendant gave Fitz the stern mother look I knew only too well.

As we were directed to first class, the flight attendant said, "Well, now that you two have arrived, I guess the plane can finally take off." The attendant flashed that painted on smile that all of them must be trained to do.

Fitz smiled at her and said, "Can ya teach me that?"

"And what exactly are we talking about?" the attendant asked with big rounded eyes over the forced toothy smile.

"How ya can say catty things while smiling like that," Fitz pointed to her face. "I'd like to learn how to do that instead of just telling people to fuck-off." Fitz made an attempt to give the attendant the same smile. "I feel like I'm not doin' it right." Fitz and the woman fake smiled at each other until the attendant walked away.

"I can't believe we almost missed the flight," I buckled my lap belt. "And an eighty-year-old-woman…on life support?" I questioned her.

"Ya said if we missed the flight, ya'd kill me. So really, ya left me little choice in the matter," Fitz gave me the fake attendant grin she was working on.

"You could have been packed and ready to go like I asked you to be," I threw the thought out there with my own fake smile.

"Ya know Janie, I'm sorry, but when Scotty hits that spot on my neck, I lose all track of the rest of the world. I think I may be a sex addict," she said like she was admitting a feared flaw.

"Yeah, I don't think you should try that as a defense," I shook my head.

"Anyway, we made the flight, with a little creative wording, and we're off to New York. And then…we'll get to see Marne!" she beamed.

This did bring a smile to my face. Fitz was my best friend since kindergarten, that's the truth. But once upon a time, we weren't just Lucy and Ethel. Once upon a time, our twosome was a threesome. Kind of like *The Three Amigos*. Or in our case, *The Three Stooges*.

Marne had also grown up to be a supermodel but lived and worked mostly in Europe. Her long legs, dark caramel skin and perfect smile had made her the toast of the industry more than once. She graced the covers of magazine after magazine and was the spokesmodel for everything sultry; from five star restaurants and luxury cars, to five star hotels, resorts and a Scotch that was twice my age.

I hadn't seen Marne in over five years. Her arrival at my twenty-first birthday had been my gift from Fitz. I don't remember some parts of that visit since between Fitz and Marne, everywhere we went drinks were paid for by people who loved the gorgeous duo.

Fitz had seen Marne a little more recently since they had done a few runway shows and photo shoots together. I'd see pictures of them on social media, hugging, sitting down to a fancy meal or at the opening of a new nightclub, while I made complicated coffee drinks for the early risers at *Spilled the Beans*. Some part of me had always been a little jealous. Not of their lifestyle, just the thought they got to see each other more often than I did. And now that I was a little freer to roam, I was afforded the time to reconnect with my old friend.

As the plane raced down the airstrip, I began my panic breathing. Flying had never been my cup of anything, but I thought I had left those fears behind in Mexico. Turns out, I hadn't.

"Remember what Tovah taught ya…for panic," Fitz squeezed my hand.

Tovah, the sister of Benny, who married Fitz's bat-shit crazy Aunt Marble, was who I was going to see. She owned a huge art gallery in New York and asked if I'd like to display (and possibly sell), some of my paintings.

When I met her on the wedding cruise to Mexico, I was a wreck. I wasn't fond of the ocean (or being up close and personal with any of its inhabitants). I didn't like flying, or boats, or heights…let's just say, feet firmly planted on the Earth's surface, I'm good with. Tovah, though, a sixty-ish widow with a zest for everything wonderful, was under the impression that you had to *LIVE* life, swallow it whole. She told me this was the only way to find my passion. And as I dangled next to her in a harness, high above the ocean, I had to agree with her…once I stopped digging my fingernails into the back of her hand and cursing loudly, that is. I still wasn't sure if I had actually said the stream of curse words out loud, or if they were just screamed in my own mind. Either way, landing, feet back on the ground, I felt lighter…like I had faced one very real fear and kicked its ass. Yet here I was again, wringing my hands and fidgeting.

I looked around the first-class cabin. Passengers in Armani suits and Prada pumps lounged in their own luxury bubble.

"I don't think me howling like Tovah would be considered appropriate, Fitz."

Fitz looked around, “Ya care what these strangers think of yer copin’ mechanisms?”

“I just don’t want to disturb anyone,” I told her.

“So, do it low! Does it not work if ya do it low?”

“I don’t know,” I admitted.

“Yer gonna have to get past worryin’ all the time about what other people think of ya,” Fitz shook her head.

“I told you, I just don’t want to be a bother, that’s all.”

“Okay,” she humored me with a sigh and head shake.

“I’m being serious,” I lifted my brows to her.

“Fine,” she said condescendingly.

“Why are you being so condescending?” I flared.

“I’m not,” she gave the palms-up and had that new damned flight attendant’s smile plastered across her face again.

“Oh my God, you are so infuriating sometimes,” I clenched my teeth.

“And yet,” Fitz pointed to the window Vanna White style.

Looking out, we were not only in the air; we had leveled off and were just cruising along.

I smiled at her, “Thank you…asshole.”

“Yer welcome…asshole,” she grinned.

2

BUMP

"What the hell!" I grabbed at the armrests.

"Calm yerself, luv," Fitz told me. "It's just turbulence. It's like we're just hittin' an air pocket, no big deal."

"How does air have pockets?" I asked in a slightly panicked tone.

"What am I, Mr. Science? I don't know it's just what I've been told."

"Great! That's helpful!" my sarcasm reared its ugly head.

"No need to get lippy," Fitz said. "Maybe we should have some champagne?"

"Why? Will that help?" I looked at her.

"I think what we should be askin' is, could it hurt?" Fitz gave me a palms-up.

Three glasses, or a bottle of champagne later, I wasn't nearly as aware or concerned by the periodic bumps. Fitz and I turned our attention to more important things.

"So, Cecil's gonna come out to see ya in New York?" Fitz grinned at me.

"He is," my cheeks immediately pulled up into a fat smile. "I really miss him," I said feeling the effects of the champagne.

Cecil and I had a rocky road getting to where we are now. My first impression of him was a spoiled rotten man-whoring playboy with no ambition who had been fortunate enough to have been born into a very rich family. It wasn't exactly love at first sight. But after Cecil decided to show me the real him, I was reluctantly won over.

He had actually come to my rescue like a knight in shining armor when my ex (the airport dumper, John), knocked me out while trying to win me back. Then I was hired by Cecil's father, Martin Callaghan, to do two paintings for him…in Ireland…at the family's manor. A lot of misunderstandings and screw-ups happened there, too, as his ex tried to sabotage whatever was budding between us. I'm happy to say, though, neither of our exes succeeded in pushing us apart. But oddly enough, if I thought about it, both of them had brought us closer together. We knew what we didn't want.

"Yer in love," Fitz's eyes sparkled.

I wasn't sure if this was from emotion, or champagne, but she and her teary eyes were right. "I am," I squeezed her hand.

"Ya must miss the hell out of each other. I can't even imagine being away from Scotty as long as you two have been parted," she shook her head.

Fitz was engaged to Cecil's brother, Scotty, and I had to agree, I didn't even want to see what she would be like if he were gone for weeks at a time, or lived *across the pond.* They had a period of unwanted abstinence in Ireland and it made Fitz go a little, well the word bat-shit crazy comes to mind. The long distance thing; me in Hermosa Beach, California and him in Ireland, was not the relationship I had dreamed of as a young girl…or an older one, for that matter. But he was worth the loneliness that distance can bring as well as the excitement of finally getting to see someone you really love.

A moment passed before Fitz piped up, "I can't believe we won't be home for Halloween. It's such a big deal at the Pub!"

I knew the truth, Halloween was Fitz's *thing*.

"And I know the Ladies of the Moon had somethin' planned for our first Halloween as members," Fitz pouted.

I tried not to show relief that we wouldn't be in attendance for whatever the Ladies of the Moon had planned. Truth is they're a great group of women. At one point, I referred to them as a coven for lack of a more accurate term. But in reality, they were just a group of women from different social, ethnic and religious backgrounds who came together to celebrate something they all had in common; the divine feminine. These women loved each other, were a support system. The fact that my introduction to them left me standing in the plastic kiddy-pool of rebirth, covered in oil, wasn't one of my finer memories. But being honest, that moment, no matter how odd it seemed at the time, had helped put me on a path to self-enlightenment and personal growth. I wish I could say that my next two run-ins were less mind-bending. But my last, I was reluctantly inducted into the group as a *Daughter of the Moon.* And in keeping with a tradition of humiliation I had adopted at all of these rituals, now I was to be named. For the foreseeable future I was to be known as Clematis. I was named so by Fitz's bat-shit-crazy aunt, Marble, who at that moment became my spirit mother.

"Yeah, I know," I said to Fitz, feigning disappointment. "But Tovah said she may have something going on for the *Holiday*, as she called it," I shrugged. I wondered if maybe she would have a party at the gallery.

Tovah was an eccentric to say the least. From the way she dressed, talked and swallowed life whole, I couldn't help but love her. But, I did have to wonder if she was going to try and get me to skydive or swim with sharks.

"Are we bein' picked up at the airport?" Fitz asked.

"Tovah said she would have a car waiting to take us to the hotel," I answered.

"Is she meetin' us at the airport?" Fitz questioned.

"Actually, she said she'd meet us at the gallery tomorrow for lunch."

"She must be a very busy woman," Fitz shook her head.

I grinned, "Well, apparently, tonight is *date night* from what she told me."

"Really?" Fitz grinned.

"Yeah. She said she has at least one a week," I smiled.

Tovah was kind of my hero, not that Fitz had lost her ranking in the least. She just had to share it now. I guessed Tovah around sixty, a slight woman with a salt and pepper faux hawk, and a one-sided grin that left me wondering if she was amused by me or just humoring me. A great art lover, she had purchased the gallery in the eighties and built it up piece by piece. Since the doors first opened, the Schumer Gallery had had the pleasure of displaying the works of some of the greatest artists the world had ever known (both alive and posthumous).

Ironically, the first time I was in New York, I would have begged, borrowed and stolen to have seen the Schumer Gallery. Instead, I was *begged* by Fitz to have photos taken by a woman/man who had *borrowed* the photo equipment from a previous employer and had my time *stolen* as I sat in a jail cell after being arrested for being part of a black market fetish ring. I was also mugged for a tiny little rubber penis by a tiny little man. If I had to judge New York by that visit alone, I would never have come back to The Big Apple.

The voice overhead asked us to fasten our safety belts and prepare for landing. This wasn't my favorite part of flying, either.

In fact, the best part of flying was the booze, and I didn't have to leave the ground to get booze.

Down the ramp we went into the craziness of the La Guardia Airport. If LAX was a zoo, this place was a jungle. People rushed everywhere and it seemed there was no *flow* to the foot traffic.

Finding our luggage carousel we waited for our bags. I couldn't help but wonder if mine had ended up somewhere else. Not because I was being negative, but because it had happened before. I spied our bags tumbling down the conveyer belt onto the other conveyer belt that sent them to the carousel where they would ride in circles until picked up.

"There they are," I pointed. Fitz and I walked up to where they would be an easy grab. But before they made it to us, a strange dark haired woman with dark glasses and a scarf over her head grabbed one of Fitz's bags and started to walk away.

"That woman has your bag!" I told Fitz.

Off like a shot, Fitz flew through the crowd of people yelling, "Stop! Ya have my bag!"

I wanted to go after her and be of some assistance but I still had to grab my bag and Fitz's other two.

I could see Fitz, her red head bobbing in-and-out of people. The small woman tried to pick up the pace, but Fitz's bags were always packed to the max and weighed almost as much as the slight woman. The woman was struggling as Fitz continued to yell, closing the distance between them. Finally a security guard decided to intervene.

Stopping the woman, Fitz was three seconds and ten people behind.

"What? Why are you stopping me?" the woman asked. "I'm an old woman!"

"That's my bag," I heard Fitz say as I and a big cart of luggage finally arrived.

"No, this is my bag!" the woman insisted.

With her huge dark sunglasses, Fitz assumed the poor woman had sight issues. "Check the tag…that's my bag, sir," she told the guard.

The security officer took the bag and looked, but said, "There's no tag."

"See, it's my bag," the woman said. "I'll be off now," she turned to walk away.

At this point, Fitz's eyes slit. "Not so fast."

The three of us were escorted out of the way so that the security guard could try and figure out who owned the bag he was lugging.

"So what's in the bag?" he asked them both.

The small older woman spat, "This is ridiculous! I can't believe I'm being treated this way," she said dramatically.

"Ma'am, I understand your frustration, but you both say the bag is yours and only one of you is correct," the security guard said. "So please what's in the bag."

"My things," yelled the woman and began to crumple up her face like she was trying to fight back tears.

The guard looked torn, obviously not wanting to make a woman cry.

"Ma'am," he said to Fitz, who had honed in on the woman's game, "can you tell me what's in the bag?"

"My undergarments are in this bag," she told him.

"That's a generic answer if ever I heard one!" the woman lifted her chin indignantly.

"Um," the guard looked uncomfortable to even have to ask the next question. "Could you be a little more…specific…?"

One of Fitz's cheeks rose, "There are six bra and panty sets, red, green, white, black, nude strapless and black strapless. Three camisole night dresses, lace; red, green and burgundy. Four pairs of pantyhose in assorted colors still in packaging, made for someone 5'8" and a half, she stared down at the 4 foot 11 inch woman. Fitz's face took on her signature evil fairy grin, "a pair of SPANX, although I don't know what for." She motioned to her perfect figure, "Also made for a woman MY size, must I continue?"

"Sir," began the woman with a look of bewilderment, "I don't know how she knows what's in my bag…this must be…some kind of scam," she asserted.

Was this woman with a set of deflated fun-bags hovering just above her navel, really going to try and pretend that she and Fitz wore the same size bra, I wondered.

I saw the look on Fitz's face; her eyes slit and her tongue found its way into her cheek. I knew this look and cautiously took a step back.

"Fine," said Fitz, "we'll do it yer way, then," she told the woman. "Sir," she addressed the officer, "in that bag you will find a silver hard cased rectangular box. I give ya my permission to open it and take a look. If she can tell ya what's in that box, I'll give her my damn bag," she stared daggers into the woman.

The officer looked perplexed as he unzipped the bag.

The little old woman with the dark glasses stepped closer to see if she could catch a glimpse when he opened the mystery case.

"Ma'am, I'm going to need you to stand back," he told the old woman. Locating the box, he made sure the woman couldn't see and he stole a peek.

I was a little perplexed as well. It looked like it could have been used for makeup, maybe an expensive makeup brush holder. But this wasn't Fitz's makeup bag and she was anal about keeping everything in its place.

I saw the security officer's eyes round as he quickly shut the box.

"Fitz's grin was sardonic as she asked the woman, "What's in the box?"

I was shocked she didn't finish that question with *Bitch*.

The guard was having a hard time making eye contact with Fitz…any of us, really.

What the hell was in that box, I wondered as the woman stammered.

"Well, ugh, this is ridiculous, I shouldn't have to answer this!" the woman said indignantly. "Obviously…," she was showing signs of panic, "it's my…eyeglass case."

"No…no, it's not!" the officer shook his head. "Thank you, ma'am," he said to Fitz and handed her back the box which immediately began to buzz in her hand.

My eyes rounded, I knew of no makeup brushes that made that sound.

The old woman made a face like she was appalled, "You carry one of those…when you travel?"

"Hence the hard cover," Fitz's eyes bored into the woman.

The officer still looked away from Fitz's eyes as he apologized and escorted the woman to the security office.

As we watched them go, I struggled to find something to say, "So I guess it's good you had one of…those...with you, huh?" was what I came up with. "That poor officer looked like he was in shock."

"Please, they do cavity searches on people with balloons of heroin shoved up their bums. Unless today was his *first* as an airport security guard, I doubt I made the *top-ten-list* of weird things he's seen. "

"It's a nice case," I offered nodding.

"Ya like it? I would have chosen the gold case, but Scotty picked it out…a gift for when we're apart," she beamed as she tucked it back inside her bag.

I had run out of things to say that would make this less awkward. The only phrase going through my head was; *Say hello, to my little friend!* "We should find our car," is the only thing I said out loud.

Outside, we saw a very irritated looking man leaning against a limo holding up a red sign that read, **O'Connelly** in big black letters.

"Hi, I'm O'Connelly. I mean Janie," I smiled.

"Nice of you two to show up," he gave us a head nod. "I've been standin' out here for half an hour," his New York accent well pronounced. "What, did ya stop off at the bar for a drink?"

My jaw dropped slightly, "Actually, someone tried to steal one of our bags. We had to let a security officer go through the luggage to prove it was ours…hers," I added quickly, not wanting to be connected to what was in the box even in thought.

"Likely story," the driver huffed under his breath like he heard this excuse every day.

"Would you like to see what I have in my bag?" Fitz asked with a smile.

I bit my bottom lip and rounded my eyes.

"Why would I want to see what's in your bag, lady?" he gave her the palms-up.

"It just reminds me of ya, that's all," she winked. "And…that I need to purchase new batteries."

The drivers face dropped as he connected the dots, "Can we just go, now?"

"My sentiments exactly," Fitz smiled as the man grumbled about her excessive luggage.

In the limo, I turned to Fitz, "Jeez, we've only been in New York for half of an hour and already we've pissed off a driver and almost had your luggage stolen. Do you think New York just doesn't want us here?"

"Yer readin' too much into it. We're one of thousands who go through this crap on a daily basis. Ya actually think we were that old lady's first victims? And this guy," she pointed to back of the driver's head, "he's just an asshole. We have those in So Cal, too."

I nodded slowly. It wasn't like others hadn't told horror stories of their visit to The Big Apple. But as of right now, we were two for two.

As we headed down into the city, I remembered the rush, hustle and bustle I had experienced last time. Bright lights drew the eye in every direction. Our driver seemed less than thrilled with the traffic as well, as he yelled at pedestrians and vehicles, alike. I noticed after several miles that he was very fond of his middle finger and shared it as often as possible.

Pulling up in front of the Ritz-Carlton, our driver seemed in a hurry to unload the bags and get as far away from us as possible. A valet called for a luggage cart and helped the driver. When all of our bags were out of the limo, the driver stood in front of us and stared.

I wasn't sure what he was waiting for until he rubbed his thumb against his fingertips; the universal money sign.

"Ah," I said reaching into my purse. Once again the driver rolled his eyes at me. Pulling out a twenty and handing it to him, he made the "*Pfff*" sound.

"I'm sorry, what's wrong?" I asked him.

"You're riding in a limo…to the Ritz-Carlton," he raised his eyebrows at me. "I waited in the airport for half of an hour for you!"

As I started to dig for more money, so embarrassed I was turning a bright red, Fitz grabbed the twenty out of the driver's hand, "Yer right, we'll probably need this to tip the bellboy," she gave him her best *fuck you* smile.

"Ah, forget yous broads," he said, spitting a loogie right next to my foot.

Fitz made a hocking sound, "No!" I told her as the driver got back into the limo.

"That guy's got a lot of nerve!" Fitz said.

"I feel stupid, I really don't know what size tip is acceptable," I told her.

"Fer that asshole, none is fine."

"But I feel bad. I mean this is how he makes his living," I explained.

"Ya spend too much time feeling bad and makin' excuses fer people who treat ya like shit!" Fitz had lost all humor by now. "Would ya tip a waitress who was not only rude about the job she was being paid to do, but insulted ya on top of it?"

I gave her the *maybe* face with a shoulder shrug.

"See, right there, that's the problem. Tipping is done in the service industry, partly because yer bein' provided with a service, true. But it also depends on whether the person is being cordial about it, at the very fuckin' least. Their job guarantees a wage… their attitude decides the tip!" Fitz educated me. "I've bartended fer years, and this is a well known fact among all service providers. So if he wants to be an asshole, he already knows what he has comin'!"

3

CHECKING IN

At the check-in desk we were greeted by a happy looking woman wearing a dark blazer and a name tag that read *Rita*, "Welcome to the Ritz-Carlton. How may I assist you?" she smiled.

"See, that's the kind of worker ya tip," Fitz said under her breath.

"Hi, I'm Janie O'Connelly and we're checking in," I smiled back.

"I have you down as a single? You'll have a guest staying with you?" she asked.

I hadn't made the reservations but I had told Tovah that Fitz would be joining me. Tovah said that she would take care of the arrangements. "Um, yes," I told her. "I'll pay the extra cost," I explained.

"Okay, and your name?" she asked Fitz.

When Fitz told the woman her name, she smiled, "Oh you have the adjoining room…already paid for by Ms. Schumer."

Really it wasn't necessary for Tovah to pay for my room, much less Fitzy's but after finding out what was in the silver box in her luggage, I had to admit, I was grateful we would have our own personal space.

We were each handed a business card by Rita, "Ms. Schumer wanted you ladies to have a town car at your disposal. You just call that number, day or night and someone will come pick you up," she smiled. I hoped the driver at our *beck and call* wasn't the limo driver from earlier.

Up in the elevator we went to the eighteenth floor. Let into our rooms, our luggage followed; my one bag plus a carry-on and Fitz's three bags and a carry-on were unloaded.

Each suite had a bedroom, sitting room, restroom and small kitchenette. It was definitely more than we needed for our short stay. But it was beautiful. Mine was done in gold and cream with a dusty rose accent wall and antique cherrywood furniture.

Fitz's room was decorated in more bold colors; burgundy and gold with a more deco feel.

If our rooms were any reflection of the way Tovah saw us, I'd have to say she was dead on. Mine: muted, subtle but classic. Fitz's: bold with some sharp edges but gorgeous.

After I gave the bellhop the twenty Fitz took back from the driver, I flung myself down on the bed. It had already been an exhausting day for me. Some part of me just wanted the king sized bed to envelope me, hold me hostage there. But I knew we had plans tonight, so getting comfortable would have to wait.

There was a knock on my door and of course I assumed it was Fitz. But when I opened the door, a good looking young man stood holding a champagne bucket and two glasses.

"Welcome to the Ritz-Carlton Miss O'Connelly," he smiled and walked into my room.

Setting the bucket down, I tried again to figure out how much to tip the young man. I almost never carried cash, and what I did have were all twenty dollar bills, so I handed him one.

He smiled at me, wished me a nice evening and shut the door

behind him, leaving me to wonder again; did I tip correctly or was he just too well trained in the service industry to make a face of disapproval?

Looking down at the champagne bucket, I noticed that this wasn't champagne.

I smiled as I pulled up the bottle; fifty year old Callaghan Whiskey. There was a card from Cecil.

"My dearest Janie…until I am there beside ya…"

Love Cecil

I let out a sweet sigh and went to the kitchenette to find ice. Another knock, drew me from my whiskey. This time it was Fitz.

"Can I get you a drink?" I showed her the bottle.

"Oh yes…yes you can!" she beamed. "I love their whiskey. It's just what the doctor ordered."

I laughed, "Are you a doctor now?"

"Yer the one pourin'," she winked.

I poured two healthy shots over some rocks and took a seat next to Fitz on the couch.

"Ah," I kicked my shoes off.

"Don't ya be gettin' too comfortable. We're meeting Marne downstairs at nine."

I guess I should have poured my whiskey into a triple latte, I thought.

"So when will Cecil be here?" Fitz asked, lifting her brows repeatedly.

I laughed, "Not for a few more days. He also has a meeting with a distributor when he does get here, so I guess I'm on my own for a bit."

"On yer own, huh? Very nice, what am I, chopped Haggis?" she grinned.

"You know what I mean," I patted her hand.

"I do!" she exclaimed, "now that you've found yerself a *shagger*, I'm tossed to the side. Never ya mind, though, I brought somethin' to keep me warm on these cold and lonely New York nights," she laughed.

"And to think, without it, we may have lost your bag," I giggled. "The look on that poor man's face," I shook my head. "Another *Classic Fitz* for the record!"

"We should probably start gettin' ourselves ready for tonight," Fitz nodded.

Perplexed, I looked down at my attire, "What's wrong with what I've got on?" I asked.

"Seriously?" Fitz made a face like she didn't believe I was questioning why I shouldn't be wearing my 501's and a baby T.

"Hey, I can accessorize and make this look good," I informed her.

"Yer in the Ritz-Carlton…" she stared at me. "Now granted, tonight I don't have to pry ya out of a band shirt…I never thought I'd get ya out of that *Panic Attack* shirt, but yer still a little underdressed for cocktails in a five star hotel."

I stared at her.

"What?" she did the palms-up at me, "I'm just sayin'."

"I just thought once I was a grown up, I'd get to make some of the rules. And on that note, I assumed that since I've chosen a muted fashion existence…"

Fitz's eyes rolled around in her head.

Ignoring her, I finished my thought. "…people would have to accept me the way I am."

Fitz thought this over while I finished my drink. Finally she said, "No," and shook her head. "It's never okay to be a train-wreck in a five star hotel. And since yer best friend is a model and a fashionista…it just reflects poorly on me," she said with a straight face.

"Asshole," I said and headed for my suitcase.

"That's my girl," Fitz nodded. "And if yer a good girl, later I'll buy ya ice cream…like a big girl."

"Shut up and help me pick something out," I huffed.

"What the hell?" Fitz said after going through my bag. "Did ya pack anything besides 501's and T-shirts?" she looked appalled.

"Yes…the black dress," I pointed at the dress hanging in the closet, "for the showing."

"And what were ya plannin' on wearin' for the rest of the trip; fer lunch with Tovah…fer dinners?"

I bit my lip, "I went for comfort," I said under my breath.

"Tomorrow before our lunch date, we shop!" Fitz informed me. "Fer right now you'll have to wear something of mine," she stormed out of the room.

I stared after her, mimicking her behind her back.

"What did ya say?" she opened the door.

"Nothing," my eyes rounded and I shook my head.

Fitz returned moments later with a halter top, "You can wear this with those black slacks ya take with ya everywhere and the heels ya brought to wear to the showin'," she laid it on the bed.

"I can't believe I have to point this out after all of these years, but you know we're not the same size, right?" I asked.

"You've worn one of my dresses before," she looked at me like I had forgotten.

"I know," I nodded to her, "and I looked like a mid priced call girl," I informed her.

"Mid priced?" she questioned.

"Yeah, it's like when you really don't look high class but still a little bit better than a street walker," I informed her.

"Ya really do think about this crap, don't ya?" she shook her head.

"And F.Y.I., I almost died in that dress!"

"Oh yer so dramatic, it was a little tight," she shook her head.

"No, trying to get out of the damn thing…I got stuck with it around my neck. I had to dance around and pull at it like a hot dog trying to release itself from its casing!"

Fitz stared at me for a moment then began to laugh her ass off, "Oh dear God, I can picture it in my mind. Oh it's hilarious!" she added, grabbing her stomach as I stood there, less than amused.

"It wasn't funny," I assured her.

"Really? Because in my head, it's fuckin' hysterical!" she mimicked what she pictured in her head.

"Ass-hole!" I said and went to try on the halter top.

I noticed that I'd need a strapless bra. If I told Fitz I hadn't brought one, maybe she would let me wear my T-shirt, I thought. But some part of me knew better. She would just tell me to go braless. I grabbed the strapless torture device and hooked the girls in. The halter was a red paisley design made out of some kind of silky but stretchy fabric that was tight in the boobs then flowed down. It kind of looked like a really short, halter hippie dress. It wasn't horrible looking but I kept having to pull the fabric back up over my boobs to keep them covered. I knew this would drive me crazy all night and said as much to Fitz.

"I got ya," she said and disappeared. Coming back into the restroom where I stood making the *not happy* face, she pulled out a roll of what looked like tape.

"You're gonna tape my girls," I asked horrified at the thought.

"No," she looked at me like I was stupid, "this is fabric tape. I'm gonna tape the fabric to yer skin, so it won't move."

I shook my head.

"What, why are ya shakin' yer head at me?" she asked.

"I was just thinking…the crap we put ourselves through!"

I didn't look too bad and wasn't as uncomfortable as I thought I'd be. Plus, the halter top wasn't going to try and kill me the way the dress had.

Fitz disappeared into her room for five minutes. Walking back into my room, she was dressed to the nines. She had on a form fitting grey silk dress that came to her mid thigh exposing a lot of leg. It almost looked like it could be mistaken for lingerie, it was so delicate. Her flowing red locks cascaded in big rings down to her mid back. Extra black lashes made her green eyes really pop.

"Wow, you look fantastic," I beamed.

"Yer turn," she said producing one of her makeup bags from behind her back.

"Oh shit," I said under my breath.

4

I (DO NOT) ENJOY BEING A GIRL

"Stay still," Fitz commanded for the tenth time. "I'm gonna poke yer damn eye out!" she threatened.

"Look, I got over enjoying this dress-up shit, when I was what…twelve? I hate this shit!" I whined.

"Look Janie, yer already beautiful, just let me accentuate it. That's what I do, I make the hot, hotter…the sexy, sexier…"

"The uncomfortable…uncomfortable-er," I said.

"Fine, we're done, although, I would have liked to get some lashes on ya," she raised her brows at me.

"Absolutely not," I shook my head, knowing it didn't really matter what I said.

Heading down in the elevator, Fitz yelled at me, "Don't pick at them?"

"I'm not," I bit back. "It's the damn glue. It feels like my top and bottom lashes keep getting stuck to each other!"

"Well, they're not. Ya just have to get used to the way they feel," she informed me.

"I wouldn't have to if you would have taken *NO* for an answer."

Fitz laughed, "Like ya thought that was gonna happen? Please *sticky-tits!* Don't pretend ya don't know me better than that."

I just shook my head, "Asshole! I feel like I have two big spiders mating on my eyelids."

In the lounge, we found a table near the fireplace. Four person tables donning lit candles made the room seem swanky in a weird way; like it was a meeting place for well-to-do swingers. I had never really been a *lounge woman.* I was used to the *come-as-you-are* pubs and bars. As nice as this place was, it seemed like kind of a quiet place for three best friends to reunite. The three of us together had a tendency to be a little loud, and a lot obnoxious. We would simultaneously make fun of each other with private jokes and then build each other back up. It was our own brand of therapy.

Fitz and I ordered a drink and waited on pins and needles.

Men in business suits were busy taking long looks at Fitz. One guy winked while another raised his glass to her, like he was in an 80's beer commercial.

Fitz smiled, "That guy keeps winkin'."

Fitz turned to see me winking as the fake lashes stuck together. "Stop doin' that! Yer givin' out the wrong signals."

A waiter carrying a tray with two Cosmopolitans said, "These are from the two gentlemen at the bar," he nodded toward them.

Fitz gave a nod of her head and raised her glass. I waved awkwardly and turned toward the wall so I could wink *flirt-less-ly.*

"Should we send the drinks back?" I asked.

Fitz made a face and then sipped her Cosmo, "Janie, they bought us a round...not rings," she gave me a curt shake of her head.

"I just don't think we should give them the wrong impression," I told her.

"That we like booze?" she questioned.

"You know what I mean, we're both taken!" my eyes rounded.

Fitz let out a sigh, "Janie," she put up her hand to proudly display her three carat rock of an engagement ring, "If they can't see this bad-boy from there, they're blind. Nothing about me says *available.*"

I looked at her lingerie dress and cocked my head.

"What?" she looked down at her attire. "Are ya saying I look cheap?"

"Oh, God no," I shook my head. "I would NEVER say you look cheap. Easy…maybe, but never cheap," I grinned.

"And now we're back to you…Asshole! Plus…I've had less people in my garden," she joked. "If numbers count…yer a floozy in 501's," she giggled.

"And now back to you…," I nodded to her, "asshole. And please, don't resurrect the garden metaphor again! I'm just now able to hear about my mother's actual garden without thinking of its double meaning."

Fitz laughed, "I bet." Fitz's attention was drawn to something behind me.

As I turned around, there was Marne. Walking toward us, a huge smile stretched across her face. She was as beautiful as ever. Even her perfect dark caramel skin and big beautiful chocolate colored eyes, couldn't boast more beauty than that smile she was wearing. Fitz and I didn't let her cross the room alone as we made a *B-line* her way and grabbed her in a group hug.

"Oh my God!" she said excitedly in the British accent I had missed hearing. "I can't believe it's been so long!" we held onto each other and squeezed.

"Seriously, you look amazing!" I told her as I stepped back to take her all in.

As we stood in the middle of the lounge, hugging, I noticed, a bunch of men's heads were turned in our direction, grinning.

When we took our seats, the bartender rushed over with more drinks. "Ladies," he nodded to us, "these are from those three men at that table," he nodded in their direction. The men smiled and raised their drinks to us. Marne and Fitz lifted their drinks in thanks. I nodded to them awkwardly, like I was a chicken with a tick. At one time, I admit, I had been used to being the *add-on* girl. And I knew I was the *add-on* girl...the one who was gifted a free drink while the guy desperately tried to hit on her best friend. I couldn't help but wonder what ploy or line would be used if the men decided to take a shot at the two models, despite Fitz's giant rock.

"I can't believe ya cut yer hair," Fitz said to Marne.

At one time, Marne had long hair that had to be relaxed and straightened. So much product and chemical had to be used to get what I had naturally; flat, straight, boring hair. When we were young, Marne used to complain about her tight curls, but I had always been jealous of them. Hence the bad, bad perm in the tenth grade. But now her hair was just past her jaw line, wild as nature had made it and she looked amazing.

We sat, drank, talked and laughed for about an hour, when I noticed that Marne had checked her watch again.

"Do ya have somewhere ya have to be?" Fitz had noticed, too.

Marne let out a held breath, "Actually...someone's meeting us here."

"Oh, yeah," I grinned. "Someone special, I take it?"

"Someone SERIOUS?" Fitz's eyebrows lifted.

Marne nodded, "Yes. Very serious," she added.

"Oh my God," I covered my mouth, "are we talking... marriage serious?"

Marne beamed and nodded. Her huge smile was all the proof I needed, I knew, Marne was in love.

"Ahhh," Fitz and I yelled and grabbed her in another group hug.

"Okay, so give, what's he like?" Fitz asked.

Marne looked like she was having trouble finding the right

words to describe her fiancé. "Well, my love is bright and smart, kind and loving..." her eyes sparkled.

Fitz nodded excitedly.

I had the feeling she was deliberately trying to leave something out. Was he already married, was he a cousin, was he just barely legal or seventy years old? What was she hiding from us, I wondered?

"My love...makes me feel...alive and invincible, safe and... unbelievably happy."

She lit up when talking about *her love*. But, I noticed, no name was used. Then it hit me...no gender was used, either. No *he* makes me feel this way or that way.

All of the sudden I saw her look toward the door and swallow hard. Even though she went back to her conversation with Fitz, she was watching a woman at the bar ordering a drink. The woman was tall, curvy; her hair was long, deep brown, pulled up into a ponytail.

Marne's eyes zeroed in on mine as I also watched the woman. I looked back at Marne and smiled.

Marne's smile was one of great relief, "I knew you'd know immediately," she shook her head at me.

"Know what?" Fitz asked us both. "Are we gonna get to meet this amazing guy, or what?"

"Or what," I said under my breath as the woman walked over to our table.

Marne stood and took the woman's hand in hers. Taking a deep breath she said, "Fitz, Janie...this is Jennifer...my love and my fiancé."

"Hello Jennifer," I said and extended my hand. "It's wonderful to meet you," I told her as she sat.

Marne let out a held breath and reached out to squeeze my hand.

Fitz...looked baffled, almost in shock. "So," she began when she found her voice, "this is…yer love…that yer marryin'?" she nodded to herself like it was just sinking in.

"Um Fitz," I said, "let's get a bottle of champagne so we can toast to the good news."

Fitz and I headed to the bar, "What the hell is wrong with you?" I asked.

"I'm just…confused," she admitted.

"Surely you have nothing against…" I started.

"Of course not," Fitz looked at me like the thought was stupid. "Look at the industry I work in," she gave me a palms-up.

"So…what has you so confused?" my brow furrowed.

"It's Marne," she said like this would make sense to me.

"Yeah," I told her, just not getting what she meant.

"We've known her since we were teens…since before any of us lost our V-card."

I nodded, "Yeah," I said again.

"Well, I guess what has me confused is, was she always gay? Did she turn gay? When, how, did this happen?" they were questions she knew I couldn't answer. "I mean did she hide it from us, or did she not know?" Fitz kept going.

"These are questions for her, if they really need to be answered at all," I shook my head.

"How can ya say that? Don't ya want to know? We're supposed to be her best friends, the three amigos," her eyes popped.

"And we are. Nothing's changed," I told her. "She's still Marne."

Fitz nodded slowly as we grabbed the champagne and glasses. Back at the table I noticed that Marne and Jennifer let go of each other's hands as we walked up.

"You don't have to do that," I shot my eyes to their hands.

Marne looked hurt, "I just don't want to make anyone uncomfortable," her hurt eyes turned to Fitz.

"Ah, for the love of Pete, don't ya do that," Fitz told her. "Ya know damn well that I'm not a homophobe! It's because it's you!"

"Oh, so you're okay with gay…as long as it's not me?" Marne fired back.

Jennifer patted Marne's hand trying to calm her.

"That's not what I'm sayin' at all," Fitz flared.

"Well what are you saying, then?" Marne asked, baffled.

"How long have ya been together?" Fitz fired off the question.

Marne lifted her chin, "Three years. And just so you know…it was easier for me to come-out to my parents. And that was *NOT* easy," she added.

"That's the point I'm tryin' to make!" Fitz flared. "We're yer best friends, right?" she pointed from herself to me.

Marne was breathing harder, "Yeah…you ARE!" her facial expression, angry.

"So why didn't ya let us make this easier on ya?" Fitz shook her head.

Marne looked confused, "What do you mean?"

"I mean, do ya have any idea how much I, we, love ya? We'd be there for ya no matter what," Fitz's eyes were round. "You should know this! Yet ya chose to hold back from us, something ya THOUGHT we'd have a problem with? Something ya THOUGHT we would see as a flaw of some kind? What the hell? Do ya know us, trust us, our friendship, at all?"

Now that Fitz put it this way, I understood where she was coming from. She wasn't upset that Marne was gay. She was upset that Marne thought she had to go through *coming out*, alone.

Marne's eyes softened and began to tear, "I was scared," she shrugged. "First I was scared of my own thoughts and feelings. I wasn't sure I trusted them." Her long dark lashes played with pooling tears. "Then I was scared of how it might change who I had always been…in someone else's eyes." A tear rolled down her cheek that Jennifer gently wiped away. "The reason it was so hard to tell the two of you…was because I couldn't handle the thought of you looking at me…differently. You two…are the *only* ones I was worried about losing," she said under her breath.

With this comment, Fitz stood, "You'll never lose me," she shook her head. "Nothin' could change the way I see ya, or feel fer ya. And if ya had told me sooner…ya would have known that," she pulled Marne up into a hug.

By now I was tearing, Jennifer was tearing, we were all just a crazy mess of estrogen and emotion.

Marne and Fitz were holding hands, "So you really don't have a problem with…who I am?" Marne asked.

"Never," Fitz informed her and kissed her cheek. Turning to Jennifer, Fitz said, "I want to hear everything…from the first meetin' to how…wait, which one of you proposed?" she asked baffled.

We all laughed.

We sat there for hours talking and catching up with each other. Jen, as she asked us to call her, and Fitz really hit it off. Jen enjoyed all the stories Fitz told about her betrothed.

When Fitz and Jen went to get another round, Marne grabbed my hand. "I need to thank you," she said.

"Thank me? What for?" I asked.

"For you! You were the one who helped me…figure out who I was?" Marne nodded her head.

"Me? How?" I asked.

"You were the reason I knew…I was attracted to women."

Now I was confused. "What do you mean?" It's not like having a hot chick attracted to you was a bad thing. But having one who was like a sister…a little weird for me.

"I was never really attracted to men. And the ones that did catch my eye were more effeminate, softer," she nodded.

This was true. In fact her first boyfriend is now married to a very handsome and sweet man who collects teacups.

"I always thought there was something…not right with my desire toward them."

I nodded.

"And always being around models and in the industry? For as long as I can remember, thanks to mom being a model, too, I was raised in the industry. Yet I wasn't attracted to the women around me, either," she shook her head.

I was following as best as I could but I just listened.

"Then…there was you," she added.

My eyes rounded as I tried to wrap my brain about what she meant. "Are you saying…you had a crush on me?"

Marne laughed, "Absolutely not!"

I let out a held breath, "Then…I don't get it," I admitted.

"I never had a crush on YOU, just on the type of person YOU are. I figured out that my attraction to women, was real, but wasn't just based on gender. I wasn't attracted to ALL women, anymore than you are attracted to ALL men. It was a certain type of woman I was attracted to," she smiled.

"Oh," I smiled. Taking this as a great compliment, I sat a little higher.

"See," Marne began, "Jen is…just real. I mean look at her!" Our eyes went to where she and Fitz stood laughing. "She doesn't care to be the center of attention. She dresses comfortably…with her hair in a ponytail…almost no makeup on…she just doesn't feel the need to try…to be anything…but happy in her own skin."

I inadvertently touched my own ponytail, and thought; that's how Marne sees me…I don't feel the need to try? I knew this was supposed to be meant as a compliment. I mean, she was in love with this woman but some part of me looked back at Jen and Fitz and thought; next to Fitz…I'm the plain donut. No sprinkles or nuts, hell, not even a thin layer of glaze. The worst part of this was that I had been comfortable this way until I saw Jen, the way Marne saw me.

As I listened to all of Jen's other attributes; smart, funny, kind, talented, loving, I still remained focused on what she was not... what I was not.

When Jen and Fitz came back to the table, Fitz asked what we were talking about.

Marne laughed, "I think I freaked Janie out for a second there by saying that she was the one who made me realize what kind of woman I was attracted to."

Fitz looked taken aback, "Excuse me, what's wrong with me?" she questioned.

"Oh, you know exactly what I'm talking about. All those women we work with? Fake eyelashes, extensions, bushels of makeup, unable to fathom eating a cheeseburger," she said to the heavens. "I wanted and am attracted to the real person she is," she leaned over and kissed Jen's cheek.

Jen glowed and smiled, "I love the real you, too, though," she told Marne. "And no," she looked at Fitz, "if she wouldn't have joined me for a cheeseburger, we never would have made it this far."

Everyone laughed, but I was stuck in my own head. Did Cecil see me as the girl who doesn't bother to try? To try and look better, to try and be more glamorous, try to be sexy...is *this* what he sees...me not trying...at all? If I was judging just by his ex-girlfriend, I'd say he chose the opposite of her, by choosing me. And as much as no woman wants to admit their boyfriend's ex is hot, she definitely was. At this moment I had a renewed hatred for her and her fake, gravity defying fun-bags.

I shook the thoughts from my head and decided to just enjoy my besties and my new friend Jen.

As the night drew to a close, Fitz and I said our goodnight's and dragged our half-crocked butts back upstairs.

In the elevator I asked Fitz, "Do you think I'm...plain?"

Fitz looked at me like she was trying to see me for the first time, "No, yer just, ya know, comfortable the way ya are."

I let out a deep sigh. Was I comfortable? I wondered.

Back in my room the phone began to ring. It was 2am, so it was either Cecil, or my mother. I laughed at the thought but I knew it was only 11pm in So. Cal., so this was actually a possibility.

"Hello my love," rang Cecil's voice. "How's my girl?"

I beamed just hearing his voice, "I'm good. How's my guy?" I asked.

"I…am missing the way yer body feels beneath mine."

A smile stretched across my face, "Mmm, I miss that, too," I told him.

"So, why don't ya crawl under the covers…and tell me what you'd like me to do to ya?" he suggested.

"Tell ya what, how about I crawl in between the sheets and tell you what I'd like to do to you?" I countered.

"How about we take turns," he offered.

I pulled back the covers and said, "Deal."

5

NEW YORK, NEW YORK

I had always been an early riser. Usually if I slept until 6am, it was a miracle. But I had been out late last night. Apparently I slept longer than Fitz could handle. At 7am, she knocked on the door. I tried to pry my fake lashes apart, finally deciding to pull them off my eyelids. Opening the door, she stood next to a breakfast cart.

"Yer favorite; Eggs Benedict," she announced pushing the cart inside.

We sat at the dining table off of the kitchenette as I tried to get my eyes to focus.

"So where do ya want to go shoppin'?" Fitz asked happily.

Eek, I thought, I had somewhat agreed to go shopping…with Fitz…in New York. The last time we attempted to do this, it didn't go as well as planned. But now that we had a car at our disposal, maybe it cut the possibility of being mugged in half.

"I have no idea. Not only do I not know anything about the stores in New York, I have no idea what I'm looking for," I told her.

"That's where I come in," Fitz smiled.

I nodded to her.

"What's wrong with ya?" she eyed me closely.

"What do you mean?" I downed half of a cup of coffee in one gulp.

"I mean, usually when I suggest shoppin', especially fer you, ya start lookin' up places that have sales on 501's."

"Well, I was just thinking…maybe I need a change," I looked sidelong at her.

Fitz's cheeks rose, "Really? I've been waitin' for ya to say this fer…years!"

"Yeah well," I acted like it was no big deal.

Fitz sat staring at me then framed me with her fingers.

"What are you doing?" I pulled my face away from her frame and slapped at her hands.

"I was thinkin' about how ya'd look with a new hairdo," she re-framed me.

"Stop that!" I insisted. "I'm not cutting my hair off!"

"I didn't say cut it off…just maybe…framing or somethin'. It's so plain!"

There was the word that I had been struggling with since last night. Plain. "Maybe…if I find a style I like…"

Fitz began to clap enthusiastically.

"I said MAYBE!" I reiterated.

"I'll take it!" Fitz bellowed.

Crap, what have I done? I shook my head.

"What time are we to meet Tovah?" Fitz looked up at me.

"Noon, at the gallery," I said.

Fitz looked like we were under the gun when it came to time, "We better get goin'," she said.

"It's 7am," I reminded her.

She let out a huff, "This is THE CITY THAT NEVER SLEEPS," she informed me.

"I thought that was Vegas," I told her in a less than thrilled tone.

I threw on a pair of 501's, a Baby T, and my Doc's. Brushing my teeth and pulling my hair into a ponytail, I was ready to go.

Fitz met me back at my room when she was ready; full face makeup, messy bun (that probably took her longer to do and perfect than her makeup), body sculpted skinny jeans, tight red half-top, black mini-jacket and a pair of black three inch heels.

I shook my head, "Heels really? Haven't we already decided that heels in New York, was a form of self-torture?"

"Fer fashion love, sometimes it's necessary," Fitz did a turn and blew me a kiss.

Fitz said this like it was a golden rule that I should have known. She stared down at my boots and shook her head.

We dialed the number on the card we had been given at the desk and waited in the lobby for our driver.

As I received a text letting me know our driver was out front, I prayed once again that it wouldn't be the same guy from last night.

Standing next to the town car was a very attractive young woman about 21-ish, I'd say. She wore the suit of a driver, but it had been tailored to snug her in all the right places. Her long black hair had been braided and ran almost down to her ass. Full bright red lips popped against her snow colored skin. Immediately, I thought, if I had been gay, this was the kind of woman I would find attractive…not someone like me.

"Hi, I'm Janie and this is Fitz," I introduced us.

"Where can I take you ladies?" she asked holding open the door for us.

Fitz piped up, "We'd like to start at Barney's!"

Our driver, whose nametag read Pam, said, "They're not open until 10am."

"Well then how about Saks?" Fitz questioned.

"Also 10am," Pam told her.

"What the hell, I thought this was the city that never sleeps?" Fitz fumed.

Pam grinned, "The city might not but the stores do."

"Damn. I was hopin' to get some shoppin' in before our lunch date," she told Pam.

"Well, all of your big department stores will be closed at this hour," she shook her head.

"I was really lookin' forward to gettin' ya into something new," she told me. "Sorry Janie."

Pam smiled at me, "I'm not sure what you're looking for but I know a few places…great fashion and products…and they won't break your wallet."

I kind of shrugged, "Sure I guess. I mean it couldn't hurt," I looked down at my attire.

Pam stared at me, "I think you look great," she winked.

As Fitz and I piled into the backseat, Fitz whispered, "Was it just my imagination…or did she give you the once-over…twice?"

"I'm sure she was just being polite. She works for tips, too, right?"

Fitz nodded like she was humoring me, "Sure, yer probably right."

As we sank deeper into the heart of New York, I could swear my surroundings began to look familiar.

Nudging Fitz, I asked, "Does this area look familiar to you?"

Fitz nodded, "I was just thinkin' the same thing."

Our last trip to New York, Fitz and I had gone to get photos taken. But not just any photos: boudoir photos. Our little adventure had taken a turn for the *worst* when the man (dressed as a woman), taking our pictures was arrested for stealing the camera equipment from a previous employer and running a *black market fetish* site. What made it 'black market' was the fact that the people being photographed, didn't know their photos were being sold for this purpose.

As we passed by the warehouse I would never forget, I shuddered at the memory of me being hauled out into the street in a dominatrix outfit. I still wasn't sure if Fitz was better or worse off, being dressed as a slutty Little-Bo-Peep look-alike in our jail cell.

A few more blocks down, Pam pulled the car up to the curb.

Opening our door she led us inside another warehouse.

People rushed everywhere, carrying boxes and stocking racks and shelves.

It seemed out of sorts; we're we supposed to just start shopping while people stocked furiously?

Fitz on the other hand, let her fashionista run wild. There were carts and big black bags for people to use so that they could shop to their heart's content. Fitz wasted no time with the bags, grabbing a cart.

Pam was also busy looking for her size in the dress aisle.

"Where do you think I should start?" I asked Fitz, who had gone into her own little shopping mode.

"Huh?" she acted surprised that I was even there. "Oh right! We're here for you!" she laughed. "Let's start with…" she cocked her head, "…dresses I think."

As we walked the aisle of dress racks looking for my size, Pam held up a dress, "I'd like to see you in this," she gave me a one-sided grin.

"I don't know if it's my size?" I said confused by why she wanted to see me in anything.

Fitz looked from Pam to me and stifled a laugh. Under her breath she said, "And ya still don't think ya have an admirer?"

"She's just being nice," I told her in a whisper.

Pam picked out another dress and held it up for my approval, "What about this?"

The dress was form-fitting, black, cut high on the legs and low in the breast. I felt like my dominatrix suit had covered about as much as this garment would.

I forced an uncomfortable smile, "I don't know if that's my style."

"Hmm, I think it should be," she gave me a sultry look.

W.T.H. was happening, I wondered.

Fitz had her back to Pam, her eyes rounded at me.

"She's just trying to be helpful," I whispered.

I took the dress from Pam then went on about my shopping. Rack after rack we searched until my cart was full. Off to the dressing room I went with my cart in tow. Fitz stayed behind to keep going through the merchandise. I didn't know how I was supposed to know if anything looked good on me. I mean, I'm the girl that has to be pried out of my 501's. How could I be trusted to know what was fashionable?

I had tried on three dresses when I heard a familiar voice.

"Did you try on the dress I picked out for you?" Pam asked through the door.

"Um, not yet," I said, staring at the tiny garment.

"Try it on…I want to see if I guessed your size correctly."

I winced and bit my lower lip. She hadn't said anything that I could take as a come-on. But Fitz making fun of the way Pam supposedly looked at me was playing in my mind.

I pulled the dress up and she did in fact have my size correct, even if the material covered less than I would have liked.

"Is it on?" Pam asked.

"Uh, yeah," I told her.

"Well…let me see?" she laughed.

"I can't get the zipper up," I admitted.

"Let me help you," she said low.

"No, I'm sure I can get it," I danced around in a circle pulling at the zipper. Banging into the wall with my elbow, I let a curse word fly from my lips.

Pam laughed again, "Seriously, Janie, just let me help you."

Reluctantly, I opened the door and started to step out as she was stepping in.

We almost smacked faces before I took a step back into the tiny dressing room. Pam followed me in and closed the door behind us. Turning my back to her, she found the zipper and slowly pulled it up. I stood there facing the mirror wondering why I let Fitz's jesting make me so uncomfortable.

"Well, turn around, let me see you," Pam said in a whisper.

When I turned, she looked me up and down then bit her bottom lip, "Mmm…this looks great on you," she leaned in.

Panic ensued; was I reading her right? Was I about to make an assumption I would feel like a complete ass for making? But before I could be absolutely sure, her lips crashed into mine. As my eyes rounded, the door to the tiny room opened and there stood Fitz. Pam backed away quickly, shock taking over my expression.

Fitz looked from me to Pam, to me again, "Um, whatcha doin'?" Fitz looked into my confused face.

Pam grinned, "I was just helping Janie with her zipper."

I had gone mute…stuck in my own thoughts.

"Ya do know she's not gay, right?" Fitz pointed to me.

Pam's brow furrowed and she cocked her head at me, "Look, if you're not interested, no big deal. But you don't have to have your friend lie for you," she shook her head.

Finally finding my voice, I said, "I'm not gay," I shook my head back at her.

Pam looked skeptically at me, "Seriously?" she asked.

"Yeah, no, not even a little bit," I rambled.

"But…when I first saw you…you gave me…the look," she cocked her head.

I thought about it and let out a held breath, "Oh my God! You know, I think I did look at you…in a different way than…I normally would. Our best friend," I pointed to Fitz then back to me, "she just *came-out* to us last night…and her girlfriend…wasn't what I would have expected…in more ways than just the one way," I gave her a palms-up. "Then when I saw you, I thought you would have been more along the lines of the type of woman I would have chosen. If I was gay," I added quickly.

Pam nodded but looked like she still wasn't sold on the explanation I gave her, "So…not gay?" she said.

"No, *if* I was, and believe me the '*IF*' is actually non-existent in me, you'd be right up my alley," I squinted my eyes at my use of this particular idiom.

She also grinned at hearing this old phrase used, "Right up your alley, huh? Well all I can do is apologize for my misinterpretation."

"No really, I need to apologize," I shook my head. "I'm very sorry if I misled you in any way."

Pam laughed, "It's okay, really. My gaydar must be off," she started to step out of the dressing room.

"Wait a minute…was it just the look I gave you that made you think…?" I asked.

"Well, the look definitely…but you also…kind of…give off the vibe," she shrugged.

I couldn't hide the look of distress on my face, "A vibe?" I asked.

"Well, a little," she said like she was trying to be diplomatic about what she must have perceived as latent desires.

"But I'm straight…like straight, straight," I informed her.

"Like I said, I must have read you wrong," she offered then passed by me to exit the tiny room.

Fitz and I dropped our bags off at the Ritz then went to meet Tovah at the Schumer Gallery.

"All I'm saying is, she said I set off her gaydar," my eyes rounded.

"Yeah well, you've never set off mine," Fitz argued.

"No offense but didn't you once date a gay man?" I asked her.

"No, I dated a bi-sexual man," she corrected. "And if anything, that should be proof that gaydar CAN go wacky from time to time," she did the palms-up.

"What if straight people don't have gaydar?" I argued.

"In the industry I'm in?" she gave me the *are you stupid* look.

"Yeah, I'm just saying…"

"Jesus, Mary and Joseph, Janie," Fitz threw her hands up in the air "Do ya have some deep longin' to be with a woman?" her eyes bugged out.

"No," I shook my head, with absolute certainty.

"Then the way some stranger interprets ya, doesn't change who ya ARE! Now can we get passed this?"

"I don't know why you're so upset with me for questioning the way I appear to others," I told her.

"Because yer fixatin'…and yer fixations become overwhelmin'!" she whined.

She was right. Since Marne had said I was her *type* of women (and she was gay), then the driver (also gay), thought I was gay, I *had* fixated.

Pulling up in front of the three-story Schumer Gallery, my heart beat quickened. "This is really happening!" I said to Fitz.

Grabbing my hand in hers she beamed with pride, "And ya deserve this, Janie," she kissed my cheek.

An older man passing by saw the kiss and said "Good for you, ladies! Out and proud!" he pushed a fist into the air and smiled, moving on.

I turned to stare at Fitz.

"That was just really bad timin'," she admitted.

I had to laugh as we walked hand-in-hand into the gallery.

The two first floors of the gallery were for the art. The third floor had been broken up into four spaces; there was a restoration room, a storage area, Tovah's office, and a good sized board room that looked more like a dining room. It had been made to look as fine as anything you would find in a mansion.

The walls were a deep colored wood. The floors, also wood, wore fine Persian throw rugs. Windows lined one whole wall making you feel both in and out of doors. The dining table reminded me of a smaller version of the table in the Callaghan Manor. I immediately began to fidget. Elegant was the word I would use to describe the room we found Tovah sitting in, reading the morning paper.

"Hey kids," she stood and welcomed us with hugs. "I'm so happy to see you. Here, please sit," she pointed to the chairs closest to hers.

"This is an amazing room," I told her looking at all the artwork. Suddenly, my breath caught in my chest, "Is that a Van Gogh?"

Tovah smiled, at my reaction, "It is," she confirmed. "I'm holding it for a friend while he's in Africa for the next year on business. Turns out, everything thing else in his estate could go up in flames and he wouldn't bat an eye. But this," she extended her hand to the painting, "is irreplaceable."

"I have to agree," I said, still in awe.

Tovah was still watching my eyes as they were drawn to some of the finest work I had ever laid eyes on, in person. "I hope you kids are hungry?" she gave us her one-sided grin.

Our lunch was served on huge silver trays and I laughed when the dome cover was removed; Bagels, lox, cream cheese, onion, tomato and capers. This was actually a favorite of mine and I dug in heartily.

After the chewing slowed to a crawl, Tovah told me that my paintings had arrived. "I'd love for you to see where they will be displayed. You'll tell me about positioning and lighting if you have any issues with the space."

I smiled, considering I painted them in a room that gets very little natural light. "I think I would be more comfortable with your opinion of the lighting," I said.

I would have liked to have more of your paintings for the O'Connelly collection. I noticed you didn't include *The Blue Woman* painting," Tovah raised her brows.

I let out a sigh, "I know. I just don't want to put her on the selling block." I told her, hoping she would understand.

Tovah nodded, but gave me a questioning look.

I got the immediate impression that this would be an issue she would bring up at a later date.

As Tovah and I spoke, Fitz had gone off into her own little world. Tovah and I stared at Fitz who was busy plucking capers from her bagel and eating them one by one.

"What are you doing?" I asked her.

"I really like capers."

I nodded, "Okay."

"I just don't know what the hell they are," she admitted.

I had to laugh.

"They taste like tiny round dill pickles," Fitz explained.

Tovah let out a laugh and nodded, "That they do," she agreed.

When lunch was finished, Tovah took us to the first floor where workers were hanging and handling fine art. Looking at some of the paintings and sculptures, I began to fidget. This was a dead give-away of my discomfort level for Fitz.

"What's wrong?" she asked quietly as we stood in front of a painting of Paris.

I tried to be coy about what was happening, but Fitz knew me better than I knew myself at times. Deciding that there was no use in trying to cover up my feelings, I said, "I just don't think my work is…in the same caliber as these other artists. I mean look at the lines…the colors…the definition."

"Yeah," Fitz said looking at the painting, "It looks like a postcard."

"Exactly," I said feeling my discomfort level rise.

"No, what I mean is…if I wanted a postcard, I'd buy a friggin' postcard. Yer work is real…sometimes raw…and absolutely fantastic. It deserves to be on this wall as much as any other paintin' here," she squeezed my hand. "Look at the paintin's ya did of the Callaghan Manor and Distillery, they prove ya can do realism quite well!"

My eyes rounded at Fitz even knowing what realism was.

"What?" she furrowed her brow, "I listen when ya prattle on about art," she grinned.

We were allowed to do a *walk-through* on the second floor where the art had a permanent home while waiting for a buyer to fall in love. A cat walk looked down over the first floor. As I looked around, I was once again bowled over about the fact that MY art was going to hang on these walls.

Tovah, who had been called away for a museum emergency, had returned. "Would you like to see your paintings?"

I covered my smile with my hand and nodded to her.

Back on the first floor, in another part of the museum, my last painting was being hung. It was a painting I had done of a woman I met in a club in Hollywood, years before.

She was a mod, as we knew them; A black-bob-hairdo, big red lips wrapped around a Camel cigarette, a rocks glass of whiskey in her hand, tiny black dress and high black boots. Sitting on a red tuck-n-rolled couch, her legs crossed as she reclined watching the band play. Flyers from all the bands that had played the club previously, hung on the wall behind her like a *Who's-Who* of 80's punk-rock.

"Oh, this is one of my favorites," Fitz exclaimed.

"Mine too," admitted Tovah.

Another was of a famous Hollywood nightclub from the street. Lots of neon was used to capture the nightlife on the strip.

And the last one was of a couple dancing at a Jazz club a little further off of the strip. They held each other close and it looked as though the gentleman was whispering something pleasant in her ear.

"Well, what do you think, Kid?" Tovah asked.

My smile stretched across my face, finding no words, I laughed.

"Yeah, that's what I thought," Tovah wrapped her arms around me and gave me a squeeze. "So the showing is in few days, but I'd really like the two of you to join me tonight at a gathering," she said.

I looked at Fitz, we didn't have any plans tonight that I knew of. And if Fitz had made plans, it was with the friend in the silver case. Marne was in the Hamptons meeting Jen's parents for the first time. I didn't envy them coming-out to her parents and hoped it went well.

Fitz gave me the palms-up so I said, "Sure."

"How should we dress?" Fitz asked.

"Tovah looked a little confused, but then noticed our very differing attire. "Comfortably," she nodded.

"My comfortable…or Janie's?" Fitz grinned.

Tovah smiled, "Come as you are. 8pm a driver will pick you up. Now I must be getting back to a phone call. I have an artist whose work will also be displayed, and he's a little… temperamental." She had searched for a word that I assumed was her polite way of saying *difficult*.

Back at the hotel, I finally got to go through all of my purchases and try them on for Fitz's approval.

"And by the way, I don't care how good ya look, I'm not gonna kiss ya," Fitz grinned.

"That was awkward," I agreed, "and…thank you," I grinned back.

Just then, Fitz's phone began to ring. Excitedly she answered the videochat with her love, Scotty.

"I didn't catch ya in the middle of playing with the friend I got ya, did I?" he asked hopefully.

"Um, no, I'm in Janie's room. Say hello, Janie," she turned the phone toward me. Scotty was blushing.

"Hi Scotty," I grinned.

"Uh, hello Janie!" his embarrassment showed all over his face.

Truth be told, Scotty and I were more alike. Cecil and Fitz were the ones who hardly ever got embarrassed by anything.

"How are ya?" he asked me, grinning.

"I'm good," I said a little confused by the WAY he asked the question.

"That's good," he said with that weird grin I had never seen before.

I gave him a grin, back. "Why? Should I not be?" I gave my head a shake.

Scotty went silent. His eyes darted, trying not to connect to mine. "No, of course not, everything is great."

My mind started running. "Why are you having trouble looking me in the eyes, then?"

"I'm not," he purposely stared at me and his smile took up his whole face.

"If it's not somethin' big, ya should just tell her, or else her mind will be preoccupied until she knows what it tis," Fitz told her fiancé.

"It's nothing!" his head shook again. "Can ya take me off speaker, Fitzy?"

I started panic breathing, what was he hiding? Was Cecil on his way here? I wondered.

"Ya see what you've done to her? Now the damn wheels are

spinnin'! I had enough trouble with the lesbian kiss!" Fitz aimed the phone back in my direction, as she walked out of the room to talk privately to her fiancé.

"The what?" I heard Scotty ask before the door closed.

I was spinning as Fitz had said. I knew from Scotty's expression that whatever it was, it was supposed to be good. But I hated surprises. Ever since I was young, they had put me on edge. Usually because my mother's surprises, that were supposed to be good, rarely were, in my book. As in: surprise, you're going to spend every Saturday during the summer at Catholic Day-Camp. And surprise, you're going to spend two weeks at Uncle Morty's and Aunt Kate's with your creepy cousin, Lenny. Now that I knew about my parent's overactive sex life (nothing I ever needed to know), I assumed I was shipped off so they could romp and play without little eyes and ears around. I shuddered at the thought. I wished it hadn't been summoned. "Broken," I said out loud to no one, "they broke me."

It was quite a while before Fitz returned. I couldn't help but wonder if she had retired to her room for a little *buzz-love* with Scotty's help as a willing captive audience. When she did come back in, she was beaming. I did love seeing her in love.

"So what's up," I asked trying not to sound panicked.

"It's nothing, really," she said coyly.

Her coyness and the way she averted looking me in the eye, wasn't exactly comforting.

"Is Cecil on his way here?" I asked throwing out the only thought I could summon that I knew *would* make me happy.

"No," she said quickly and pretended to check her makeup.

"He is coming, though, right?" I asked.

"Oh yeah, far as I know his plans…are still the same," she still dodged my stare.

"So…can you at least tell me if it's a good thing?" I gave her a desperate palms-up.

"What?" she pretended to have no knowledge of my suffering.

"Fine," I shook my head. "We'll just go down and eat," I added.

Down in the dining hall, I was still a mess of *wonder*. As we sat at our table, menus perched in front of us, I couldn't stop my mind; *what the hell is going on?* was front and center.

Finally dropping her menu and looking in my direction, Fitz's eyes focused in on my face. It wasn't a look of concern for my feelings that she had turned on me. This was a look of wonder. "Janie, are ya feelin'…itchy?" she asked.

At first her question perplexed me, "Why would you ask me that?"

Then I saw Fitz's eyes round as she winced, "Oh God no," she said.

It didn't take me more than that to realize what was happening. Fitz and I rushed past our oncoming waiter into the ladies room. There I stood staring in the mirror and watching hives take over my face.

"Are you kidding me?" I yelled. "How come wondering about what Cecil is doing, always breaks me out in hives?"

"It's not as bad as all of that," Fitz said, but she was still wincing as new bumps rose and reddened.

"What am I supposed to do?" I asked her. "I can't show up at Tovah's with huge red itchy bumps and blotches! And I certainly can't take an antihistamine," my eyes bugged out remembering (or not remembering rather) my run-ins with them.

"Mum said that you weren't takin' the non-drowsy kind in Ireland. Maybe ya won't have the same reaction to those?"

I remembered what I had put, not only Fitz and Miss Elanor through, but, eventually the whole family as they had to start a search party to find me. "That's kind of a big gamble to take, isn't it? I seem to be…misbehaved under their influence."

"Boy, that's an understatement," Fitz cocked her head.

"Not helping, Fitz," I assured her.

Fitz said, "Okay, calm yerself. We'll get ya the non-drowsy pills, and then I'll stay by to yer side the whole time. If ya start to act weird, I'll get ya out of there, double time, okay?" Fitz offered a solution.

We purchased non-drowsy antihistamines from the gift shop. Heads of the rich and elite turned in my direction as my face and neck turned into a tomato with tiny bumps.

Back in my room, Fitz said, "It can take up to an hour to work effectively."

I looked at the time on my phone, half of an hour until we were supposed to be picked up. "It'll be cutting it close," I said, "but we have to try. I don't want to make Tovah feel like I'm making excuses not to come."

"Well, good part is, if ya show up lookin' like that, she'll know an excuse wasn't the case," Fitz continued to wince.

Fifteen minutes later, I asked Fitz, "Any better yet?"

She gave me the smile she learned on the plane from the attendant, "Not too bad, will be right as rain in no time!"

"I'd believe you if you'd wipe that damn plastic smile off of your face," I huffed.

"And I'd be able to, if I wasn't lyin' my ass off," she shuddered.

"How bad can it be?" I asked walking to the mirror. My eyes bugged out of their sockets.

"It's not…that bad?" Fitz said this as a question.

"Not that bad? I look like I need a Phantom of the Opera mask…for both sides!" I turned my head back and forth so she had the whole view.

"Well, ya need to try and calm the hell down," Fitz raised her voice. "If ya keep focusin' on it, it'll only make it worse! Now do ya feel…weird at all?"

I was trying to breathe long and deep relaxing breaths, I shook my head. "No, I feel normal."

"Well at least that's a good thing," she insisted.

I poured myself a drink.

"Do ya think that's a good idea?" Fitz asked.

"It calms me," I took a sip.

"Ya, but if ya are gonna go rouge, do ya think ya need a buzz-on, as well?"

She made me sound like I would turn into a crazed super-villian. From what she and Elanor had told me, I was just obnoxious as all hell.

"I'll be fine," I assured her. "If anything was going to happen, I think it would have by now."

As my bumps and rash started to subside, we were texted of the arrival of our car.

"I wonder who our driver will be tonight?" Fitz asked. "Will it be your lesbian lover or the guy who tried to spit on ya?"

"Do you really want my hives to start over?" I asked her.

Seeing the parked car, I held my breath. Popping out of the driver's seat, I was shocked to see a woman in her seventies, I would imagine: ample, a tight gray bun perched upon the top of her head, square spectacles over round cheeks and in a British accent, she said, "Hello ladies! I'm Elsa." She raced to embrace us both.

"Oh," I said hugging her back.

She put me in mind of every fairy godmother I had ever imagined. Not that I had ever pictured one in a chauffer's uniform, but it was a new millennia and the economy was tight.

As she backed away from our hug, she saw the hives slowly dissipating, "Oh ya poor dear," she gave me the sad grandma look. "Well, don't ya worry about this, I know how to fix it," she smiled and caressed my cheek.

As Fitz and I piled into the back of the town car, Elsa got into the driver's seat and we were on our way.

I started to breathe deeper, casting off everything that had me stressed-out, as best as I could.

A few minutes passed before Elsa got the ball rolling by asking what had upset me so, that I had broken out in hives.

I really didn't want to go back through it and risk another bout of the stress-induced bumps and blotches, so I just said, "Boyfriend." Her being a woman, I was certain that would be enough of an answer.

"Oh, ya poor thing! Ya wretched, wretched thing," she added.

I couldn't help but wonder if the word *wretched* was used differently in Britain. I shot a look to Fitz.

"I can see ya wear no ring unlike yer friend," she shook her head.

I thought she was going with the '*you can walk away anytime*' approach. "No, I don't," I agreed.

"And yet," Elsa began, "I can see by yer face that ya have laid down and played the whore for him," she made a clicking noise with her tongue. "Disgraceful," she added.

My face dropped as Fitz looked from her to me with questioning eyes.

"Well, ugh, I…we have um, had relations," I said. Not knowing why I felt the need to say anything at all.

"And see, yer face…those marks…that's God…trying to force the Devil out of ya," Elsa informed me. "For your lustious sins," she added.

I wasn't sure where grandmotherly went, much less fairy anything. And lustious? Was that even a word? My mind was spinning again.

"Hey, she's in a committed relationship!" Fitz flared. "They're in love!" Fitz looked at my face to see whether or not I had started to blotch anew.

"Oh no, ya can't be one of those women…who believes that a

man will buy a swine if he can cut himself off a piece of rump from time to time," Elsa warned.

My eyes were popping from my head.

Fitz, on my defense team pointed her finger at our driver and said, "Hey, she doesn't let anyone near her rump!"

I whispered to Fitzy, "Not helping," I gave my head a shake.

"I think perhaps I should pray over ya," Elsa said. "For yer damned harlot soul," she looked at me in the rearview mirror.

Fitz's jaw clenched, "Not necessary!"

Elsa began despite the resistance she was encountering. "Dearest Lord, please let this poor wretch of a *HO*, find her way to yer knee…to learn to love herself, cherish herself and keep her *open to the public legs*, closed for repairs!"

I was so dizzied by Elsa's prayer I couldn't even speak, as my eyes blinked furiously.

"Please make it known that she is not the devil's teat, allowing the miserable to suckle upon her, use her and degrade her like Satan's pole dancer," Elsa asked for an *Amen* to which she received silent horror from me.

"Now ya look here, ya batshit old prune," Fitz began. "Don't ya dare say another word against Janie, or you and I will have it out in the street. I don't even care if yer old enough to have breast fed Moses, you'll still be picking up yer dentures off the ground!"

The louder Fitz yelled at Elsa, the louder she conversed with the Big Guy upstairs.

"Make her vow," Elsa yelled to heavens, "and if she breaks it, may her hair fall out…"

My brow furrowed.

"…may her skin sag from her face, like the jowls of the St. Bernard…"

I shook my head, *no*.

"…and may her nipples drag the floor!"

My eyes went wide with a visual that was horrifying. I couldn't decide if I saw the boob stretched long and the nipples touching the floor, or just regular boobs with incredibly long nipples. Either way, it was a terrifying flash from my brain.

Fitz yelled as loud as she could, "I'm not toyin' with ya, old lady! I'm about to throw away my teachin's of respectin' my elders. I'm warnin' ya fer the last damn time…yer about to see the wrath of an angry Irish woman!"

"And were here now," Elsa said sweetly as she pulled to the curb. "I hope you ladies enjoyed the ride. There's an online evaluation where ya can rate yer experience."

As Elsa came to open our door, all I could think was W.T.F. just happened? Opening the door, she smiled that grandmotherly smile again and wished me well. Was she crazy I wondered, senile, possessed by *who knows what*, when behind the wheel?

Fitz jumped out of the car, her lips pursed, her hands balled into fists, she huffed through her nose.

Elsa said, "Keep a good eye on her, ya don't want to be known as a whore for the company ya keep," she smiled.

As Elsa turned to walk back to the driver's side, Fitz said, "That's it old lady!" she lunged, both hands going for the elderly woman's throat. I had to move quickly and hold Fitz tightly around waist to keep her from tearing our driver to bits. "Come back here," Fitz demanded, "I'll drag yer nipples across the ground!" Fitz yelled as the car pulled away.

Letting go of my hold on Fitz, she spun on me and yelled, "What the hell was that all about? Why didn't ya let me at her?"

"Like I know?" I yelled back and shrugged. "Plus…I can't let you beat-up a woman old enough to be your grandmother!"

Fitz shook her head, her breathing wild like a caged animal.

"The fact that you would beat up a woman in her golden years for me…is enough," I nodded and hugged her.

When we released each other, Fitz said, "Hey…yer rash is gone!"

"Really?" I asked as Fitz dug in her purse for her compact. Looking at my clear face, I couldn't help but wonder…did the medicine finally kick-in? Or was there a devil in me that had been expelled by the crazy old woman?

Fitz looked around like she was considering the same thing, "Thanks for not lettin' me have at 'er, after all," she shuddered.

6

YOU'VE GOT TO BE KIDDING

Standing out in front of the building where we were to meet Tovah, my face squished up.

"What's wrong?" Fitz asked.

"Well, I don't think this is her home," I said looking at the old building that looked like it was once a warehouse.

"Guess we won't know until we go inside," Fitz shrugged.

I tried the door but it was locked.

"Try the intercom," Fitz suggested.

Looking to my right, I did see an intercom. Buzzing, a voice said, "Hello."

"Um, hello, this is Janie O'Connelly and Sarra Fitzpatrick…to see Tovah Schumer."

The door opened on some kind of automatic swing. Walking inside, candles lit a long hallway. As my eyes adjusted, I could make out crimson carpet below our feet. Paintings lined the walls, but in this light, I was having trouble getting the full pictures because of where the candles were placed. I slowed to look at one a little closer; a woman stood on a grassy knoll, nothing but blue sky above and flowers surrounding her, her arms were raised above her head. With her eyes closed, she looked as if she may be praying. The picture stirred…something in me, but I couldn't be sure what. Down the hallway Fitz and I went slowly.

"Do ya notice anything strange about this hallway?" Fitz asked.

"I notice *a lot* strange about this," I answered her.

"No! I mean, there's no doors…that lead to…anywhere."

Fitz was right. Shouldn't a building this size, have more than just one long, ill-lit hallway leading us to…wherever the hell we were going to end up?

"It's kind of creepy," Fitz shared her thought.

I had to agree, this seemed a little odd.

As we moved further in, we heard something and stopped dead in our tracks.

"Is that…chantin'?" I asked Fitz.

We both turned our heads to listen, "Sounds like it," she said after a moment. I noticed that neither of us rushed to take another step. "Yer sure this was the right address and that crazy old lady didn't drop us off with some kind of *de-whorin' cult*, right?" Fitz asked.

"No, this is the right place," I assured her.

"How well do we know Tovah?" Fitz wondered out loud.

I gave my head a shake, "Guess we're gonna find out."

As we moved closer to the double doors at the end of the long hallway, the chanting was louder. Whatever we were hearing, was happening behind those huge wooden doors.

Fitz thought it necessary to remind me, "Remember, I don't have to be fast. I just have to be faster than you."

"Well, you should be comforted by the fact that you are," I told her. "Are we gonna do this?" I waited for a reply.

Knocking, the chanting stopped. Turning my ear to the door, I could hear footsteps approaching. My heart began to race as I turned my concerned eyes to Fitz's. As the doors were opened, a cloaked figure curled her pointer finger to us in a come-hither gesture. One of my brows lifted as I considered running. Fitz, sensing my fight or flight inner battle, pushed me ahead of her.

A huge candle-lit room was presented to us. Cloaked figures stood in a circle, with their attention focused our way. Just as I had made up my mind that running my ass the hell out of there was a great idea, I heard Tovah's voice beckon us, "Hello ladies. Come."

Walking inside the grand room, I could make out no faces beneath their hoods. I wasn't even sure which figure was Tovah's, until she started walking toward us and lowered her own hood.

"Don't look so nervous, Clematis," she said.

My eyes rounded, hearing the name Clematis made me nervous for a totally different reason. The look of shock on my face made Tovah smile from ear to ear.

"Welcome. We are the New York chapter of The Ladies of the Moon," she explained. "All of her daughters are welcome," she nodded to us.

Fitz beamed at the idea of being recognized as a Daughter of the Moon. I, Clematis, was a little less thrilled.

As we were introduced around, I began to worry. I had enough trouble remembering the names of the women in our small group. But there seemed to be about fifty women before me, all wearing purple cloaks with their feet bare.

"You look stunned," Tovah said to me.

"I had no idea that there were more…chapters…of The Ladies of the Moon…so I also had no idea you were a member," I shook my dazed head.

Tovah grinned, "This is where Marble met Benny. She was here for one of her spiritual classes and was invited to a gathering…as a fellow sister. I was so taken with her personality, her soul, I asked if she would like to meet my brother," she smiled. "And as you know, the rest is beautiful history…with a future."

I had no idea that Tovah had played a role in Aunt Marble and

Benny finding each other, either. From the look on Fitz's face, neither did she. I was starting to think that The Ladies of the Moon may have many secrets that we weren't aware of.

"We do things a little differently here," Tovah told us. "Each chapter does things their own way. Our chapter is the largest in the U.S., and we're gaining on Ireland and France."

My head was spinning, this…whatever it was, was nationwide, worldwide? As my thoughts swirled, one thought busted through all of them; would I be known in small groups around the world as…Clematis?

As if Fitz could read my thoughts, and I was sure she could, she gave me a *ha-ha* grin. Under my breath I said, "Asshole."

"Come ladies, we're going to chant," Tovah told us.

Becoming part of the ring, Fitz and I stood with Tovah between us. Joining hands, one woman began to chant. I had never heard this chant done, had no idea what they were saying or what language was being spoken. As others joined in and raised both their voices and the vibration around us, a young woman stepped into the circle. Her head fell back, eyes closed, her arms stretched out to her sides with palms up, she began to howl. Not the *wolf howl* I had done with Tovah in Mexico, but more like a low moaning.

At first, I made a face, like I didn't understand what she was doing. But then, while watching her, her moan turning into a wail, I *felt* her. I could see great…energy, swirling around her, through her. I watched as it entered her body, moved its way through her and then shot out of her palms, to the heavens. I was seeing differently; these waves of energy that she sent into the *beyond* were coming from the women on the outside of the circle. The woman in the circle was *taking* from the other women…what I perceived as great sadness or despair. The emotions; feelings pulled, cycled through her and then they were released. Rising up, they disappeared.

I watched in quiet awe as the energy was *pulled out* from one woman after another. The woman in the circle seemed to be blindly drawn to people who needed her, turning toward them and moaning as the different colored light was transferred from them to her. Then a different kind of light, a different color, a different feeling, traveled out of her…into them.

After a while, she turned to me. My breath caught in my chest. Some part of me wanted to run. I had no desire for her or anyone else to play in my energy. But then, I felt as though my arms and legs became very heavy, my head dropped back, my eyes closed. A stirring inside, an overload of emotions were moving to the surface of me. From my feet, I felt them rising upward, like tiny bubbles under my skin, to the top of my head. Slowly I began to feel lighter as this unexplainable weight was being lifted and pulled from me. A voice, soft and sweet rang through my mind, "Let it go! It's okay to let it go," I heard it say. And yes, I wanted to let it go. I stopped fighting and gave it willingly to the abyss. Within moments, I felt so light, almost like I could float on the air surrounding me. The next thing I felt, I will never find the right words to fully describe it; but a rush, a rush of gold, warm, ecstatic, joyful energy replaced the space that had been left bare by my release. I had felt this before, at Diane's, and was no closer to explaining it now. I found it hard to stay upright. Every muscle relaxed and was drowned in peace and love. I wanted to lie down, to sleep. Fighting the urge, I forced my eyes to open so I could watch the last of the women in the circle be liberated from what I can only describe as…suffering.

After The Ladies of the Moon applauded the woman who had been in the center of the circle, they began to cluster into smaller groups to talk amongst themselves.

I stood there, still staring and blinking trying to grasp my own thoughts.

Tovah smiled, "There's someone I'd like you both to meet," she said to Fitz and me, beckoning us to follow her.

Walking toward the young woman who had done the *pulling* of energy, I smiled. She seemed to be no older than twenty-one. I would guess her about five-four, short dark hair in a faux-hawk with big blue eyes and a half grin.

"Ladies," Tovah announced, "this is my niece, Tovah," she beamed, "but we call her Vah."

"It's so nice to meet ya," Fitz extended her hand. "I am Rose," she introduced herself by her group name.

"It really is wonderful," I added, "I'm…" I didn't want to say it.

"This is Janie," Tovah grinned at me.

"Oh, you're the one with the unfortunate name," Vah said, shaking my hand.

Fitz laughed at me.

"Well think of it this way," Vah added, "there are lots of Irises and Daisys worldwide. But as far as I know, there is only one, Clematis."

I sighed, "Oh, to be an original…of something horrible."

Everyone had a good laugh, including me.

"I did try to get Marble to reconsider the name, but she was absolute in her choice," Tovah gave me that one-sided grin.

"So yer Tovah's niece? That makes us family now," Fitz told her.

Vah smiled, "Yes we are."

"One of the sadder things your Aunt Marble and I have in common was the inability to reproduce. And since her mother passed," Tovah reached out to caress her niece's face, "I had asked if I could be allowed to try and stand in for my sister."

"You've made her proud," Vah said, "and me," she added.

It was beautiful to see how close Tovah and Vah were. My mother and I, although getting closer now, have to really work at our finally budding relationship. Then again, had my mother been more like Tovah, it may have been easier from the *get go*.

"If you don't mind my asking," I began, "you don't keep the energy you pull?"

Vah smiled, "Why would I want to do that?"

"What I mean is…how do you release it?" I asked.

"Really…I'm not sure," she shook her head. "I'm a *drawer*."

I had never heard this expression. It sounded quite straight forward, but I couldn't be sure. "Is that like a channeler?" I cocked my head.

"Not quite," she smiled. "A channeler allows others to come through her or him…to speak through them. I, on the other hand, just pull negative energy and ask that it be taken and properly discarded. Then I ask that the empty space be filled with love and golden light."

I nodded like I understood. And I did understand the *concept*…but not the *how*?

"Ya seem so…young. Have ya been doin' this long?" Fitz asked.

Vah thought, "I am young in this body," her smile was matter-of-fact. "But I've been doing this since I was about seven," she looked to Tovah for confirmation.

Tovah nodded.

"It was after my mother passed. We were all so…broken. I couldn't stand to see my father or Benny, or Tovah, so sad," she gave a small nod to her aunt. "I asked if I could lay hands on them and pray," she laughed. "I think they humored me, my need to try *something* to help with the pain. But from the first time I did, they said they felt better. I saw the energy leave them, run through me and release itself…"

"From your palms," I said.

Tovah and Vah turned their eyes to me.

"You saw?" Vah asked, with that little half-grin passed down to her by her aunt.

Now I was nervous, was I not supposed to? "I did," I told her.

Tovah wore that same one-sided grin and nodded to me.

Fitz looked confused, "Is that…bad?" Fitz asked the question I had wanted the answer to, but didn't want to ask.

"Not at all," Vah gave her head a shake. "It's just rare."

Fitz beamed for me, "She is definitely that," she took my hand in hers.

Vah smiled again, just like her aunt Tovah and said, "It was wonderful to meet you, both. But now if you'll excuse me, I need to talk to one of the ladies before she leaves. I hope to see you again." She offered us each a hug and moved off through the crowd to where a woman stood alone looking rather blue.

"Wow, she is something, Tovah," I said.

"She's so grown up. At twenty-one, I was a bit more unsettled and wild," Fitz grinned.

I laughed, "At twenty-five, you're a bit more unsettled and wild,"

Tovah beamed with pride, "She is the love of my life. And I'm glad you two came tonight. You ladies get to see how we do it on the East Coast."

After we mingled a bit more, people started to excuse themselves and we weren't far behind.

Sitting against the back wall with the blue woman, Vah, held her hand. I couldn't hear what was said, but I did get a feeling from the woman. I felt she was holding onto something… something she couldn't release. I could almost see the healing golden light circling around Vah, with nowhere to go. Vah didn't push, didn't try to force her light, or drag the woman's energy from her. I heard a voice in my head clear as a bell chiming, "*What we choose to hold on to…* " repeated itself over and over.

Just as we were about to dial for the car and roll the dice on whatever dysfunction our next driver would have, Tovah offered us a ride to the Ritz-Carlton. I was very grateful that I wouldn't have the lead role in an exorcism or *de-whoring*, or whatever else awaited us.

In the back of Tovah's limo, she asked me, "Are you nervous for the showing?"

I let out a sigh, "I really haven't had the opportunity to be nervous about the show," I admitted.

Tovah gave me that one-sided grin. "Other things occupying the mind?" she questioned.

"Just…the man, I guess."

"Well, I don't need to remind you that stress shows itself on the face and in the eyes," she patted my hand, "not to mention the *drawing* I saw you receive tonight."

I let out a heavy sigh, "I know. I won't put too much blame on him for that, though. Most of that…was all me," I confirmed.

"Everything will work itself out. Until then, don't allow yourself to be refilled with negativity. Breathe and try to relax. Hell…have a drink, if it helps," she instructed.

I smiled, "Thank you. I WILL try, and possibly have a drink or two."

The rest of the way, we spoke of other things. Mainly we spoke about the New York chapter of The Ladies of the Moon. This was the first chapter in the U.S. and was brought here by Tovah's grandmother. I never thought I would feel so honored to be a part of…well, anything. But I found out that it was in fact a great honor to be invited into the fold that was almost one hundred years old here, and even older in Europe. Tovah came from a long line of strong women who were revered as wise women and healers. I came from a long line of women who made pot roast on Sundays and could get any stain out of anything. It was our superpower.

"Don't forget, ladies, we have a gathering on the 31st,

Halloween, whatever you want to call it. I hope you'll attend," Tovah cocked her head at us.

Fitz was thrilled with another meeting of the *Ladies*. I, on the other hand, had had more…interesting encounters with them. I knew if I tried hard enough, I could pull off a smile that wasn't saturated with fear.

As we said goodnight to Tovah and headed upstairs, I felt my bag vibrating. I hadn't looked in my purse or at my phone for hours. It was Cecil. I hit speaker, and as soon as Fitz heard me say, "Hi Cecil," she began to grin. But it wasn't the grin I was used to, it was bigger, excitedly beaming.

"Hello my luv," he said. My flesh rose just hearing him call me love. "I'm countin' down the days until I get to see ya. This whole *an ocean away* thing is startin' to become very overrated."

I worried when he said this. Would it eventually become so overrated that he didn't want to do it anymore? I forced a thin laugh. "I miss you, too."

"Are ya alone?" he asked slyly.

"Nooo, Fitz is with me."

"I could give ya some privacy if ya want," Fitz yelled in the background. "Maybe ya should go shoppin' with Scotty next time…for Janie."

I shot her a confused look.

"What do you mean?" Cecil's voice changed, it echoed concern. "What did Scotty tell ya?"

Fitz's eyes rounded, "No, I meant since he bought me a… travel companion, Janie might need a…little friend as well, that's all."

Cecil let out a breath, "Oh that, yeah. Got to hear about yer airport run-in. Well played, sister-to-be."

I was confused by his initial reaction and why he sounded so relieved when she clarified what she was talking about. "Not necessary," was all I added to the conversation.

Both Fitz and Cecil laughed, then Cecil said, "Tell ya what, if we shop fer that, it'll be a *we* thing, okay?"

"Can we talk about…anything else?" I suggested.

"I miss you," he said.

"Me too. I love you," I said.

"Aye, I love ya, too…to the moon and back."

Letting out a lonely-hearted sigh, I hung up. Back in my room I turned to Fitz, I said, "So what was that all about?"

She gave me the round eyes of pure innocence, "What do ya mean?" she asked.

"Oh please," I poured us each a shot of whiskey on rocks glasses and searched the mini-freezer for ice. "You gave me the same look when you knew David Spellman was going to ask me to prom. You gave me the same eyes when you knew my parents bought me the Schwinn cruiser I always wanted," she looked away from me. "And, ya gave me that same face when you knew that John had started thinking about marriage."

Fitz's newly widened eyes shot back to mine.

For a moment, we just stared at each other, "No," I said it as a question and began to shake my head slowly.

"I didn't say that," Fitz shook her head back.

Eyeing her closely; her breathing changed. I could tell that she wanted to look away without me knowing what her *looking away* meant.

"No," I said again. Walking over to and slowly sliding down onto my bed, I had to keep my suddenly weakened legs from dropping me on my ass.

"I didn't say that," Fitz repeated as she pled her case, shaking her head vigorously.

"Well, what are you trying to say then…or not trying to say? You KNOW I hate surprises."

"Please Janie, any thoughts I have, are purely speculation. I have no real knowledge of what's goin' on."

"So Scotty doesn't actually *know* anything?" I eyed her closely.

"No, everything he has is speculation, too!" her red hair was vibrating, she shook so hard.

I could tell she was being honest. I had to come at this a different way. "So, what are your…and Scotty's…speculations, then?"

Fitz swallowed hard, "I don't want to ruin a surprise. As ya just pointed out, I've ruined plenty fer ya!" she spat, using defensiveness as her weapon.

"But…as I also pointed out, I hate surprises."

"I knew you were gonna throw that one back. I don't know why I thought that angle would work, I mean, I've always had this problem…"

I cut her off, "Deflecting? Really? You thought that would work?"

Fitz huffed, "I was changin' the subject. By the way, two years of high school psychology…doesn't make ya an expert!"

"No, but twenty plus years of friendship, does make me a *Fitz-pert*," I argued.

Fitz let out a long sigh while she mentally struggled back and forth about whether she should say anything. "Okay, I'll tell ya what I *know*. But only because I don't want ya to spend the next few days covered in hives."

"Should you pour me another drink?" I asked as I pounded the first one.

"Umm, maybe, yes," Fitz nodded.

She took my glass, pounded her first whiskey on ice and poured us two more. Walking back to where I sat, she let out a deep breath. "Okay, so Scotty told me that Cecil talked to his dad."

I nodded.

"I guess his dad told Scotty that Cecil asked if he could go through his mother's jewelry."

"Okay," I shook my head. "You think it's something…for me?" I cocked my head.

"Well, who else would it be for?" she asked like I was either stupid or at the very least, dim. "Anyway, she has a large collection of jewelry from Martin, her mother, even her mother's mother."

"Well that's sweet, but I don't need anything," I offered.

"Oh fer the love of God, I know ya don't need anything…but maybe he *needs* to give ya something," she raised her brow to me, trying to pull me along her train of thought.

Suddenly my eyes went wide, "You don't really think…" I couldn't even finish the thought out loud.

I pounded my second drink as Fitz began nodding. "Now we're on the same track. Thought I was gonna have to pull ya there in a little red wagon."

"No," I shook my head.

"I'm just telling ya what Scotty told me, that's all."

"But Scotty didn't say anything about marriage, or an engagement ring, did he?" I tried to keep my breathing calm.

"Well, no, we both just assume," Fitz shrugged.

"No," I said again.

"What's with all the *NO*? Think about it, we'd be married to brothers. It'll be just like we planned when we were young, remember? Wait, would you say *no*, if he asked ya?" Fitz looked bewildered.

"We haven't been together long enough to talk about marriage!" I gave her a palms-up.

"So what? Neither were Scotty and me when he proposed," she reasoned.

"Yes, but as you well know, I've subconsciously tried to make someone the right one in every relationship I've ever had. Doesn't that alone, mean I should slow down, make sure, be ready…for forever?"

Fitz mulled this over, "Ya do have the worst track record."

"Right?" I emitted, bypassing any offense I could have tried to take from her comment. "I'm just not sure I should trust my *picker*, anymore."

"Cecil's a great guy…" Fitz trailed off.

"They all were in the beginning," I argued. "But once we got to really know each other, spend real time together, that's when I noticed how different we really were, and I tried to accommodate their likes and dislikes from there."

"We'll have to agree to disagree on the thought that they all started out as great guys. But ya know yerself better now. Ya know ya shouldn't have to completely change yer needs or throw away yer wants for someone else." Fitz threw her hands up in the air.

"I know. And I won't do that again, but some part of me wants…more time before he becomes the one, if he is the one. You get it?"

"Ya know what? …I do," she nodded.

"You never had to worry about that with Scotty because you have that magical quality. You always knew…what you were looking for…and would never settle for less. You always knew *you* better. I'm just learning what I want and need from another person."

Fitz hugged me, "I do get it."

"So…do you think Cecil would understand, I mean, if he did propose?"

Fitz bit her bottom lip and thought about it.

"Fitz you are aware that you aren't saying anything, right?"

"I just don't know. Some men…they're so temperamental. I don't really see that in Cecil, but I can't say for sure that it wouldn't wound his ego or pride…or make him change his mind."

I let out a sigh.

"It's a hard call," Fitz pounded her drink then pointed to mine.

I too took what was left of my drink, down in one gulp before she set off to make us a third.

"That thing ya said, about not trustin' yer *picker*, do ya still feel that way?" Fitz asked as she poured.

I thought about it, "Not as much. Now that I know *me* better and I understand why I did the things I did…I don't think I have that same fear now with Cecil, that I should have had then with the others."

Fitz's head bobbed up and down as she handed me my drink and took a seat next to me, "Yeah, ya should have. You've come a long way baby," she lifted her glass to me.

I raised my own glass, "Isn't that from an old cigarette ad?"

"Ya want somethin' original, yer gonna have to wait for a few more drinks."

We sat silently for a bit then Fitz piped up, "What did ya see tonight, at The Ladies of the Moon meetin'?"

I pondered how to describe it, "Kind of like…smoke," I cocked my head.

"Smoke," Fitz repeated.

"It was being pulled out of the women. Well, not all of them, just a few."

"Did she pull…from you?"

I don't know why I was embarrassed to say that she had, but I did tell her.

"But not from me?" she questioned.

I shook my head no.

"Hmm," Fitz took a sip of her drink.

"Why? Are you…stressed?" She hadn't said anything about stressing.

"I am," she said seriously.

Now I was worried. Had I not been there enough for her? Was she just waiting, hoping I would ask? I started to feel like a bad friend, not to mention an asshole. "What's wrong?" I put my hand on her shoulder.

She pulled out her phone and started going through pictures, "Here it is."

I took her phone and my eyes rounded, "Is that your new wedding dress?" I asked, sure that her and her over the top, eccentric Latin designer, Rudolpho, had come to an understanding about her dress; not Flamenco! I couldn't tell exactly by the picture…was I seeing it wrong?

"Is that a gold and silver mini-skirt?" I finally asked after weighing all other possibilities in my mind.

"No," she shook her head slowly and stood. Taking my glass from me she headed back to the kitchen to pour two more. I raised one brow. I was already quite relaxed from the first three drinks. Whatever this picture was of, it required a fourth whiskey?

"So what is…it?" I asked.

She let out a long sigh, "I took Scotty to meet Rudolpho. They got along famously, just as you'd expect from Scotty, right?"

I nodded. Scotty was a great man, even tempered and fun-loving. I couldn't imagine someone not getting along with Scotty.

"Well, Scotty decided that Rudolpho should make his wedding attire as well," her eyes closed.

Looking back at the picture, my mind began to open. "Is that…a gold and silver…mini-kilt?"

"Oh, it tis," Fitz whispered and took a sip of her drink like it would calm her.

I didn't quite have the words to explain how I felt about this, so I began laughing my ass off.

"It's not funny," Fitz scolded me.

Looking back at the picture again, I said, "The hell it's not! Scotty's going to look like he belongs in a gay Irish chorus line!"

"Oh, but ya haven't heard the worst of it," Fitz flopped down next to me.

"Oh my God, there's more?" I whimpered through strained breaths.

Fitz gave me a sidelong look, "Yeah, all his groomsmen are to wear the same thing."

With this I laughed even harder. My side hurt, I was having trouble breathing, when all of the sudden, it dawned on me. My laughing slowed as I thought about this. "Oh no, Cecil is his best man!" I exclaimed.

"Still feel like laughin'?" Fitz asked.

My head started shaking, "Oh this is gonna be horrible," my hand covered my mouth. "Why don't you just show Scotty? I'm sure he'd veto this," I pointed to the picture.

"Ya'd think, right?" her eyes rounded at me.

"No," I said. "You're kidding!"

Fitz took another drink, "He loves it. Black tux coat…with a silver and gold plaid mini-kilt," she stared off across the room, bewildered.

Studying the photo closer, I asked "How *mini* are we talking about here? I mean a traditional kilt comes to the knee."

"Aye," she said.

"And this hits…where?"

Fitz shuddered, "Mid-thigh."

My eyes rounded as I got another mental image in my head. With this, I started laughing all over again. Not only was I picturing Scotty, I was picturing Cecil as well. In my mind, they were standing together, featured on a gay Irish dating site; labeled the Merry Irishmen. I said as much to Fitz, through my gasps for breath. At first I thought she couldn't see the humor in it. But then in true Fitzy fashion, she began to roll with laughter.

"Jesus, Mary and Joseph," she spat through her own rolling. "Do ya think Martin will wear one as well?"

All I could do was snort as I slid off the bed.

The last thing I remember was me cracking up as Fitz break danced and did '*the robot*' to '*Egyptian Lover*'.

7

I KNEW BETTER

I felt the hangover long before I opened my eyes. The skull pounding reminded me that I did in fact have a brain…and it was pissed. I had no idea what time it was. As the sun poured through my window, I hissed like a vampire caught in the light. I assumed the lump under the covers beside me was Fitz. Still a little drunk, I teetered off toward the mini-kitchen in search of water.

As I pounded my third glass of agua, I heard Fitz moan; a long pain filled moan. Pouring us both a glass, I headed back to the bed and handed her the first step in the hangover recovery process.

Sitting up, she reminded me why I didn't go crazy with makeup. Fitz looked like a red headed raccoon. Fighting her tongue free from the roof of her mouth, she said, "I'm dyin'."

Digging through my bag, I found the ibuprofen and handed her three. Step two of the hangover recovery process, had been administered.

"Was I breakdancin' last night?" Fitz asked.

"You were," I said picking up the phone and waiting for room service to answer.

"Thank God," she breathed, "There's a good reason why every muscle in my body hurts."

When room service answered, I ordered 2 Bloody Marys; doubles and extra spicy. Step three of the hangover recovery process was well under way.

"Not to worsen the delightful feelin' of death creepin' in, but have ya givin' any more thought to the Cecil thing?" Fitz asked holding her skull.

"I don't think I decided much last night except that I will never be on Dancing with the Stars," I admitted.

"Yeah, what were ya tryin' to do?" her face squished up.

"Poppin' and lockin'," I threw up some finger signs and struck a pose. "But I think the fact that you thought I was having a seizure and kept trying to roll me on my side, means I'm not very good at it."

Fitz gave me a nod of her head, "If I were tryin' to be gentle, that's how I'd put it."

Slamming the two Bloody Marys, I then ordered two Mexican omelets with the hottest hot sauce they could find. After eating, step four was complete. Now all we could do was wait for the pounding to subside.

Fitz had crawled back into bed, her eyes closed. I wasn't sure if she was going to fall back asleep and really didn't care. Her phone began to ring and one eye popped open.

"Where is it?" she asked.

"The kitchen, I think."

"I'll pay ya one thousand dollars…to go get it for me."

Getting her phone and checking out the display, I said, "It's Scotty."

I wasn't listening to their conversation as I refilled my water glass. All of the sudden Fitz jumped up and headed for the door.

"Where are you going?" I asked her backside.

"Gonna go get rid of my hangover," she bolted out the door.

I was pretty sure what that meant and I couldn't help but grin. Since Fitz had shared hangover cure #5 with me, I had to agree, it worked better than steps 1-4 combined. I realized that I, too, would benefit from some hangover relief.

I had finally bought a new phone that had all kinds of new capabilities. Although it didn't flip closed, something I had loved about my last phone, it did have video-chat. This technology was probably only new by my standards. It was 3pm in Ireland and I thought maybe it would be a nice happy ending to Cecil's day. I had never been the dirty girl. Yeah, Cecil and I had sexted and even had phone sex, but this video-chat could take our playtime to a whole new level. Quickly I fixed my makeup and hair, slipped off my clothes and got under the covers. Dialing his number, his secretary told me he was just finishing up a call with New York and asked if I would hold the line.

I switched the call to video and there I sat, trying to hold a sexy face and wondering why the *hold* music was the song *Spanish Flea.* I tucked the satin sheet around me so both of my legs were bared, but my good stuff was covered. I pulled the sheet down to look inviting, but not enough that my girls were on display. After a few minutes on hold, I began to stare off into space. I decided that I would give him another minute or so before I hung up. If he was too busy, I understood. The next thing I knew, I could hear Cecil calling my name. I had apparently fallen asleep. Coming to, I smiled, "Hi luv," I said. "I was just thinking about you and…"

Cecil cut me off, "This is actually a private call, Wanda," he said to his new secretary. "Can ya take the video off the screen and send it to my phone."

Cecil was standing in a room with a table full of suited executives. Hands flew to their mouths as they all tried to stifle grins and laughs.

"Oh my God," I yelled and pulled the covers over my head, while trying to press the *end call* button. Every time I hit *end call,* the phone would say *call ended* for one second, then it would flash *dialing*. I was so horrified, not just by what had already happened, but also by my phone's desire to keep my humiliation going. Finally I just threw the phone across the room, wrapped the sheet around me and ran into the bathroom.

Two minutes later, I heard my phone ringing. I was scared to answer it as I peeked my head out the bathroom door. Sneaking-up on the phone, the screen read *Cecil*. I winced before picking up the phone and answering.

"Janie, luv, are ya there?"

"I am *sooo* sorry," I blurted out. "And *sooo* embarrassed," I added.

Cecil chuckled, "Ya have nothin' to be embarrassed about. Wanda thought it was the business call that had been dropped, callin' back. That's why she sent ya to the conference room."

"Oh my God," I thought I was going to be sick. "I am so sorry," I said, again. "I just thought, ya know, spice it up!"

"Aye, that ya did," he laughed. "But ya needn't be embarrassed or sorry about that. Yer beautiful, Janie. And as I told everyone in the meetin', yer my favorite view."

"I'm sure it just came off as so…slutty, not to mention…unprofessional."

"Actually, some of the suits in the room are from Japan and speak little English. Their interpreters led them to think this was a spot for our upcoming commercial."

"What?" I asked completely baffled.

"Yeah, *Callaghan's Whiskey, It's Almost This Good*," Cecil laughed. "Or," he added, "*Callaghan's, What Does Yer Friday Night Look Like*? They loved it. You may have given us a new pitch."

I shook my head, "Maybe no more video-chat…at least, not naked and trying to get video-laid."

"Oh really, is that where that was headin'?"

"It was supposed to," I admitted.

"I don't see any reason why it shouldn't continue on that way."

I had to laugh.

"I'm switchin' to video…I wouldn't miss this for the world."

After all was said, and done very well, he said, "That was almost as good as bein' there. I can't wait to see ya, love," he said seriously.

"Me either," I grinned, still blushing.

We exchanged our "*I love yous"* and hung up. I had to admit that I did feel much better, if you excluded that whole two minutes of pure humiliation and embarrassment, which I knew, I never would.

When Fitz came back in, she looked just as bright-eyed and bushy-tailed as I expected her to be.

"Okay, so now I can start my day," she smiled.

"Me too," I added.

Fitz eyed me, "Wait a minute," she stared into my face. "What did ya do?"

"What do ya mean?" I asked as innocently as I could.

"I mean ya look…different…relaxed."

I shook my head, "Just waking up…did some stretching…a little cardio," I added.

Fitz nodded, "Oh yeah?" She walked over to my coffee maker, "Got a good work out, then, did ya?"

"I did," I nodded.

"So it didn't have anything to do with ya posing seductively in front of a whole board room?"

My jaw dropped as she hit brew on the machine. "Oh my God," I began. "How?" was all I could utter.

"Scotty was on the conference call, too," she laughed. "Seriously did ya think he wouldn't tell me? Of course he felt sorry for ya, because he knows how modest ya are and prone to embarrassment. So he told me I needed to come to comfort ya," she shook her head. "He still doesn't know how we work, does he?" she gave me the evil-red-headed-fairy grin.

Covering my eyes I asked, "You're gonna torture me with this, aren't you?"

Fitz picked up her freshly poured cup of hot coffee, "Aye, every chance I get."

"I'll make you a deal, you don't tell EVERYONE we know about this…and I'll stop making fun of you for dating a gay man," I threw the offer on the table.

"Bi," she corrected me, then thought for a moment before she said, "Nah. Now that I'm engaged, no one cares who I used to date."

I let out a heavy sigh. She was right about that, "Shit."

My phone began ringing immediately, "It's mom," I said.

Fitz just shook her head, "It's like she can sense a disturbance in yer morality. I've always said the force is strong in that one."

"Hi mom," I rolled my eyes. "What's up?"

"Not a lot. Your father and I were just wondering when you would be home from New York."

"Um, we're coming home the day after the showing so Saturday. Why?"

"Well, we'd like to maybe do Sunday dinner at Betty's house with her, Larry and his two boys…I can't remember their names."

"Walter is the older one," I informed her. I had never properly introduced to either one of them. But Walter had accompanied Betty and my parents on that fateful night when my mother became the Queen of the lap-dance on social media.

"Oh that's right. I don't know why I can't remember his name!"

I was going to offer *blacked-out* as a possibility, but decided to let it go. "Yeah, I guess that would be fine," I said. But I had a question gnawing at my brain; a flashback from who mom USED to be. "Um, this isn't some kind of setup, right?"

"Oh no. I'm done trying to find you a man. Plus you have the Basil guy, right?" she asked.

"Cecil," I corrected.

"Well, it's not like I've ever met him," she huffed.

Here we go, I thought. This is where she goes back into Mom mode.

"Speaking of that, *when* am I going to meet this young man?"

"Not sure," I shook my head as Fitz began to giggle.

"Well, it's just weird that I haven't met him. That's all I'm going to say."

"He does exist, mom, dad's met him," I reminded her.

"I know…and your father…liked him, I guess," she added.

"Yes he did," I agreed.

"It would just be nice if I had met him, too, that's all I'm saying."

I wanted to remind her that she had already said *that's all I'm saying,* once before, but she was already in fighting mode, so I let it go.

"Tell ya what, mom, as soon as he's back in the U.S., we'll have dinner, okay?"

"Okay," she said like she wouldn't be holding her breath.

I closed my eyes and took a few deep breaths.

"What are you doing?" she asked.

"Deep breathing, mom," I said.

"Why?"

"It helps with stress supposedly," I explained.

"Well I don't know what you have to be stressed-out about, but if you think it helps. By the way, is Fitz there?"

"Absolutely," I said. Fitz who had been laughing at me under her breath stopped when I held out the phone to her. "Mom wants to talk to you," I painted on my attempt at a flight attendant smile.

"Hey Mrs. O, how they hangin'?" Fitz asked.

I shook my head ready to hear my mother blow-up through the receiver. Instead Fitz laughed.

"Well that's what they make bras for," she joked with my mom. There was a pause before Fitz said, "No, with yer complexion, ya need more orange than pink or brown."

One of my lips curled like an angry dog.

"Right," Fitz said. "But I still get better results if I start at the apple and move up the cheek bone."

There was another pause, followed by laughter before Fitz said, "Okay, talk to ya soon, bye," and hung up.

I stood shaking my head.

"What? What's the face for?"

"I just can't believe that you and my mother…get along, now. It's just…mind-bending."

"Are ya pissed? Ya look kinda pissed!"

I tried to weigh exactly what I was. Eventually, I came up with, "Kind of."

"At me?" Fitz's brow furrowed.

"No, I'm mad that she treats you better than she treats me."

"Fer twenty plus years, yer mother was a thorn in my side. I'd think you'd be happy to have us mendin' fences!"

"I am, I really am," I nodded my head. "It's just…she's been horrible to me for twenty plus years, too. I just don't see how she can change the way she treats you, a complete 180, and yet she still treats me like this! It's like she's seen the error of her ways with you…but not with me."

"She has," Fitz said sympathetically. "It's just goin' to take her time. She thinks that treatin' ya like yer all grown up, means ya don't need her."

A heavy sigh pushed its way out of my lungs, "I do need her… I always will but what I need from her as an adult is…" I thought about it, "I need her to be supportive, respectful of my choices and to give her opinions only when asked for them. I need her to be more like Mum."

Fitz began laughing, "Right, ya need my Mum, the Mum who tried to potion ya. The Mum who *DID* ambush her son with dates, did potion at least one of them, and constantly meddled in his private life."

"Why doesn't, didn't, she ever meddle in your life that way?" I asked her.

"In Mum's opinion, her boys needed more guidance than her girl. She said I was always so stubborn and determined she didn't worry about me the same way. Plus, just bein' honest, it's different with mothers and sons."

"Oh come on, you really believe that?" my eyes rolled.

"Aye, just like I believe fathers are different with daughters. Mothers protect their sons from women with certain womanly traits they see, know and don't like. Fathers protect their daughters from…everything."

I did have to agree with that one. My father was my backbone. I always knew how much he loved me and how proud he was of me. I couldn't help but wonder, though.

"What? Yer makin' the face," Fitz pointed out.

"Well," I cocked my head, "it's just…do you think my mom would have had an easier time…mothering, if I had been a boy?"

Fitz cocked her own head and looked off as if trying to picture my mother with a male child. Suddenly her face squished up and her whole body shuddered. "Eewww!"

"What?"

Still shaking she said, "All I could see…was yer cousin Lenny. *THAT'S* what I think she would have produced if ya had been a boy."

Inadvertently my own face squished. The thought that I could have turned out to be a dead-bug-collecting, fecal-specimen-stealing freak that wasn't allowed to use the stove, made me grateful of my gender in a whole new way.

My phone began to ring again and I was almost scared to look at it. Had Mom forgotten to say something that could irritate the hell out of me? Looking at the screen I smiled; *Betty* illuminated the screen.

"Hi Betty!" I answered. Betty was my landlord, but oh, she was so much more than that to me. And now that she and my mother had become friends, she was even *more* than what she had already become in my life: she was a special person, a great friend and a much needed buffer against my mom's insanity.

"Hi Puddin," she said in the Southern accent I loved. "How the hell are ya in that Big Apple?"

"I'm good…really good."

"Really," Betty asked again for confirmation.

"I am, why, what's wrong?"

Betty paused, "I just got a call from yer mama."

"Yeah?" I put her on speaker so I could make myself a cup of coffee.

"Are you and Cecil okay?"

First thing I noticed; Betty got Cecil's name right. "Yeah, we're great, why?"

"Hmmm, well yer mama said you wanted to meet Larry's boys?"

I shot a look to Fitz and slowly shook my head.

"I guess I just got the wrong impression. You know I do that sometimes, read somethin' wrong."

"I don't think you read anything wrong, Betty. I think mom is hoping I'll find someone to date that doesn't live an ocean away."

"Oh…so she's meddlin', again?"

"I'm afraid so. I'm sorry Larry and you have been dragged into her….bat-shit craziness."

Betty laughed then went quiet for a moment. "Ya know honey, there's more than one way to skin a cat."

I was confused, "What do you mean?" I asked her.

"Well, suppose I do set up a dinner."

"Why? I mean I'd love to properly meet Larry's sons, but I don't see how it would help derail her."

"You leave that up to me," Betty said.

"Okay," I told her, a little worried about another battle of wills between Betty and my mother, although Betty fared quite well.

"Don't you worry Puddin, I got this," Betty laughed.

"I'm going to just say thank you in advance."

"Yer welcome, Puddin, you have a great day."

"You too, Betty," we rang off.

"I wonder what Betty's gonna do?" Fitz grinned.

Shaking my head I said, "Probably best not to think about it."

"Agreed," Fitz said. "Now let's get dressed and go see New York!"

This time around, I wanted to see all the sights I missed the first time we came to New York together: The Empire State Building, Central Park, The Statue of Liberty. I was ready for a day of sightseeing. I threw on my favorite 501's, my Panic Attack band shirt and a well worn pair of Chucks.

When Fitz saw me, her jaw dropped, "Ya can't go into Saks lookin' like that!" she bellowed.

"Saks? I thought we were going to go sightseeing?" I was baffled.

"We are! I have it all mapped out," she looked at her list, "Saks, Barneys, Bloomingdale's, Dior…"

"No," I shook my head.

"Why?" Fitz whined.

"I want to see the real sights!" I told her.

"What? Like a giant park? You've never seen a park before?

And the Statue of Liberty looks exactly the same in person as it does in the movies," she gave me a palms-up.

"Your family, my family, came through New York to become American Citizens. The Statue of Liberty welcomed them here. For God sakes, you yourself came through this way as a child! Doesn't that…stir anything in you?"

"Yeah…the fact that I've seen it before," Fitz gave me a palms-up.

"But I haven't," I argued.

"Fine, if we go to the statue, can we go to Saks?"

I smiled, "Fine."

Outside, the weather was a bit overcast. I loved the fact that the seasons were changing. A crisp chill made me sniffle as I tucked my hands into my jacket pockets. Fitz dialed for a car and we decided to wait for its arrival in the lobby. When a car pulled up out front, I held my breath.

"We haven't exactly had good luck with the drivers so far," I told Fitz.

"That's funny," Fitz said.

"Why?"

"I think ya could have gotten lucky with one of the drivers," she grinned.

"Yeah, that's hilarious."

I heard the door to the driver's side open and close, but I couldn't see…anything. Finally, I saw the top of a white-haired head, bobbing toward the back of the town car. Around the back of the car, came a little old man. As I tried to break my own stare, I noticed Fitz's dropped jaw. I couldn't tell if it was his lack of size or abundance of age that held her attention.

"Hi," the little old man said, "I'm Barney!" he held out his hand.

His blue eyes were somewhat magnified by his glasses. A full head of pure white hair didn't do anything to take away from the fact that this man had to be eighty years old if he was a day.

"Hi," I said, nudging Fitz so she would close her mouth. "I'm Janie and this is Fitz," I pointed to her.

"What?" the man turned his ear to me.

"Oh shit," Fitz said under her breath.

"I'm sorry, I have a little trouble with my right ear," he yelled.

I nodded and repeated our names a little louder.

"Oh, Amy and Bits, nice to meet you!" he shook our hands.

Fitz sent me a sidelong look. "We're gonna die in this car, aren't we?" she said through her teeth like a ventriloquist.

"I'm sure we'll be fine," I assured her. "Just…smile and nod."

"Welcome to New York," Barney yelled. Moving over to the door, he fought with the handle a bit before getting it open. "I have a little arthritis in my hands and feet," he explained loudly.

"I take it back…we *ARE* gonna die in this car," I said quietly as Fitz's head bobbed up and down.

Sitting in the back seat, Barney turned his small body around so we could barely see his eyes over the seat, "Okay Amy and Bits, where did ya wanna go?"

Since today was all mine, I told him, "I'd love to see the Frick Collection." I pronounced each word slowly and loudly. "Do you know where that is?"

Fitz rolled her eyes at the thought of spending the day at an art museum.

Giving me a smile he said, "I sure do! As you wish." Without even looking he cranked the wheel left and pulled out into traffic.

Cars and cabs behind us laid on their horns and stomped their brakes as Fitz's and my eyes rounded with heart jolting fear.

"Do ya think he can see over the bloody steering wheel?" Fitz panicked.

"I don't know! I can't see his head over the seat," I grabbed onto the *Oh Shit* bar as Barney made a quick right. The ass end of the car whipped around and fishtailed before righting itself.

Half a block in front of us brake-lights lit up the back of the cars we were quickly approaching. Fitz laced one arm through mine and held on for dear life. With her other hand, she crossed herself. "Jesus, Mary and Joseph, *GO LIMP*!" Fitz yelled, as I squeezed my eyes closed tightly, just waiting for impact.

Being thrown forward was the next thing I felt as Barney braked as hard as his tiny legs would allow. The car came to a screeching halt just inches from impacting the back of a bus.

"I'm a little colorblind, too. I just missed that one by a cunt's hair," Barney said to us over the seat.

Fitz's eyes narrowed as mine rounded, "What did that old man say?" Fitz asked.

As offended as we both wanted to be, it would have to wait as the traffic was moving and we were off again. I swear Barney was driving with both feet; one on the gas and the other on the break. The word *merged* couldn't be used to describe the way he pulled onto the expressway; he just kind of sailed across three lanes of traffic as I held my breakfast down by sheer will. Fitz had turned a pale shade of green and was swaying back and forth. She had the look; not often seen but well known by me; she was going to puke.

"I wish these people knew how to drive," Barney yelled from the driver's seat. I saw a tiny hand float up to the window giving a one fingered salute to the people he passed. I was sure people saw the hand, but not the driver.

"Oh Jesus, hold on Fitz," I yelled to her.

"What in the hell do ya think I'm doin'?" she threw her hands in the air in pure exasperation. Right as she did, we hit a pothole at top speed.

Being bumped up off her seat, she hit her head on the roof of the car. Grabbing her head with one hand and wincing, she reapplied her grip on the door.

"Oh my God! Are you okay?" I asked as I righted myself.

"Make him stop," Fitz said to me as she cupped a hand across her mouth. "I don't care if ya have to put the old man in a sleeper hold. I don't care if ya have to cover his eyes so we slam into the back of someone, just make his blind ass stop movin' this damn rollin' coffin!"

"Barney," I yelled at the top of my lungs, "we need to stop!"

"Where do you want to shop?" he yelled back.

Fitz shook her head and rolled down the window to get some much needed air.

"NO! We need to *STOP*," I yelled again.

"We're almost there," Barney yelled.

Off the expressway we flew, leaving horns beeping and people cursing in our wake.

"I don't care where we are. Just make that crazy son-of-a-bitch stop the bloody car!" Fitz pled.

"Barney…STOP!" I yelled again.

As he bounced off the curb and skidded to a stop, he announced, "Here we are!"

I took a few deep breaths and patted Fitz on the back. "Where are we?" I asked.

"Where you wanted to go," Barney said with a pleased grin.

Taking a look around, it didn't look like we were in the right place at all from the street views I had seen on the internet. "This doesn't look right," I told Fitz. "We're at the Frick Collection?" I asked Barney loudly.

"Yeah, The Prick Collection!" Barney yelled.

Fitz found her voice, "The what?"

As Barney pulled away, he yelled out the window, "Bye Amy, bye Bits."

Fitz shook her head, "The Prick Collection," she read the sign three stories above.

"How? How did this come to his mind, but the Frick Collection, didn't?" I wondered out loud.

"Seriously," Fitz was still a bit wobbly. "Any man who uses the term *a cunt's hair* as a gage of measurement, it shouldn't surprise ya too much. Well, should we go in?" Fitz asked.

My face squished up, "Why?"

"Because we don't have a ride, because I need my stomach to settle before we try to find another ride, because there's not another damn thing around here! Pick one!"

"I just can't help but wonder…" I raised my brows.

"Think of it this way, at least it's somethin' we know we both like," Fitz shrugged.

Walking into The Prick Collection, I wasn't sure what to expect. Was it a bar? Was it an adult toy shop? A whore house filled with male prostitutes?

As we entered a waiting room of sorts, a spunky looking brunette approached us wearing what looked like a magician assistant's costume gone steam-punk. A black leotard was covered by a short-waisted, long sleeved green and black striped satin jacket with tails and knee high boots covering her black fishnet stockings. Sitting perched on the side of her head sat one of those tiny little top hats with a fishnet veil covering one eye.

Her full red lips curved into a grin, "Welcome ladies to The Prick Collection!" she announced with a flourish. "If you'd be so kind as to follow me, we'll get your Prick adventure underway. Step right up," she announced like a circus barker, "and see Pricks throughout history. It's just ten dollars for a walk through and twenty if you choose the interactive tour."

One of my eyebrows rose at Fitz, "Interactive?" I questioned. "What the hell kind of place is this?" I asked under my breath.

Fitz's head shook, "Not a clue, but I'm pretty sure I don't need the interactive Prick tour…not another one, that is."

We each paid our ten dollars then were led behind the blood red curtains with the steam-punk brunette as our guide. It was dark in the next room, but tiny lights on the floor outlined a walkway.

Stopping at our first red lighted square, she began her spiel. The first display case was suddenly illuminated to reveal...something. I knew what the shape was…but…

"This is an early-times alternative Prick, or dildo for all of you prim and proper types," she winked at the horror my face showed.

I shot a look at Fitz who was closely eyeing the…tool.

"As you can see, the outer layer is made of well broken-in soft leather," the girl smiled.

"What's the inner layer made of," Fitz asked with gusto.

"The inside is a piece of steel, forged and shaped to replicate a man's member," the woman smiled. "The thin leather outer layer was designed not only for a woman's comfort, but so she wouldn't hurt herself if her play became rambunctious."

That thing looked anything but comfortable. Medieval torture device was easier for me to believe, I winced at the thought.

Fitz stared, "Is yer who-ha currently tryin' to slam-shut, because mine has hung a no-entry sign at her door."

I nodded and whispered, "I'm thinking of buying knee-shackles so my legs can't open."

"I thought ya already owned a pair of those," Fitz cocked her head.

"Hey! Don't forget, in the experience department, I bypass you in numbers, as you've become so fond of pointing out."

"I don't think having sex with five of the Seven Dwarfs constitutes experience. More like providing a social service to the mentally, emotionally," she began to laugh, "and physically inept," she curled her pinky at me.

"I didn't tell you that so you could use it against me!"

"Let's face it, Janie girl, me usin' it against ya, is the *only* way ya would ever have felt that one," Fitz gave me the evil-fairy-grin.

I had to laugh, "You're an asshole."

"Yep…your asshole," she batted her eyes at me.

The next hour or so, we saw *friends* made from steel, wood, marble, stone, fabric and even one made from a corn cob. All the way through history, we walked through centuries of mock-members, all the way up to today; vibrating plastic and latex. Our guide was very animated as she told stories of women throughout history that lived by and even died for, the right to their *O*. One woman had even been buried with her long-time, well-used companion. At the end of the tour, she invited us to peruse and enjoy the gift shop.

Standing in the gift shop, staring at framed pictures, coffee mugs and even wine glasses with The Original Prick on them, I finally asked Fitz, "What do you think the interactive tour means?"

"I'd pay a hundred bucks to never find out!" Fitz said under her breath.

Fitz had had her fill of bad drivers for the foreseeable future and decided we'd take our chances with a cab. As the cab pulled up, both Fitz and I leaned down to inspect the driver before committing to another ride from hell.

The man was about our age; well groomed hair and attire, wearing a pair of glasses, his blue eyes shined as he asked if we were the ladies who called for a cab. When Fitz said "*Yes,*" the man exited the cab and raced around to open our door. "Ladies," he said with a smile.

Comfortably in the back seat I asked Fitz, "Where to now?"

"Did ya still want to go to that Frick place?"

The look on her face told me that this was the last thing she wanted to do. "No, let's go to Barneys."

"Really?" she asked like I had said I had given her a puppy for Christmas.

"Yeah," I patted her hand.

The truth was, Fitz didn't have a weak stomach or get motion sickness. So for her to turn green on our last ride let me know she needed happy shopping therapy.

As the cab pulled away from the curb, our driver, who introduced himself as John, asked where we'd like to go.

"Barneys," Fitz replied clapping her hands.

After a short while, I noticed that the driver was stealing glances at us in the rearview mirror. I couldn't help but wonder if Fitz and I were blocking his view out the back window. Scooting further to the right side, his eyes followed. Fitz, who was busy texting, hadn't noticed that she, we, had become our cabby's fascination. I averted my eyes and watched the world whizzing by.

As we hit traffic and slowed to a crawl, I could see the Statue of Liberty out in the distance. Two trips to New York and I still hadn't laid eyes on her up close. Right then, she went on my bucket list.

That feeling you get of being watched, drew my eyes back to the rearview mirror. Again our cabby was staring. Being more than accustomed to the looks Fitz received everywhere we went, I was less accustomed to being the one receiving the stare.

Shifting uncomfortably in my seat, our driver, John, said, "You're Janie O'Connelly, aren't you?"

I couldn't hide my surprised as my brows met my hairline. "Um, yes," I said.

"I thought so," he nodded and smiled.

"I'm sorry, do we know each other?"

"No, no, I've just seen some of your work," he shook his head.

This confused me even more "My work?"

"Yeah, you have an upcoming show at the Schumer Gallery, right?"

Fitz beamed with pride for me, "She sure does."

"Yeah," John nodded, "I get museum updates from all the

major galleries. Online, they have a sneak-peak of one of your available paintings with a picture of you as a featured artist."

I was shocked, "I didn't know," I shook my head.

"Yeah, it's an invite for all of the big buyers and true art lovers. I love your work, by the way. I mean, what I saw of it," John said.

"Wow, thank you!" My cheeks began to blush a little. But to be honest, this was really exciting for me.

"Of course, it's wonderful to meet you. I'm actually going to the showing, myself. Maybe I'll see you there?" he said.

"I'd like that. I'm most likely going to be really nervous, so having a familiar face there, especially one who likes my work, will be much appreciated."

John smiled, "Absolutely."

I could tell by the look on Fitz's face how proud she was. Taking my hand in hers, she gave it a squeeze.

Three hours later, we left Barney's. Fitz was loaded down with all the bags of her purchased therapy. I offered to carry a few of them to lighten her load.

"Okay," she prepared to hand me a couple of her bags, "but what do we do if a tiny man tries to mug us?" she asked.

I stuck my tongue in my cheek. True; I was mugged by a tiny man the last time we were in New York. True; Fitz was ready to hunt down said tiny mugger and beat him within an inch of his tiny life. Considering what the tiny mugger had stolen (a tiny rubber vibrating friend) well, ironically, to die for it…I wasn't willing.

"I scream my friggin' head off!" I told her.

"No!" She pulled the bags back from out of my reach, "These," she shook the bags, "are from the fall line. If someone tries to mug ya, ya need to go *Janie-Ground*-and-*Pound-O'Connelly*, on their ass. Nothin' less," she shook her head. "Do ya understand?"

I let out a sigh and shook my head. "Yes," I nodded. "I, Janie O'Connelly, am willing to lay down my life, ready to die for your

Jimmy Choo's. I will not have died in vain if you are still able to wear your Chanel Pantsuit to my funeral."

"I get the sarcasm yer wavin' around…but I'm glad to know that ya understand what page I'm on," Fitz grinned.

By the time we got back to the hotel, Marne had texted letting us know she and Jen were back in New York.

Text from Marne: Back in New York…all went well (it read with several smiley faces). Drinks?

I was more than ready for a little more Marne time. Although I loved the one night the four us had spent catching up, one night in five years, just wasn't enough.

"Are ya gonna tell Marne that Cecil might propose?" Fitz asked while pinning up her long red mane.

"Why?" I shook my head.

"I don't know, I mean we're supposed to tell each other everything."

"I'd rather not tell her about a hypothetical possibility."

"Oooh, big words comin' out," she smirked. "Does that mean that the thought still has ya wonky?"

"I've been trying not to think about it, to be honest. I mean, if I said *yes…*" I trailed off. "But if I said *no,* would he ever ask again…if the time was right and it turned into a *yes* in my head? Would he dump me…think I didn't want him at all?" My breathing changed to my well known panic mode.

Fitz turned to look at me, "Okay, calm yerself, now! I don't need ya to go through another bought of hives. Breathe," she instructed. "This really does set ya on the edge, doesn't it?"

Just then the phone rang. I showed Fitz the name of the incoming caller.

"Speak of the Devil," Fitz eyes rounded.

"Hi," I said a little breathless.

"Hi. Ya okay?" Cecil asked.

"Yeah, why?"

"It sounds like ya were doin' yer panic breathin'?"

I had forgotten that Cecil had seen me do this before when we had a misunderstanding or two during my stay in Ireland.

"No, I'm good," I told him trying to get myself back to a place of control.

"Well, I think yer better than good."

I smiled. "So you'll be here soon? I'm so excited."

"Me too, but try and save some of that excitement for when ya see me," he laughed. "I have a surprise for ya."

"Oh," I said, my brow furrowing. "I'm not really good with surprises," I admitted.

"You'll like this one," he promised.

I winced, "Could you give me a hint?"

"Let's just say…it's about the joinin' of hearts."

"Umm, okay," I turned frightened eyes to Fitz, who stood there giving me a palms-up.

"I love ya, Janie," he said.

"I love you, too, Cecil."

When we hung up, Fitz practically pounced on me. Her eyes wide, "Well, what did he say?" she asked.

"He said it was about hearts joining," I trailed off.

"Okay, so what else could that possibly mean?"

"I don't know…but I hope there is one."

I didn't know who the designer was but Fitz wore another dress that I thought looked a lot like a slip. It was a very pale baby blue, which oddly enough worked very well with her snow colored skin and flaming red hair.

When we were young and Fitz had just started out as a model, she and I had our color charts done. Oddly enough, all the colors they said I shouldn't wear were dead on. True, I could wear the pale yellow I had been warned against, but only if I was rockin' a tan, because if not…I looked like a tall, drowned-out banana. But

Fitz, she always looked amazing, even in colors they swore she wouldn't.

Pinning the sides, she let the length of her red mane go wild. As she turned to me, she said, "Yer Turn."

A few well placed bobby pins and one big barrette on the back of my head, she gave me a messy…well, it wasn't a bun…a messy bunching? I looked in the mirror and squished up my face.

"It's the style," Fitz told me. "You've seen models wearin' it in all the new magazines."

"Yeah…and it looks good on the models," I said. "On me, it kinda looks like…I tried…but not too hard."

"Good. That's what it's supposed to look like." Fitz turned me toward her, "What are ya gonna wear? And before ya even think of sayin' 501's and yer Panic Attack shirt, know we are goin' to a big club!"

I let out an already exhausted sigh, "The dress you picked out, I guess."

"Red or white?" she cocked her head to one side.

"Does it really matter?" my face squished up.

"Shhh, I wasn't talkin' to ya!" she looked off as if picturing the outfits.

The red dress would work with my hair style according to Fitz. Whereas the white, would demand a more refined do. I chose the red for this reason alone. I didn't want her to insist on a hairstyle change.

Fitz looked at the completed ensemble. "Ya need a smoky-eye."

Already exhausted, Fitz and I headed out into the night in search of a cab. There was more than just a chill to the air for this Southern California girl. I zipped my jacket up to the top and pulled the collar around my neck, tightly. We were still avoiding our town car service with more than good reason in our minds.

The doorman asked if we needed a car and before he could hail a cab, one pulled up in front of us.

Bending down to see if our cabby looked like a serial killer or sex offender was no longer a good judge of crazy. At this point we'd settle for the low bar of being able to see over the steering wheel and not trying to perform a *slut-orcism.*

Fitz and I shared surprised looks when we noticed it was the same cabby from earlier, John.

"Oh hello, John…right?" I said surprised, scooting across the backseat so Fitz could get in.

"How weird is this?" Fitz asked. "There has to be a one in a million chance of us stumblin' across ya again."

"You'd think, huh?" our cabby turned his head and smiled. "So where are you ladies heading off to tonight," he asked.

"Well John," I said, "we're going to Bangherand."

In the rearview mirror, I saw his brow raise, "Okay," he pulled off into traffic.

Fitz's phone began to play a Barry White song. I turned my head to her, confused as *Can't Get Enough of Your Love, Babe* was sung.

"What?" she squished up her face. "I gave Scotty his own ring tone."

I nodded. I don't know why, but Barry White wasn't who I thought of when I thought of Scotty. I began to mentally go over *who* I thought I would associate with him. Lost in a weird thought, the cabby, John, asked me something.

"I'm sorry, what?" I said being pulled back to reality.

"You live in California?" he asked.

Cocking my head, I answered, "Um yes."

"Oh, I wasn't trying to be weird. It's on your bio…that you're from California."

"Oh, yes, I am."

"Is that where you got your big break in the art world?"

"Well, I wouldn't exactly say I'm part of the art world but it is where I got my first break, at a small gallery in comparison to The

Schumer. The Rein?" I asked like maybe he had heard of this gallery.

"And the Schumer...how did you get from a small California Gallery to the Schumer in New York?"

I wondered how I would describe Tovah: A mentor, friend, friend of the family or family of a friend? "The owner is newly-acquired family of my best friend," was what I came up with.

"Oh...so a little nepotism?" he nodded his head.

I wasn't sure how to take this comment. "Well, no, she didn't decide to carry my paintings until she saw them."

"But the *reason* she saw them was because you both know the same people, right?"

I thought about this, "Well, that's probably true," I said a little wary of his line of questioning.

Fitz's loud laugh broke the new weirdness between me and the cabby.

"No, you hang up," I heard her say in her most sultry voice. "No, you!" she said two seconds later.

8

BANGHERAND . . .

As we pulled up in front of Bangherand, I noticed a long line of women waiting to enter; only women.

I said an awkward *good night* to our cab driver and waited on the curb while Fitz paid the fare.

I heard our names being called and noticed Marne waving at us from behind the ropes. “Come on!” she yelled and waved us forward as *line-waiters* gave us the evil eye. I started to protest line skipping, but as Fitz pointed out, Marne wasn’t in line.

Standing at red rope barring off the front door, Marne told a hulking man with no neck that we were with her and Jen. The hulking man pulled the rope aside and attempted a smile that was frightening as all hell.

“Have fun ladies,” he said in a voice so high pitched, my eyes rounded.

Passing him, Fitz whispered in my ear, “Steroids.”

“You’ve got some pull here, huh?” Fitz asked Marne.

“A bit, this is Jen’s club,” she grinned.

My eyes rounded and Fitz laughed.

Walking in, you were on the upper level. A double staircase, one on each side, wrapped their way down against the walls leading to the huge dance floor below. The floor looked like frosted glass that changed colors with the beat of the music. A huge bar on the lower floor, that looked really far away, lined the whole back of the building. The lower story was for everyone who was lucky enough to even gain entry and the place was packed. The upper story had another security guarded walkway that led out over the middle of the crowd below to a private bar and seating area.

As we approached, another hulking man smiled and leaned in to kiss Marne's cheek. I couldn't hear what was said, but he smiled to Fitz and me, as well, stamping the back of our hands. I looked down to see the word *PRIVATE* scrolled in black ink.

Onward we followed Marne on the walkway that hovered above the dance floor below. Behind heavy black curtains was a more intimate room with a smaller, manned bar and four plush purple velvet booths.

Jen smiled and stood as we approached. After hugs and hellos were exchanged, we sat. It was much quieter in this room. I assumed the room had to have been seriously soundproofed not to hear the music blaring below.

"Wow Janie," she said, "you look fantastic!"

"Just a little of Fitz's magic…and then a little more," I laughed.

"Yeah, Marne's tried to play dress-up with me a few times, but I just can't pull it off," she grinned to her love.

"You always look fantastic," Marne leaned in for a kiss.

Fitz and I both made the "*AWE*" sound.

"So this is your place! It's amazing!" Fitz told her as a round of Cosmos made their way to the table.

"Thank you. I do love it. Everything but the name," Jen's eyes rounded.

I went over the name in my head. Fitz must have been doing

the same thing because our eyes rounded at the same time and we laughed out loud.

Marne laughed at our faces, "A little on the nose."

"Well maybe not the nose," Jen took a sip of her drink. "But when I bought the club, the name was already well established. I've seen too many businesses doing well then crash when they switch owners. I bought the club as well as the name. I did have the three dots after the word *and,* removed."

"So you didn't make a lot of changes?" Fitz cocked her head.

"Nope. I have the '*if it ain't broke…don't fix it'* attitude when it comes to business. Too many people buy a place because of how well it's doing then run it into the ground thinking it can still be improved upon. Our profit margin has jumped twenty percent in the last two years by doing nothing more than a little extra advertizing."

I nodded as if I had a better idea of business than I did. "You sound like you know what you're doing. Of course I must admit my business knowledge is limited."

"Oh, this is just one of her enterprises," Marne's eyes went wide. "She owns a coffee house, a small boutique downtown, a day spa and a novelty shop."

I laughed, "A novelty shop?"

"What is life without laughter?" Jen smiled and shrugged.

"Here, here!" Fitz raised her glass.

After a bit, I needed to use the ladies room. As so often happens in the world of women, Fitz joined me.

While Fitz and I washed our hands, I asked her, "Did you hear any part of the conversation I had with the cab driver, John?"

Fitz gave her head a little shake, "No, why?"

"I think… well, he basically said I was only invited to be part of the Schumer showing because of nepotism."

"That's ridiculous," Fitz chortled. "Tovah's not even related to ya!"

"No…but she is related to you," I cocked my head.

"So what?"

"It sounded like he was implying that I, my work, didn't belong in the Gallery," I told her.

"Why are ya worried about what he thinks? Tovah is the one ya had to impress and ya did. It's that simple," Fitz gave me a palms-up. "Are ya doin' that thing again, where ya find some way to suck the joy out of a moment you've worked so hard for?"

My tongue found its way into my cheek as I stared at her.

"Oh, I'm sorry, did I hit that nail directly on its head?" she gave me her flight attendant smile.

I had to laugh, "You're right," I nodded. "I guess I still can't believe that I'm worthy. "

"Well stop it. You've worked too hard, not to mention yer gettin' too old, to always be questionin' what ya deserve. And just a thought, I think the name *John* may be cursed for ya. Avoid the Johns," Fitz said as two women entered and raised their brows at me.

Walking back from the bathroom, skirting the dance floor, I felt someone grab my hand. Fitz continued ahead of me through the crowd as I turned to see Pam. Out of her chauffer's uniform, she was even hotter. Her dark hair was flowing free and long, skinny jeans and a red halter top made one well aware of her curvaceousness. A pair of high and tall black boots made her and me the same height. "Funny bumping into you here!" she yelled.

I smiled and gave my head a shake. Leaning in so she could hear me, I pointed to the top deck. "My friends are here."

"Oh yeah? So you're not here on the prowl?" her lips curved into a smile.

I had to laugh, "Nope, I'm still *not gay, Janie*."

"Does that mean you won't dance with me?" she yelled over the music.

I looked up to where Fitz, Marne and Jen stood looking over

the railing and clapping me on. I knew when I saw Fitz whisper into Marne's ear, exactly what she was telling her. I saw Marne's head go back as she laughed and whispered in Jen's ear. All three of them gave us the thumbs-up.

"Your friends seem to approve," Pam grinned.

I shook my head, "Sure, why not," I shrugged.

Pam and I hit the overpopulated dance floor. She pulled me through the crowd until we found enough room to move. All of the sudden it dawned on me…I can't dance. Leaning in, I let her know my personal shame.

"I have no rhythm," I yelled.

She looked skeptically at me, "None?" one eyebrow rose.

"None," I confirmed.

"Then you're lucky I'm here," she took my hands in hers and raised them together over our heads. The music was fast but she began to writhe, slowly at first, as I just stood there. "Side to side," she yelled eyeing my frozen hips.

I began to try to follow, watching her hip movements. "It's lucky you're holding my hands," I yelled. "So I don't do the *finger-gun-thing*."

"Seriously?"

"It's my *go-to*," I confirmed. "Or maybe like a fist-pump thing," I made a fist and pushed it over my head.

Pam gave me an amused look before shouting, "Yeah…don't do that!" she said seriously. "I'm positive now…you *sooo* aren't gay! I'm not sure you could pass for straight, either," she laughed.

"I have to have a strong partner to make me look good," I informed her.

"And you think only a man is a strong partner?" she shot me a look.

"Well, to be honest, I haven't danced with a lot of women," I shook my head.

"Well, then hold on!" Pam grinned as she swung me out away

from her body then pulled me back. As I twirled back into the nook of her arm, I laughed. I could hear Fitz let out a loud whistle from above. Overhead, my friends cheered us on, clapping and howling.

As the music changed from a techno beat to a Latin sound, she began moving, "Watch my feet," she yelled. One foot in, shake, shake. One foot out, shake, shake. Spin then back to one foot in. I was following pretty well while concentrating on not stomping on her feet with my size nines. "It's like a complicated Hokey Pokey," I yelled to her. Pam brought my arms back up over my head then pulled them down around her. Off we went in a circle as the floor cleared to give us some room.

Now people had moved back making an open circle, just watching us. I threw my head back and laughed as I spun then she spun. I was having a great time as all the smiling faces whizzed by. I had finally stopped concentrating on her feet and was just moving. With Pam as my partner, I didn't feel nearly as spasmastic as I usually did on the dance floor. I looked up to try and see the girls and was alarmed to see them racing down the stairs. As I went around in a circle, I had to spin my head around to keep them in my focus. I was busy wondering why they looked so…

I felt my messy-bun being grabbed. I was being pulled backward by my head. My eyes bulged, what the hell was happening? This was my only thought as I spun to see a beautiful Latina woman wearing her '*angry*' like a mask. As the crowd moved even further back, I was still very confused.

Pam started to protest to which the Latin woman pointed her pointer finger at her, "In my club?" the woman yelled. Although to be honest, I wasn't sure which one of us she was yelling at, or what her question meant.

"In *MY* club," I heard Jen yell as she, Marne and Fitz made it to my side. Snapping her fingers in the air, the blaring music stopped.

"What the hell is going on?" I asked Marne who was closest to me.

"My guess? This is either your friend's girlfriend or her EX," Marne said.

"That's right, she's my *EX*," Pam said advancing.

"And you thought…?" I left the question hanging in the air as I pointed to said Ex.

Security was moving in but just kind of *hanging-out* on the sidelines, waiting for Jen to give them the signal.

"You want her?" the beautiful Latina Ex in the red dress asked me. "Then we handle this the right way!" Her dark brown eyes bored into my frightened blues.

I was confused about which angle to explain this from. I ended up pleading my case with, "I'm not gay!"

There were some "*awes*" from the crowd.

"Oh, so you're one of those? White girl curious, are we?" she threw out a label I didn't understand.

I shot questioning eyes to Fitz, who shook her head '*no*'.

"No, I mean I'm not curious," I shook my head, still not 100% sure what this term meant.

"Yeah, that's not what I'm getting from you," the Latina woman crossed her arms, looking me up and down.

My face squished up, "Huh?"

"She's not gay…or curious and she's not after yer girl," Fitz stepped forward, apparently understanding the label and not liking the attitude I was receiving.

"And I don't know why you think you have a right to care anyway?" Pam folded her own arms across her chest. "The one who's caught cheating…doesn't get to have an opinion on what her *ex* does."

The large circle of women, "*Ooohed,*" as their heads began to shake and fingers wagged.

Yep, I was up to speed, now. I had inadvertently danced my

way into an unwanted love triangle.

The Latin woman stepped toward Pam, "Can she love you…as I do? Can she hold you…as I did?"

I stood there shaking my head '*no*', damn sure I wasn't the one.

Pam didn't respond.

"Look, you can either leave," Jen said, "or you can handle it *OUR WAY*." The look on Jen's face was no-nonsense.

For a moment the Latina woman thought about her choices. I stood there wondering what the hell *OUR WAY* meant. I shot my eyes to Fitz who gave a palms-up, but looked like she was ready to kick someone's ass if need be. I had seen that face too many times in the last twenty-something years to question its meaning.

"Will you agree to the terms?" the Latina woman asked Pam.

Pam set her jaw, "If you win…I will listen to what you have to say," she told her EX.

Holy shit, we were going to fight? This was what I was thinking, while I tried not to look too panic-stricken or like I was about to pee myself.

"Fine," the beautiful Latin woman said. "A dance-off it is!"

My eyes bulged as my head cocked forward, "Excuse me, what?" I asked.

"You and I are going to dance…for Pam's heart," the Latin woman said dramatically.

"No," I heard and shot my eyes to where the voice had come from. "You'll dance against me," Jen told her.

I stood there, dumbfounded as Marne began to grin devilishly.

"I should have to dance against the woman who is the threat!" the woman stated.

"As she said, she's not gay. I can vouch for that," Jen told her as she pulled off one heel at a time, "She's no threat."

Again some in the crowd, "*Awe'd.*"

Fitz leaned over to whisper in my ear, "It seems ya have a bit of a fan club."

I had never felt so wanted and so confused in my whole life. Had I set off other people's gay-dars, too? WTH?

"She's willing to listen to you…if you beat me," Jen said standing barefoot in the middle of the dance floor.

The woman thought for a moment staring at Pam then said, "Fine."

As the circle pushed further back, Marne whispered in my ear, "Yer gonna love this."

Jen stood there, unbuttoning her white button-up shirt and handed it to Marne. Now standing in her black boot-cut stretch pants and a red camisole, the music began to play. It rang out, "*At first* I *was afraid…I was petrified…*" Jen pulled herself in slow motion up onto her toes like a ballerina, just standing, perched on the tips.

"How the *HELL*…can she do that…without ballet shoes on?" Fitz asked Marne, completely dumbfounded.

"Fifteen years of Ballet, Modern, Pop and Jazz," Marne shook her curls and smiled from ear to ear. "Prepare yourself to be amazed."

Up on one barefoot Jen went, a pirouette, made everyone *gasp* and "*Awe*."

I was still nervously watching her toes, waiting for them to break.

As the music picked up its pace, "*And now* you're *back,*" Jen broke into a walk-around the circle as she shook her money makers. She made it to the far end of the circle where we stood, mouths gaping open, and pointed to the Latina woman.

The Latina woman began to Ricky Martin's *Maria.* She took the floor in a slow full body grind that made all the women *howl.* Her hips moved as the rest of her body stood completely still. Her eyes bore into Jen's.

My eyes rounded, my head cocked; how the hell did she do *THAT*?

The Latin woman gave the floor back, pointing to Jen.

Jen moved into the circle as Enigma began to play; *Sadeness*. A slow rhythmic body shifting; like a snake slowly releasing itself from its skin, Jen pushed her head back and let the music guide her. Down she pulled her rubber band, letting her long dark hair free as she grinded just her hips in a forward motion. Only her arms and hips moved. Everything else just kind of…stayed put.

Marne, along with Fitz and others, let out howls of approval.

"Jesus Christ, that's sexy," Fitz tried her hips to see if she could do the same move. "I'm gonna surprise Scotty with this one."

Now her whole body joined in; I could do this, the body-wave, but not the way she did it. (Hers didn't look like a fast air hump that was out of rhythm with the music.) This looked like something you'd see done…with a partner. I had to admit, what I hadn't seen in Jen before was the *SEXY.* Ironically, the same thing I didn't see in me. But it did exist in her…abundantly.

I watched as Marne's eyes stayed fixed on her. I saw great love, huge amounts of pride…and some definite yearning.

"Holy crap," Fitz said to Marne.

Marne smiled, "I know. She's the whole package."

The Latin woman was given the go-ahead, as *'Egypt Egypt'* played. I watched as she went freestyle: Front Steps into a Drop, Up-rocked, Cabbage Patched, Jelly Rolled, then began Popping and Locking.

"See, that's what it's supposed to look like," Fitz yelled to me. "Not a seizure," she shook her head.

I shot her the *you're an asshole* look that we so often exchanged.

Jen took the floor to Bow Wow Wow's, *I Want Candy*. She did some *cheer* moves before running across the floor: A Cartwheel, into a Walkover, into a Round-off, down into the Splits.

My jaw just dropped as the crowd went wild. Into a Handstand she pushed herself up and let her legs fall slowly out to her sides, just holding herself there.

"Oh yeah, she was a gymnast, too," Marne grinned.

With amazing form and control, she eased her body down until her nose almost touched the floor, then slowly she rose back up into a Handstand. I just stood there, shaking my head. Lowering one leg at a time, she just...walked-over into a standing position. The crowd circled Jen and cheered. I wasn't sure how this worked exactly, but I assumed this *huddling* meant she had won.

The Latina woman dropped her head. Oddly, I felt bad for her. I didn't know if she was a cheater, but I did know that she had publically tried to earn the chance to explain.

As I watched, Pam walked over to her. They just stared at each other for a moment, before Pam extended her hand.

Finally, I turned my attention to Jen as she made her way through the crowd. "That...was friggin' amazing," I told her. "And thank you for stepping up to defend my honor."

"Well, I'm not sure your honor was at stake," Jen laughed.

"Oh, it would have been, if she had danced," Fitz laughed.

"That's mean," Marne scolded Fitzy.

"No," I said wrapping my arms around Fitz and Marne, "it's just accurate."

We all had a good laugh at my pathetic dancing skills and headed back up to the private room above.

"Can ya teach me how to do that one thing with yer hips? That snake thing?" Fitz asked Jen.

Well into the wee hours of the morning, Fitz, Jen and Marne danced as I held up dollar bills.

Saying our goodnights, I made sure that Marne and Jen planned on coming to the showing at the Schumer, before Fitz and I got into a cab back to the Ritz.

Checking my messages, I had a voicemail from Mom. Biting my bottom lip, I pushed play. Listening and waiting for her rant to end, I said, "Huh?"

Fitz stopped singing the high part of *Bust a Move*, "What's wrong?"

"It's mom. You know how she wanted me to have dinner with Larry's sons…"

"Yeah?"

"Well, she doesn't anymore. She called them pervs and sex addicts," I shrugged.

"Well, I'm guessin' she'd know a sex addict," Fitz laughed.

"That's just it, she doesn't think she and dad ARE sex addicts. Can you imagine how bad," my eyes rounded, "his sons would have to be for mom to think that they are?"

Fitz thought for a minute then busted out laughing. "Betty said she was gonna take care of this for ya?"

I nodded.

Fitz laughed even harder, "I can't wait to hear the story that goes with this call," she pointed to my phone.

When she put it that way, I started laughing, too.

When we pulled up in front of the hotel, it didn't immediately dawn on me, but we had an uneventful cab ride home. I wasn't sure if it hadn't been a trip from hell, or if Fitz and I were too Cosmo'd out to notice. I paid the cabby while Fitz stood on the sidewalk busting a move. Shutting the cab door, I got that *stared-at* feeling again and looked around. There, huddled up against the side of the building, was John, the cab driver. When our eyes met, he just held my gaze; no smile, no readable expression…no blinking. I felt ice water run down my spine.

As Fitz hit the high part, "*You want it…you got it*," I tried to grab her flailing hands.

"What?" she barked; upset that I ruined her solo. Her eyes following my line of view, she squinted. "Is that John the cabby guy?"

I gave a small nod.

"What the hell is he doin' here…and why is he just starin' that way?"

"I don't know."

"John! Hey John," Fitz yelled, walking toward him.

"Fitz no!" I grabbed her arm.

"What," she batted at my hand. "I wanna find out why he's standin' here at three in the mornin', starin' at us like that," drunken Fitz told me.

"That stare *IS* the reason I don't want you to confront him," I told her.

"Nonsense, I'm gonna go find out!" Fitz took one step toward him.

Back-stepping, the darkness of the alley swallowed John whole. Fitz stopped in her tracks. "Where the hell did he go?" she asked, her buzz quickly subsiding.

"I don't know…but we're not gonna follow him to find out," I shook my head and pulled Fitz with me toward the hotel's entrance.

In the elevator, Fitz asked, "What exactly has he said to ya?"

I went over everything that was said, as well as how I interpreted what he said. "I could be wrong, right? I mean, my interpretation could be off?"

"Well fifteen minutes ago, I would have said you were actin' paranoid…but after that whole…*Matrix* bullshit he just pulled?" her head shook. "What is his obsession with ya?"

"I'm really not sure."

"He said he saw some of yer work along with a bio…?"

I cut her off, "One painting on the Schumer Gallery site."

"Then I think that's where we need to start." Fitz pulled her phone from her clutch and began searching.

The first few sites were completely normal; advertizing the Gallery and showing some of the works that had been featured and sold. Fitz and I looked at the prices some of these pieces sold for and our eyes rounded.

"How many zero's followed that two?" she asked.

"Six," I told her.

"Holy crap…that's a lot of money."

I nodded.

I saw my bio; sad to say, it wasn't all that interesting. The Jazz painting was used as an example of my work.

Still scrolling further down, was an article about a disruption at the Schumer Gallery the previous year.

As the story read, the Gallery was having a private showing, by invitation only, when a large package was delivered to the owner, Mrs. Schumer. Upon receiving the package, her doorman noticed that the package was moving on its own and strange sounds, a chirping as the door man described, was coming from the large box. The delivery man, who was dressed in a courier's uniform for a local company, never asked for a signature, disappearing quickly after delivery. The police and animal control were called to the scene. As the package was unwrapped, a cage of frightened squirrels was revealed. A call to the courier showed no packages had been sent to The Schumer from their company. Animal control later put Mrs. Schumer's (an avid animal lover) mind at ease telling her that all of the squirrels were well, healthy and had been released into Central Park. With no other information and no real harm done, the incident was written off as a prank.

Fitz and I stared at the article long after we both finished reading. Finally Fitz spoke, "What. The. Hell?"

"You think…?" I just left the question hanging in the air.

Fitz pondered, "I don't know, but we're sleepin' in my room. I don't want ya to wake to a squirrel's head in yer bed."

As tired and buzzed as I was I had a hard time falling asleep. I kept seeing John's face; his crazy, non-blinking, staring face. Maybe Fitz was right, maybe *Johns* were a curse for me. Scarier thought was just how many people named their children John. Johns were everywhere.

9

HAPPY FITZ-O-WEEN

I was awakened with a start. Grabbing my chest and trying not to yell *earthquake*, I spied Fitz jumping next to me on the bed.

"Wake up," she sang, "It's Halloween!"

Sighing and pulling the covers back over my head, I curled into a ball.

"Wakey-wakey," Fitz sang louder as she continued to bounce.

"What time is it?" I asked with my eyes still closed.

"9am," she said with gusto.

I should have known better. If I had been thinking about it, I would have taken my chances with the possible psycho, slept in my own room and barricaded the damn door. Fitz was the late sleeper. Fitz was the *angry-morning-person* at 11am. Fitz was the one who could kill someone and get away with it, claiming temporary insanity if her sleep was disrupted. Everyday…but Halloween, that is.

"We've been asleep for five hours," I pointed out.

"I know!" Fitz voice was breathless from her continued

bouncing, "there's only fifteen hours left of All Hallows before the veil closes," she announced.

Halloween had always been Fitz's day. Christmas, St. Patrick's Day, hell, even her birthday took a back seat to October 31st. During our lifelong friendship, I had been dragged to parties in full costume, scare houses, corn mazes, pumpkin patches, graveyard tours and even séances where overly imaginative people yelled, "What was that?" to absolutely nothing. I knew that today, the scenery might be different, but I was still going to be dragged in search of spooky fun and displaced ghosts.

When we were eight, Fitz's older brothers had told her all about the legend of Bloody Mary. So of course they told us that the upstairs bathroom mirror would be the best place to see her. There we stood, in the dark, and called her name three times. Suddenly, in the darkened glass, a face of a beautiful woman emerged. Her white dress and long black hair were flowing, as if in a breeze. Her eyes looked around like she was searching for something, someone. The feeling I got from her was desperate, frightened. She leaned toward us, making our eyes round. As her lips parted, you knew she was about to ask you for help, assistance of some kind. Fitz and I stood paralyzed by fear and wonder as her mouth fell open wide…quickly she turned into a demon; her teeth turned to fangs, her skin turned green, the once brown eyes turned into hollow black sockets, her hands raised to us. We were sure she was coming for us. She was going to come out of the mirror and get us, dragging us back into the Netherworld she lived in. Fitz screamed and punched the glass…I passed out cold…and peed a little.

When I came to, Barry had my head on his lap and Mum was wrapping Fitz's bloody knuckles. Da stood nearby reading his older sons the riot act. I had never seen him so pissed. Turned out that the two older brothers, Danny and Andy, had been taking cinematography. What better way to try your hand at film making than to scare the living hell out of your little sister and her best friend?

I had to laugh at the memory. In fact, thanks to the brothers, I no longer let my own imagination run wild, believing instead that there was always a logical explanation for everything; everything… except Fitz still jumping on the bed. This defied logic for me.

"Okay, stop!" I threw the covers off of me. "I'm up. But if you want me awake, you're going to have to get me coffee," I told her.

Fitz's face beamed before she scurried off to the coffee maker. "What are we gonna do today?" she yelled from the kitchenette.

"Have you completely ruled out sleep?" I whined.

Fitz came back into the bedroom holding out a cup of coffee for me. "Janie," her eyes filled with awe, "today is the one day a year that the veil between the living and the dead is at its thinnest! It's the day when we can communicate with all the souls that have passed on before us."

"Right," I answered.

"And, I've found a spooky fun way to celebrate Halloween and get ya some clarity on the Cecil thing!" she announced.

"Pray tell," I took a careful sip of my hot coffee.

"We're gonna get ya a psychic!"

"We're gonna get me one? Are we planning to kidnap a psychic? I mean, if we could, wouldn't that mean she's not a very good psychic?" I yawned.

"No! Ya know what I mean. We're gonna go see one!" she ran out of the bedroom.

Staring after her, I yelled, "Was that conversation over?"

"See," she came back in the room and handed me one of those small pamphlets you saw littered all over the city.

"*Readings from the other side* with *Madame Tiffany*?" I questioned.

"What?" Fitz looked taken aback.

"I don't know," I shook my head. "It's like I wouldn't go to Dr.

Barbie for a Pap."

Just then Fitz's phone began to sing '*You Are the Wind Beneath My Wings*'. I stared at her phone, hoping this wasn't Scotty's new ringtone.

"Hi Mum," Fitz answered switching to speaker.

"Ahh," I nodded; that made more sense.

"Hello my babies! Happy Halloween!" Mum yelled through the phone.

"Happy Halloween," Fitz and I said in unison.

"How is New York treatin' ya this time around?"

"Well Janie hasn't been mugged and we haven't been arrested yet," Fitz laughed as I shook my head.

"So I heard ya met the New York chapter of The Ladies of the Moon…how was that?"

"It was really…" Fitz searched for a word.

In my head I went over my own list: odd, crazy, weird…

"It was awesome," Fitz beamed. "Why didn't ya tell us?" she asked her mother.

"I figured it would be a nice treat for ya both."

"Aye," Fitz laughed.

"What do ya have planned for All Hallows?" Aunt Marble's voice chimed in?"

"Hi Auntie," Fitz yelled into the phone.

"Hi Aunt Marble," I added.

"What are ya supposed to call me?" Aunt Marble said to me I assumed.

"I mean, Hi Mum," I corrected.

Aunt Marble began to gush in what sounded like sobs, "Oh ya make me so happy, my little Clematis!" she yelled.

I sat there shaking my head as Fitz laughed behind her hand. "I'm so glad…you make me happy too, Mum," I told my spirit mother.

"Oh Marble, try to pull yerself together," said Mum in her

truly loving way. "So what are ya girls doin today?"

"I'm takin' Janie to see a psychic, Madame Tiffany!" Fitz tried to say the name with as much mysticism as she could.

There was a silence before Mum repeated, "Madame Tiffany?"

"What the hell is wrong with Madame Tiffany?" Fitz gave me a palms-up.

"Madame Tiffany, it just sounds like someone who runs a cheerleadin' camp," Mum told her.

"Or a brothel," Aunt Marble added.

"Yeah, or one of those," Mum added.

I gave Fitz a palms-up back, "That's all I'm sayin'."

"That's..." Fitz searched for a word, "Name-ist!"

Everything went silent around her as I gave her the *really* look.

Mum broke the silence, "Anyway Janie...it's why I'm callin' ya; as ya know, Aunt Marble has been learnin' how to throw the bones."

Now Mum was met by silence, but if she could have seen my face, she would have seen confusion wrapped in a level of fear.

"Um, I wasn't aware of that," I said as Fitz and I shook our heads at each other.

"Well, she has been," Mum confirmed.

"What kind of...bones?" Fitz broke in, looking a little worried, too.

"Well they're supposed to be animal, but we found some plastic ones at the spiritual store on Second Street, so she's usin' those."

I just shook my head.

"She's worried...for ya, Janie," Mum added.

"Me?"

"I am, my dear baby," Aunt Marble piped up.

"Everything is fine," I assured them both.

"No, Marble's afraid somethin's comin'," Mum said.

I could hear Aunt Marble beginning to sob softly in the

background.

"Okay…what is she worried about?" I asked as Fitz had gone into her own world of fear.

"Ya need to warn her, Marble!" Mum told her sister.

Now the sobbing was even louder and tortured, "I can't...I can't say it!"

Mum let out the sigh that let me know she had taken the reigns in this conversation. "She saw ya…burned…as a witch!"

Fitz's hand covered her mouth, her eyes rounded.

Silence engulfed me as one brow rose up. "Ugh…you do know…that I'm not a witch, right?"

"Well of course I do, dear. But what she saw…there's no way to dismiss it," Mum told me.

I had to disagree with this comment…I was already dismissing it.

"Maybe she should throw the bones again?" Fitz asked.

I couldn't help but see that Fitz seemed genuinely worried, which made me worried…for her. Aunt Marble, as much as I loved her, was bat-shit crazy to say the least. Somehow the vision of her; her hugely magnified eyes behind huge framed glasses, decked out in a muumuu, rolling the plastic bones she bought at basically a spiritual/novelty shop…I wasn't feeling the overwhelming sense of doom she was seeing.

"She's rolled them seven times…they always say the same thing," Mum announced like I had just been handed my irreversible fate.

"Mum, I'm sure I'm fine," I told her.

"Were you speaking to her or me," Aunt Marble sniffled.

I let out a sigh, "Both of you, both of my Mums," I added.

"Please, please be careful my girl, we're protectin' ya from here," Mum let me know.

"I will," I told them both, "and thank you," I added.

We exchanged *I love you's* and Fitz hung up her phone. Before I even had time to respond to how ridiculous the call was, Fitz ambushed me in a tight hug.

"Yer not leavin' me!" she ordered.

Hugging her back and humoring her need to worry, I told her, "I have absolutely no intention of leaving you."

"Promise!" Fitz's watering green eyes bore into mine.

Sticking out my pinky, she locked hers around mine. "I promise," I told her. "You do know...that this is Aunt Marble we're getting this information from, right?" I needed to clarify.

"It's not that I *BELIEVE* Aunt Marble is right...it was just the thought of bein' without ya someday...it hurt," she explained.

"So you don't think I'm going to be burned as a witch," I laughed.

"With me by yer side?" her brow furrowed. "I'd like to see someone try!"

"Funny...I'd prefer they don't."

Out on the street, New York didn't seem like it was celebrating Halloween at all. Business men and women in suits rushed about. Cabs crowded the streets and huge clusters of people moved here and there and everywhere. I shook my head, sure that I would never get used to how busy the city was.

Taking our chances yet again with the driving service, we waited on pins and needles. When the black town car pulled up, Fitz and I both took a deep breath and held it. Out of the driver's seat, stood a very attractive man; I'd guess him about thirty, dark eyes, dark hair, nicely built and a smile that made him very easy on the eyes. He wasn't wearing the usual uniform. I was no expert, but if I had to fathom a guess, I'd say a well tailored Armani was holding his bull sized shoulders.

"Hey ladies, the name's Vito," he said with a Brooklyn accent, "you called for the car?"

"We sure did," Fitz smiled.

Looking Fitz up and down, he said, "You are somethin'!"

I noticed Fitz blush a little, which was unlike her, "Thank you," she scooted across the back seat.

When he looked at me, his head cocked, "Wow, you're a tall one, aren't ya? I'd like to see ya in a dress. Maybe black…no, red," he nodded.

I couldn't hide my confusion, "Um, I'm not big on dresses," I said.

"I get it," Vito nodded, "you're the *Accept me the way I am* girl. That's kind of hot, too."

"O-kay," I scooted into the backseat.

As Vito pulled the car away from the curb, I asked Fitz, "Did you tell him where we were going?"

"No. You didn't?"

I shook my head.

"Um, Vito," Fitz began, "did ya want to know where we wanted to go?"

Vito laughed, "That's a good one. We should be there in about twenty minutes; unless the tall one wants to stop off somewhere and get a dress or somethin'."

I assumed I was the tall one he was referring to, "Why would I want to do that?" I asked him.

"Hey, honey, like I said, you're a good lookin' girl. I just think you'd make more money if ya, ya know, dressed up a bit."

My worried eyes shot to Fitz. "Make more money?" I mouthed to her.

"Vito, what do ya mean by make more money?" Fitz asked.

"Well I assume you don't do it for free?" Vito laughed.

"Do what, exactly?" I asked.

Vito got quiet as he pondered the question. "Hey, if you two's are cops and I ask if you're cops…I think ya have to tell me. It's the law, right?"

Dropping my jaw, realization had hit.

"I think ya may have picked up the wrong girls?" Fitz

told him.

Vito's eyes shot to me in the rearview mirror, "Ah geez, of course I did! Now it makes sense…why you're dressed…like that."

"Hey," I said.

"You hey? Me hey! He's saying I look like a call girl!" Fitz barked.

"Well, he's saying I don't look good enough to be a call girl!" I barked back.

"Hey, hey, ladies…I'd *do* either one of ya," he put his hands in the air.

With eyes slit, Fitz said loudly, "*CURB*!"

I wasn't a hundred percent sure if Fitz meant *pull over*, or if she planned on introducing Vito's face to the curb.

As the car pulled away, leaving us God knows where, all I could do was shake my head. "So is it all of the drivers in New York that are crazy, or do we somehow attract them to us?" I asked.

"Not sure," Fitz raised her hand to hail a cab.

As a cab pulled up, we both leaned down to inspect the driver. An East Indian man smiled at us, "Where can I take you?"

The uneventful ride and its lack of crazy made me want to hug Mr. Anand when we exited the cab in front of a place named *Realizations*. Considering how weird this could be for him, I just tipped him really well, instead.

Walking into *Realizations*, it was exactly what I would have expected. The main room was for selling wares; candles, crystals, CD's of metaphysical music, display cases with jewelry, wands, pipes and bells. There were long tables which held prayer rugs, drums, Tibetan bowls and mojo bags. Across the back of the building were shelves with books ranging from getting in touch with your psychic self to self-help books and Tarot decks. Chimes and wood carvings hung from the ceiling along with pyramids, orbs and what looked like phallic symbols being ridden by demons or gods.

As Fitz and I waited for Madame Tiffany, people brought their purchases to the checkout desk. I watched as an older lady in a gown strewn with magical symbols, unloaded her cart filled with incense, candles and small packages of what looked like weeds and flowers onto the checkout counter.

Fitz *Ooh'd* and *Awe'd* at everything she saw, purchasing a white candle, shaped like wings, that came with a small pamphlet describing a protection spell.

"What are you gonna do with that?" I asked her.

"I'm gonna do a protection spell for ya," she added.

"Ah," I nodded, humoring her.

"Don't scoff; a little added protection can't hurt ya."

Out of the corner of my eye, I saw a blonde woman walking toward the checkout. She looked about eighteen, long pigtails stood out on both sides of her head. Her makeup was dramatic in the sense that there was a lot of it. She wore a denim mini-skirt with a long sleeved cotton shirt, rainbow tights and a pair of UGGs.

"So, yer gonna wanna go counter clockwise," she nodded to the lady she was accompanying to the desk. "Reverse is necessary for this particular thing," she added.

I shot Fitz a look; what were the chances this wasn't her; Madame Tiffany? I watched her blow a huge bubble with her gum and suck it back into her mouth. I was ready to walk out even if I had to do it dragging Fitz behind me.

"Janie?" the young woman called out, looking around for her next appointment.

I whispered in Fitz's ear, "See, if she's such a damn good psychic, why doesn't she know I'm Janie?" I questioned.

"Come on, chicken. She's over here," Fitz said, pushing me toward Madame Tiffany.

As I drew nearer, she smiled, "Hey," her head bobbed up and down.

"Ugh...hey," I said back.

"Follow me," she took off toward the other side of the building that had dark curtains separating *reading rooms* from the sales floor. Down a long hallway were six tiny rooms; three on each side. Pulling back another curtain I was ushered into a tiny room that had a table with a chair on one side and two on the other.

"Have a seat," she popped her gum again before pulling the wad from her mouth and sticking it to the underside of the table.

Fitz saw the look I shot her and prodded me forward to a seat.

Pulling out a deck of cards, she began to shuffle, "So I'm gonna need you to concentrate on a question you want answered while you shuffle the cards to your heart's content," she nodded at me.

"I don't really have a question?" I admitted. "I'd prefer it if you just," I shook my head, "read me?" I gave her a palms-up.

"Oh, you're old school...I can dig that!" She laid down the deck of cards and reached under the table pulling out a huge crystal ball sitting in a three pronged dragon stand.

Working hard not to let my increasing irritation show, I bit my bottom lip.

"Oh yeah, I see some shit," her blonde pigtails bobbed up and down. "you should probably just walk everywhere...or maybe try the subway."

Fitz piped up, "Yeah, we've had some transportation issues."

"Yeah well, the best way to sidestep the inevitable...avoid cabs," she made a strange snort laugh, like she was amused with herself. I, on the other hand, was not.

Madame Tiffany's face crinkled up, "I see a woman...but she's...blue," she cocked her head.

"Does she look like me...but with a blue face?" Fitz asked excitedly.

"Mmm...maybe. There's a lot of blue," she scrunched up her nose. "Do you know any other blue people?" she asked me.

Eyes slit and head cocked, I said, "Not really, no."

"Movin' on," said Madame Tiffany. "Oh, this is cool, you're an artist! Ya know I do some really intense macaroni work, like on crepe paper or sometimes poster board."

I nodded, "Ah."

"So you have a big night happening," Tiffany confirmed.

"She has an art showin' at the Schumer Gallery!" Fitz offered.

"Is this like…live art? Because I'm seeing live art," she put her palms-out at me like a mime.

"Mine isn't," I shook my head. "Not completely sure about the other artists."

"Right," her head bobbed up and down some more.

Sitting in complete silence, my eyes shot around the tiny room just…waiting for her to say anything else.

"There's a surprise coming your way," Madame Tiffany's over-colored eyelids pulled back as her eyes rounded.

"Is it a good surprise?" Fitz inquired.

"Mmm, that would really depend on who you asked," she responded.

"Okay," I let an exasperated breath escape me, "let's say me, the person this is happening to…is asking," I tried to keep my cool.

"Right…then, no. This isn't good for you," her head shook. "There's a lot of negativity and misunderstanding…" she looked deeper into the ball, "and a little *cray-cray* involved. It's a total mess," she gave me the *bummed* look.

I shot Fitz a look. I wasn't sure if she was getting the same feeling that I had; this reading was so vague, I could apply it to almost anything that had happened or was going to happen.

"Is everything gonna to be okay?" Fitz asked in a frightened way.

"Yeah, I think so. But you really need to avoid fire," Madame Tiffany's head bobbed harder.

Fitz's eyes practically popped from her skull, "Did ya hear that?" she grabbed at my sleeve.

"Sitting right here. Got it," I nodded.

"Would ya happen to see if she's dressed like a witch when fire is an issue?" Fitz asked the crystal ball.

Tiffany looked harder into the orb, her eyes slit. "Ya know… maybe," she said like this helped in some way.

"Okay," I smiled and stood. "Thank you so much for… everything," I gave her a palms-up.

"Totally…anytime!" Tiffany responded.

As Fitz and I turned to get the hell out of there, Tiffany asked, "Your Irishman…"

With this, my head spun back in her direction.

"Does he have a brother…I mean another one…not the one she's dating?" Tiffany pointed to Fitz.

Okay, now she had my attention and Fitz's, I noticed. "Um, not that I know of," I stared at her…waiting for her to reveal something about the Callaghan brothers.

"Just my luck, right? The spirits said there were only two of them," she sighed. "Well, it's time for my lunch," she stood.

As we walked back to the front desk, Fitz asked in a panic, "Do ya have yer lightnin' bolt with ya?"

Patting my pocket I nodded, "Right where she always is… when she damned well feels like it," I added.

"I think I should buy ya a mojo bag, ya know, to wear for some added protection."

"What? And make my lightning stone think she can't do her job? I'll have none of that," I humored her.

"I'm not kiddin', ya heard her. She knew about the guys…and the fire thing…and me being blue!"

I let out a sigh, "I'll give you the *guys* thing, but everything else…was really vague. Plus, she said everything was going to be fine."

"She said to avoid fire! The same exact thing Mum and Aunt Marble said!" she added.

I thought about that. Mum and Aunt Marble had also told me that Fitz's crazy sister-in-law, Mona, had been throwing the symbols of *The Watchful-Eye* at me with her hands. The two of them were sure Mona was a dark…something, and was trying to curse me. I'd give them the *she's a dark something* (something being a bitch), but when I asked her about the symbol she had made at me, she confirmed *MY* thoughts on the matter; "I was calling you a giant pussy!" she said with that hateful smile she so often aimed my way. Plus in general, how many people *shouldn't* avoid fire, I wondered.

"I'm sure I'll be fine," I gave my head a shake.

"I don't know," Fitz wondered out loud.

"What?" I gave her a palms-up. "You'll be there to protect me…how much safer could I be?"

With this comment she gave me a serious nod, "Aye, tis true," she said like a seasoned warrior. Providing we weren't attacked by rats, snakes or a really big lizard, I thought to myself.

Fitz had already pre-searched every Halloween event that was happening in The Big Apple today and of course, she was like a kid in a Halloween candy store.

"So now, we head to a Halloween street festival down by the waterfront," she showed our cabby the destination on her phone.

The cabby nodded and off he sped. I was no longer worried about fast driving as speed now held no candle to erratic driving. It seemed all was well as we moved along. Just as I was lulled into a false feeling of calm, my phone rang.

My phone played the same old tune, as I checked the readout; *MOM.* I really needed to give mom her own ring tone. Taking a huge cleansing breath, I answered.

I didn't even get in a hello before mom went *full-mom* on me.

"You are never to see those boys of Larry's, do I make myself clear?" she barked.

"Hello mom," I said, knowing full well that my not immediately acknowledging her rant would in fact drive her nuts. "What's up?"

"Those boys," she started in almost hyperventilation mode, "I have never been so shocked in all my life!"

"You don't say?" I added for effect, but I had heard her say this a million times at least since I was a child. "What happened, mom?" I finally asked.

"Well, Betty and Larry invited us to dinner, but your dad was feeling a little under the weather, so he begged out…"

"Is dad okay?" I interrupted.

Very dismissive of my concern, mom quickly said, "Oh, he's fine!"

"O-kay, continue," I shook my head.

"Well, I went because I knew your father was fine," mom clarified. "He was just gassy and I assume he didn't know, that I knew, a boxing match he wanted to see, was on at seven…"

My head bobbed up and down as I tried to stay focused on the drawn out conversation. "Right," I added so she knew I was still listening.

"Well, I was hoping that maybe one of his sons would, you know, would be the kind of man you might like…to meet," she added as my eyes rolled around in my head.

"Well, his oldest son, the one who showed up on time," she added, "he showed up to dinner in…" she stopped like she couldn't even finish her thought; like it had sucked her dry to think about it.

"What mom? He showed up in…?"

"*DRAG*," she said, like the shock should have made me cry out with…I don't even know what.

Silently I began to laugh. Fitz saw my face and leaned in close so she could hear the conversation.

"Aren't you shocked?" mom yelled to my silence.

"Now…when you say drag…" I let the question hang in the air.

"I mean FULL-DRAG," she yelled, "… a dress, heels…for god sakes, a full face of makeup and a long blonde hookie wig!"

Fitz and I were trying not to laugh out loud, "Hoochie," I corrected.

"Whatever it's called, what do you think of his son *dragging*?" mom asked horror stricken.

"I'm shocked, mom!" I said with as much fake shock as I could muster.

"Then the other one, the younger one…"

I grabbed my stomach which already hurt from holding my laughter, "Drag?" I questioned.

"Oh my God, I wish!"

Fitz threw her hand up to her mouth, trying to stifle herself.

"He seemed perfectly lovely, especially in contrast to his… brother," she spat. "But then, his shirt wasn't buttoned all the way up…"

I couldn't even imagine where this was going.

"Well, I didn't mean to, but every time he moved to grab a serving tray or serving spoon, his shirt fell open a little. I couldn't help but see!" she announced defensively.

"Right," I nodded, still only able to force out one word responses.

"Well, he caught me looking!"

"At…his chest?" I couldn't imagine why this was a big deal. I mean a little on the creepy side, kind of, but not full pervert or anything.

"No. He was wearing…" she paused.

"Yeah?"

"Well what I thought was some kind of newfangled exercise

gear…was a leather bondage vest."

Fitz moved away from the phone so she could muffle the laugh she could no longer hold back.

"He caught me staring and asked if I wanted to see it. Before I could say anything, he stood and started unbuttoning the rest of the buttons," her voice quivered.

I was mentally picturing not only the view of Larry's son revealing his fetish, but my mother's face painted with sheer horror.

"The vest had rings on it…and holes that his…nipples popped out of…and they have earrings through them!"

I couldn't hold it any longer, I snorted so loud and hard that it hurt my nostrils.

"Are you laughing, Janie? Because this is NO LAUGHING MATTER!" she yelled. "He's a sex addict, and apparently one of those SNL people."

"S&M, mom," I offered.

"WHY DO YOU KNOW THAT?" she yelled louder, making Fitz cross her legs so she wouldn't pee herself.

I wasn't sure how to answer this, so thinking nothing could make this any worse than it already was, I looked at Fitz and winked before saying, "Porn!"

"OH MY GOD, are you a sex addict, too? Are you an M&M?" mom panicked at the thought.

"No mom, not at all. I learned about it in Catholic School," I lied. "It was on the list of what good Catholic girls should avoid," I added.

Mom was taking some deep breaths, "Well thank God your school taught you about these things. I'd hate to think of you being lured into this stuff and not knowing the dangers."

I wasn't sure what exactly mom thought she knew about S&M, but from what I had been told, it was a consensual act.

Fitz was still laughing behind her hand and whispered to me,

"Oh dear lord, I wish I had a picture of ya in that dominatrix suit, now!"

My face contorted with noiseless laughter. "My Christmas card," I whispered back.

While I was busy trying not to crack up and mentally thanking Betty from the bottom of my heart, I couldn't help but notice the car next to us. The feeling of being stared at was back and it wiped the smile off of my face. In another cab that pulled alongside of us, was John the cabby.

Sucking in my breath, I slapped my hand at Fitz to get her attention. Fitz looked past me to see what I was seeing. There he sat, driving, but only taking glances at the road in between staring at us.

Mom kept talking as Fitz's and my eyes rounded.

"I guess that Cedrick guy is better than either of Larry's sons," mom huffed.

Normally I would have been offended that she once again messed up Cecil's name, but at the moment; creeped-out was taking precedence over ticked off. "Glad to hear it mom, I gotta go," I hung up the phone and stared some more at the scary cab driver.

Fitz was feeling *all the creepy* I was feeling, "Does he ever blink?" she asked me.

"I don't know," I felt the ice water run down my spine again.

"Um, excuse me," Fitz tapped the shoulder of our driver, "Would ya mind speedin' up a bit?"

Our driver, whose name I couldn't have pronounced if I tried…and I didn't want to offend him by trying, asked, "NASCAR?"

Fitz looked at me and shrugged, "Um, fine."

Off of the passenger seat, the man pulled a ball-cap. Showing it to us first and smiling, my jaw dropped; Good ol' #3, Dale Earnhardt.

"Oh shit," Fitz said under her breath as the man pulled the cap on his head, locked both hands onto the steering wheel and slammed his foot down on the gas pedal. Off we shot, like a bra being unfastened after a sixteen hour shift.

Watching, like a deer caught in the headlights, the ass-end of the car in front of us grew closer and closer. As we approached fast and without even a sign of braking, our driver quickly switched lanes at the last possible second. I turned to look where John the cabby had gone. One car length behind and two lanes over on the right, he, too, darted in and out of the traffic. I took a glance at Fitz and she looked frightened, but I couldn't tell if it was the driving or the scary stalking cabby that had her eyes popped out the way they were.

"Are you okay?" I yelled to her.

"Yeah," she yelled at me, "I'm bloody peachy!" she had a death grip on the door and our driver's headrest.

Again Fitz and I were thrown sideways as our cab shot into another lane. As Fitz slammed against me she yelled, "By a cunt's hair! BY A CUNT'S HAIR," she screamed frantically as we just squeaked past a cab on our left. The gentleman sitting in that cab's backseat, a perfectly groomed business man, lowered the phone he was talking into and dropped his jaw as our door handles almost rubbed his.

Our driver, still going at top speed, looked back at us and smiled. "I. LOVE. NASCAR," he pronounced each word slowly, determined to say it correctly.

On my left, I saw a cab pulling up neck and neck with our cab; there he was again, scary John. But now he wore a smile so sinister, my breath caught in my throat. Grabbing Fitz and pointing, she turned her less than happy face his way. With as much Fitzy-ness as she could still muster, she flipped him the bird.

John's brow rose at Fitz's display.

"Pull over," Fitz instructed our driver.

"Oh God, are you gonna be sick?" I asked as the car slowed.

"Nope," she said with Fitzy gusto, "I'm gonna kick John the Cabby's ever-lovin' ass!"

Jumping out of the backseat even before the car came to a complete stop; John's cab rolled by and just kept going.

"Get back here, ya piece of lousy shite!" Fitz yelled.

A short, thin man in his 30's, with greasy slicked back black hair and a circa 1980's jean jacket over his AC/DC shirt, passed us. In his nasally New York accent, he told Fitz, "Why don't you shut it, fire-pie!"

Fitz's eyes narrowed, she broke into a dead run. The man's eyes rounded as he dropped his grocery bags and bolted.

I yelled after her, but she and the man were gone. I proceeded to pay our NASCAR cabby for yet another ride from hell when all of the sudden, I heard a man yelp loudly from down the block. "My eye, my eye," he bellowed.

I started to run toward the noise just in time to see Fitz walking back wearing a look of utter contentment.

"Are you okay?" I breathed.

"*Fire-pie*...that's the last time he will *EVER* utter those words," she nodded her head. "I have half of a mind to steal his groceries, too," Fitz added, looking at the strewn bags. "SPAM...who eats that crap?"

"Black Pudding," I reminded her.

"It may be an Irish thing, but it sure as hell isn't a Fitz thing," she winced. "Come on, let's get to the waterfront."

We were only a few blocks from where the party/gathering was to take place. As we got closer, people in costumes of all kinds littered the streets going to and coming from the six block long festival. Unlike many Halloween parties that seem to have no rhyme or reason to their costumes, all the ones I saw had a definite theme: Magical and Mystical.

10

A FUNNY THING HAPPENED . . .

Some were dressed as witches and what I assumed were warlocks if that was the right word. Others were wizards, sorceresses, fairies, gypsies, banshees, sprites, ghosts, mythological creatures and gods, and there were even a few dressed as characters from well known kids books that adults had fallen in love with, too.

Each booth had something unique. One sold witches brooms and cauldrons in every size. Another sold intricate knives and long swords that would take two hands to hold. Others sold incense, herbs, crystal balls, jewelry and clothing straight out of the middle-ages. In short, the festival was just like a bigger, outside version of the store we had just left.

Everyone seemed to be having a good time as mock battles stirred up in the middle of the street out of nowhere. Actors had been hired to look as patrons; picking fights with one another over wenches, ale, what have you. They would challenge each other to battles and duels for the onlooker's entertainment.

The music which was primarily done with drums, flutes and

small harps, boasted some great tales sung by men and women dressed as Lords and Ladies.

If it weren't for the skyscrapers in the background and all the food trucks parked behind makeshift storefronts, you'd almost believe you had stepped into a magical world.

As Fitz and I passed a huge cauldron with a head dunked in it, she squealed with delight. When the man brought his cold wet head out of the water, Fitz's face fell seeing it was in fact apples they were dunking for.

"That's not how we do it at the pub," she pouted.

I knew she would be a little nostalgic for her family's yearly traditions at Fitzpatrick's pub. I rubbed her arm and said, "Not everyone is Irish enough to bob for beers. Plus that guy," I pointed to the wet-headed chap, "is like fifteen."

"That's when I learned to Bob for Beers!" Fitz's pout deepened.

I smiled, it was ginger beer we bobbed for, but yes, we were in the pub for a Halloween Festival when we were fifteen.

At the very far end of the festival a stage had been erected. The curtain was still pulled as a thin man wearing a sorcerers robe picked people out of the crowd to join in on the merriment. As the man drew near, he tapped my arm, "How about you, lovely? Would you like to take part in a skit?"

I crinkled up my nose, "No thank you."

"Ah come on," Fitz insisted. "Have some fun!"

"I'd rather just…watch," I gave her a palms-up.

"Yer bein' a *stick-in-the-mud*! Go on, enjoy." Fitz pushed me toward the sorcerer with blue gown and long white beard.

"It's gonna be fun," the sorcerer promised. "Come on, assist me." It had to be hard to make the *puppy-dog-eyes* beneath fake bushy white eyebrows, but he did.

I forced a smile, "Okay," I let him take me by the hand and lead me to the stage.

Staring back at the crowd that was now staring at me, I began to fidget. I had no idea where to stand or what to do with my hands. I was put just off stage until I received a cue.

"What's your name, honey?" whispered the sorcerer.

"Janie," I told him.

"Okay," he turned and walked back out onto the stage and began to tell a story of long, long ago.

I could see Fitz from where I stood out of direct sight. Her eyes spied me and she waved like a proud parent watching her child at a school talent show.

"Long, long ago, a sorcerer sat in his castle…" he began. "He stood over his cauldron, alone and weary. A wish, he threw to the sky; I wish for a beautiful woman to spend my days with…to love and adore." Magically a cauldron appeared.

A rope with a cauldron attached was pulled from one side of the stage to present the cauldron to the onlookers.

As the sorcerer stood over the cauldron whispering magical words, I put my hands in my pockets to keep from wringing them.

Removing the cauldron's lid, a plume of smoke rose. "What attributes should I wish for?" he asked the crowd. "Should I make her…skinny as a rail?" He picked up a potion jar from the table then shook his head, no. "Then we'll use no *skinny and frail*," he put the jar down, as the crowd chuckled.

"Should I make her plump in the rump?" The sorcerer grinned slyly and made ass-grabbing motions with his hands. Nodding, he said "We'll need *hubba bubba lumps* to make her rump plump," he grabbed another jar which looked like it held cubes of sugar. "Only one lump?" he asked the crowd.

"NO," the crowd yelled.

"Well, maybe two…will do?" he tapped his chin. "But I like me a plump rump…round, you see!" he nodded, "so not one will do, or two, maybe three!"

The crowd roared.

"And now what about the bumps…ya know, the lumps on the

front?" he looked off like he was deep in thought. "Tiny?" he grabbed another jar, "not with that hiney!" he shook his head before setting it down. "Or should I make them gigantic?" his eyes rounded as he pondered. "Should I make them gigantic? Enormous? Titanic?" he used his arms to display boobs so huge, he then staggered off kilter. "Although it would be fun to nestle in such lumps," his face went dreamy.

The laughter of the crowd again rang out.

Then a look of horror crossed his face, "But certainly I would cease to breath in THOSE epic bumps." His tongue then lolled out of his mouth as if dead.

"I'll make them perfect, perky and round, not ever so tiny," he made the tiny sign with this thumb and forefinger, "or touching the ground," he stomped around stage pretending to carry a set of huge boobs about.

I was cracking up with the crowd when I was handed a black witches hat and a wand made out of a gnarled piece of wood. "Put it on before you go on stage," said a young stagehand.

"And now on to her glorious lips," he let out a sigh, "this is my favorite part. If she uses them well, she'll surely win my..." he looked down towards his crotch sexily, "heart," he feigned a look of embarrassment. "I like the top lip curved like beautiful hips," he made the female form with his hands. "I like the bottom lip full, just like I like her..." a devilish grin made his eyes slit "personality!" he tried to look innocent. "I do love my lips to have a full, warm, engaging, never has a headache...um...personality," he was drawn back to himself.

The crowd roared again. His expressions were so hilarious I almost forgot that at some point, I would be expected to walk out onto that stage. A slight woman with dark shoulder length hair and emerald green contacts walked herself up to me.

"Hi, I'm Morah," she smiled sweetly.

"Janie," I smiled back.

"Okay, so, he's going to finish his song, throw a handful of something in the cauldron; there'll be a flash-bang of smoke, then you'll arrive on stage behind the plume, wearing the witch's hat."

I nodded, "Okay," pretty sure I could do this. "Then what?"

"Oh, well he's gonna thank the universe for you…then he'll pretend to get handsy…you just lightly smack his check, look appalled, use the wand like you're casting a spell then strut off stage," she flashed a white smile.

I had all of this down except for the strut-thing. I couldn't strut in Converse, I thought. Then it dawned on me…I didn't really strut well in heels, either.

I listened to his song; it was hysterical as he begged the universe for a woman to liking, "Let her be a doll," he threw in some herbs as he sang. "Let her know what makes me tick…and if you can swing it…make sure she likes…" his eyes rounded for effect as a slide whistle emphasized his unsaid words.

Laughter rang through the crowd.

As the sorcerer grabbed several different potion jars, he sprinkled a little from each onto the fire, "Big blue eyes…with love they will stare…flowing long tresses…of gold colored hair. My own sexy plaything," he humped the air, "with an angelic smile," he folded his hands into the position of prayer. "And please makes sure…she loves herself some doggie…" he pursed his lips and covered his mouth like he said a naughty. "I mean…make sure she's a…dog person," he corrected and winked for the crowd then dumped all the contents from that jar into the cauldron to the screams, whistling and clapping of the audience.

"Okay," said the slight dark haired Morah, "get ready!"

I put on the witches hat and leaned out just a little to see Fitz, waiting for the sorcerer's song to end.

The look on Fitzy's face changed as she cocked her head at me and dropped her jaw.

As I began to walk on stage to the roars of the crowd, I saw the sorcerer throw the handful of something into the cauldron. A flash so high and loud caught me off guard and stopped me before I hit my mark. Fire sprung from the cauldron making even the sorcerer step back in dismay. Eight foot flames erupted upward, catching the pulled back stage curtain aflame. Everyone "*Oooohd*" until they realized that this wasn't part of the show. People backstage began to rush about.

Through the crowd of rushing stagehands and smoke, I heard an Irish accent scream coming my way, "No!"

Before I could even see what was going on, I was tackled by Fitz. Covering my body with hers, she yelled, "I won't let them burn ya as a witch!"

We could have been a mile from the contained flames for as far from me as they actually were. Underneath the weight of her body smashing into mine, I said, "Thanks Fitz," as the fire was put out by someone casually walking past, spraying a fire extinguisher.

The crowd hadn't moved and as the smoke cleared they began applauding seeing that the sorcerer had not only received one woman for his *casting*, but two! As the sorcerer helped Fitz up, then me, the onlookers yelled and whistled.

"Take a bow, ladies," said the sorcerer to us. Joining hands, the three of us bowed to our audience.

When all calmed down a bit I told the sorcerer, Malcolm, that I enjoyed the play very much before the *exploding cauldron* thing.

"I don't know what happened," he said. "I've done this show a hundred times. It's just supposed to be a small flash-bang, then I get a little handsy, you wave the wand…turning me into a toad."

Fitz raised an eyebrow, "Hear that, Janie…never happened before."

I nodded knowing this was a sign for her, that I wasn't quite ready to accept as a sign. "Yes, and as you can see…it all worked out fine…everything is okay."

Malcolm stared at the two of us, confused by our conversation.

"Well, I'll need to get new curtains, but yeah, I guess the ending worked out okay."

As Fitz and I enjoyed the rest of the fair, I had to ask her, "So now can we put all of this *burned as a witch* behind us?"

Fitz thought for a moment as she licked her *Magical Night* ice cream cone. It was really just blueberry ice cream with edible gold glitter. "Yeah, I think we can safely say we averted the fate Mum, Marble and the psychic saw," she nodded.

I grinned a little at her take on things. "By the way, thank you again for coming to my rescue."

Fitz grabbed my hand in hers, "If yer goin', I'm goin' with ya! That alone should be enough fer God to keep a close eye on ya… and the devil to side-step ya," she laughed.

I laughed, "I'd have to agree."

The rest of the fair had great wares being sold. But I had to remind myself that whatever I purchased had to fit in my luggage. I bought a few small trinkets for Mum and Marble; tiny fairy necklaces with different colored glitter. I knew my mom wouldn't really appreciate anything from a new-age fair. I pictured giving her a medicine bag; I could see the horror on her face as she took it to the church to be properly discarded after being drenched in holy water. I loved my mother and had grown fully aware of her stringent outline of good and evil from my very first Hail Mary. But I did have to wonder if she ever considered the fact that according to her own beliefs, God had made all the stones and herbs that the medicine bag contained. This to me was logic…to my mother…it was sacrilege.

As I pondered what to get my mother, my phone rang. I couldn't help but wonder if my thoughts had set off the *mom signal.* Looking at the name flashing across the screen, I let out a grateful sigh; it was Miss Betty.

"Hi Betty," I sang into the receiver.

"Hi yerself, Puddin! How the hell are ya?"

"Better now...and I think you may have had a hand in that," I giggled.

"Boy yer mama's mouth sure did drop when Larry's youngest boy showed her his bondage gear," she laughed. "Complete with nipple rings," she added.

Laughing I said, "It must have been quite the sight. I would have paid money to see it."

"Well, I did snap off a picture for ya. I'll send it to ya," she laughed.

"Well, tell the boys *thank you* for me. And for going that extra mile...I mean, Drag? William must have a great sense of humor. Most men would freak out if you tried to get them into ladies clothing."

"Not him," Betty said.

"No?" I questioned.

"No Puddin, he actually *DOES* a drag show once a week down off of Vine in Hollywood."

I pondered; was William gay? Did he feel like a woman trapped in a man's body? Or did he just like women's clothes? This could go so many ways. And regardless of how it went, he still looked better in a dress than I did, I'm sure. "Is he..." I just left the question hanging in the air, reluctant to accidentally cause any offense.

"No, he's straight. And his girlfriend, cutest little thing ya ever did see, by the way, she dresses like a man and they do a skit together. It's really funny. Ya need to come with me to see it, sometime."

I grinned, "I would absolutely love that."

"Now the other one...with the bondage gear...I don't know what his thing is, and I find it's better not to ask," Betty laughed.

I couldn't help but think about it for a moment, "I'm with you on that one," I agreed.

"So is everything else goin' well?" she wanted to know.

I explained to her about the mess-up with the Frick Collection, and she howled with laughter. I told her about the *gay dance off* I was almost dragged into and how that ended.

"Oh honey," she giggled, "the strangest damn things happen to ya!"

"Speaking of strange…" I told her about the odd cab driver.

Betty went silent for a moment. So silent I almost thought we had been disconnected then she "*Hmmm'd*."

"What? What are you thinking?" I asked her.

"Well, Puddin, I'm thinkin' I should get ya a gun," she told me.

My head started shaking furiously, "No, I don't feel…safe with a gun."

"You feel safer without one?" she asked.

This I had to ponder, "I really don't know."

"Well, when ya get home…I wanna take ya to the range. Just so you can get some idea of what it's like. If yer still uncomfortable, I'll never bring it up again. But ya may still get a Taser in yer stockin'."

I laughed, "Fair enough. I miss you."

"I miss you, too, Puddin. Come home soon."

"Will do. Keep an eye on my mother," I giggled.

"Will do," she giggled back and rang off.

After updating Fitz, she cracked up, "I want to go to the drag show, too!"

"I'm pretty sure you were included in the invite," I told her. "Betty loves you."

"I love her, too," Fitz beamed. "Hard to believe just a few months ago, she was just yer landlady. Funny how things change! Ya know we have to bring yer mom, right."

My eyes nearly popped out of my head, "Oh now it'll be even more fun!"

We walked and shopped a bit more, "Where to now?" I asked.

"What time are we to be at Tovah's?" Fitz cocked her head at me.

"Nine," I answered.

"We better head back!"

"Now? It's four o'clock, Fitz."

"Well it's gonna take me awhile to look just perfect in my costume."

"Ah, the surprise costume you brought...and won't let me see!" I raised a brow to her.

"Why would that surprise ya? Every year I pick a costume and keep it secret until the big reveal," she said dramatically.

"I brought a costume fer ya as well, although now, I'm not sure it's a good idea."

I had to laugh remembering some of her costumes. She really did go all out. One year she had a casket wheeled into the pub. Suddenly the lights went out and shrieks played over the speakers as she re-enacted the rise of Dracula's Bride.

My brow furrowed as I considered what it could possibly be. "Well, you already knew I wouldn't want to dress up."

"Stick in the mud," she said under her breath.

"But out of curiosity, what did you have packed for me?"

Fitz let out a deep breath, "Witch's costume."

I held back a giggle and nodded, "Yeah, I've had enough of pointed hats and wands for the day."

Just then my phone dinged letting me know I had received a message. Looking at the screen, I almost peed myself. Turning the screen toward Fitz, she busted up. "I'm gonna need that framed!" she said seriously.

"Hell, *THIS* is my Christmas Card this year!"

There stood my mother with Larry's sons, one on each side with their arms around her: one in full drag, and yes, stunning. The other just in his bondage vest and a pair of tight black briefs, that left absolutely NOTHING to the imagination. And the best part, even though mom looked appalled and slightly offended, she was looking down at bondage-boy's package. But as Fitz pointed out after her laughing slowed, mom was probably just trying to make sure it wasn't coming after her.

As Fitz and I pondered calling the car-service vs. a cab, we decided on the subway. True, I hadn't had a great subway experience (being mugged and all), but we had gambled on other modes of transportation that had turned out to be every bit, if not more, nerve-racking.

The subway ride was completely uneventful yet still very entertaining. Fitz and I made up a game we called, *Everyday* or *Holiday*? We had to try and decide if people were in costumes or if this was their natural state of being. In New York on Halloween, this kept us quite busy.

Back at the hotel, Fitz locked herself in her room to prepare for tonight's festivities. I still wasn't sure if we were supposed to dress up for the occasion, but that wouldn't stop Fitz. Honestly, it was one of the reasons I loved her; she did what she did, no matter how it looked to other people. This part of her personality had always drawn me to a place where I could be an observer of, but still wasn't fully immersed in or blessed with, the IDGAF mentality she had in spades.

I showered and shaved the parts of me that mattered, dressed and ordered a burger from room service. After I had chowed-down so hard it left my tummy bloated, my phone rang.

A smile spread from my face to everywhere else when I saw Cecil's name.

"Hi," I said.

"Hello luv, how's my girl?" he said. Normally hearing him say this made me feel all warm and fuzzy, but something in his voice put me on guard. "What's wrong?" I asked.

Letting out a sigh, Cecil started apologizing, "I'm sorry, I won't be able to make it there until the night of the showing."

I actually felt my smile drop and my shoulders droop, "What's going on?"

"I have to fly into Tennessee for a meetin'. Seems our whiskey is causin' a stir. A few of the distributors who want to carry Callaghan's are bein' met with some resistance from shareholders. I have to go and pitch the products, myself. Schmooze, I think is the word someone came up with for this crap."

"Well, I'm sorry that I won't get to see you sooner, but you will be here for the showing, right?"

"Aye, and so will Scotty," Cecil said.

I hadn't thought of that. I wasn't going to have to be the one to tell Fitz Scotty wasn't coming early, either, was I? From the next room I heard Fitz yell, "What the bloody hell!"

"I'm guessing Scotty is telling Fitz, right?" I asked.

"I believe so, yes," Cecil said. He was unaware that this particular ball was being dropped right now, if I wasn't mistaking.

"I really am sorry, luv. How's everything else goin'? Been mugged yet?" he joked.

"Not yet," I sighed. I wondered if I should tell him about the creepy cab driver. But I couldn't see any reason to make him worry. "I miss you so much!" I said.

"I miss ya, too…somethin' awful."

"Um, speaking of something awful," I hesitated.

"What's wrong?"

"My mother wants to meet you." I wondered if this would be where I got the "*It's been nice knowing ya*," speech.

"Well, I assumed that at some point we'd meet. I don't see why this is a problem?" he told me.

In my mind, that was the problem…he didn't understand. "She's just…difficult," I summed her up with one very fitting word.

"More difficult than Ms. Elanor was fer you and Fitz?"

I pondered the question with great thought. Ms. Elanor had

been quite the thorn in our sides. More like a poison dart, at one time. I even told her she reminded me of my mother. But she had come full circle and I enjoyed her now. Could I even hope for the same with Cecil and my mother?

"Janie luv, are ya there?" his words broke me from my thoughts.

"I'm here. Mom's…just kind of judgmental …critical … overbearing…and prudish…"

"I got it. If I'm on my very best behavior, everything will be fine, I'm sure," he laughed.

"Do you have a best behavior?" I joked.

"You should know that better than anyone," he joked back. "I seem to remember some of my best behavior was presented in yer bedroom…"

I giggled and felt my cheeks warm a little.

"…and then some more on yer couch…then there was a bit in the shower…and then a bit more in the kitchen…"

"Okay, I got it," I couldn't stop smiling.

"And yer gonna get more, I can guarantee that!"

"So you're okay with meeting her?"

"I insist. I want to see what you'll look like in twenty years… see what I'm gettin' myself into," he laughed.

When he talked about *twenty years*, the fear of him proposing came back from wherever it had been hiding.

I forced a laugh and said, "I do love you."

"I love ya, too. See ya as soon as I can."

"Okay, I look forward to it…more than anything."

"Soon my luv," he told me then hung up.

I made an ugly pouty face and allowed myself to feel sad for a moment. I really had missed him. If I had to compare the excitement I felt; it was a kid counting down the days until Christmas. And this kid had just been told that Christmas had been pushed back to the 27th.

I didn't get to wallow long, or go over the adult version of my Christmas list, before I heard a thud. It sounded as if something had hit the door, hard.

Rushing to the door, I heard Fitz let out a colorful curse word. Opening the door, she almost took me down to the ground. The door had been holding her upright from what I now understood.

11

THE TRICK: NEVER GROW UP

There she stood, bent over; long red tresses flowing wild. When she finally was able to stand, I got the full picture. Fitz was a mermaid, complete with a clamshell bra and tail. Her skin had been painted a blue-green and her face, my God; her eyes were huge black sockets, her mouth had been painted to look like a skeleton's but with fangs. Streams of crimson ran down the sides of her mouth. More fake blood had dripped down onto her blue-green, clam-shelled breasts. I had to hand it to her; she looked positively fright-inducing…until she tried to walk. Baby stepping like a toddler, with its legs tied together at the knees, she shook and shimmied her way into the room.

I couldn't help but laugh, "How the hell are you gonna walk?"

"Just like this," Fitz said defensively.

"So…we'll get to Tovah's by next Tuesday," I joked.

"I'm not in a jokin' mood," she said like I should be able to read her horrifying face. "Did ya get the call yet? The one sayin' that our men won't be here till the night of the show?" her eyes rounded…I think.

I nodded, "Yeah, Cecil called me," I tried not to sound as bummed as I was.

"I had this all planned out; I was goin' to seduce him," she gave me a serious look.

I was all for seduction, but in this get-up?

"Then when I had him…beggin' for me to finish what I had started, I was gonna make him promise me that he wouldn't wear that damned kilt fer our weddin'!" she laid it all out.

I began laughing, "Why don't you just ask him not to wear the kilt?"

Fitz tried to sit on the bed, but her unbending legs started to cause her to slide. Catching her, I pushed her up until she was in a laying position.

"Pour me a drink, will ya?" she laid there like a colorful sequined burrito from the waist down.

I smirked, "This should be fun to watch!"

Handing her a drink, she raised up her head just enough so she could *lip* the rocks glass. "I can't tell him because he loves Rudolpho," her skeleton painted bottom lip pushed out making her look like she had a severely pointed under bite.

"I'm just gonna go out on a limb here and say that he loves you more."

"Yeah but it would be a *tit for tat*, that way. He wouldn't feel like he was givin' without gettin', ya know?"

"I think there will be plenty of time to…um…give…before the wedding," my head nodded.

"Yeah, but I had this whole routine planned out. And after this," she tried to look down at her body, "I'm not ever gettin' back in this thing!"

"So if you're so miserable, why don't you get out of that; change into something comfortable?"

"I'm green Janie! This took…hours…I'm wearin' the damn costume!"

"You did say you had a witches costume…a witch could be green," I lifted my brows.

"Nah, it's in yer size. It'll never fit me. No offense."

"None taken…asshole."

Fitz sighed deeply, "I guess we should call a cab…or the service and head to Tovah's," she suggested.

We still had an hour until we were expected at Tovah's for… the festivities. I couldn't understand why we were leaving so early. But when I tried to get Fitz to the elevator, it became hilariously clear. Moving three inches at a time, she shuffled her feet in a forward motion. I had to hold on to her so she didn't go off balance and fall flat to the ground. Some sick part of me kind of wanted to watch her try to stand from a laying position. In my head, she would look like a beautiful dolphin…trying to erect itself on its tail. I said as much to Fitz as I laughed at the vision in my head.

"Asshole," she said as we moved five whole feet closer to the elevator.

Ten minutes later, Fitz was breathing hard from the exhaustion her forced tiny steps caused. I had had enough of the shuffling. "That's it! Turn toward me."

"What? I'm almost there!" Fitz bellowed.

My eyes bulged as my head shook, "No, you're not!" I told her.

Turning toward me she asked, "What are ya gonna do?"

Putting my shoulder down around her waist, I lifted her in what was supposed to be a fireman's carry, but of course she couldn't really…bend, so I just carried her sequined ass all the way down the hall to wait for the elevator. By the time I set her on her uni-foot I was breathing hard.

"Have you gained weight?" I huffed.

Fitz's eyes rounded at me, "EXCUSE ME!" she barked. "I'm almost all muscle, except fer my fun bags, I'll have ya know. And everyone knows muscle weighs more than fat!"

"Well, I'll have you know that I've been carrying you for YEARS and this is the first time it's been a struggle," I panted.

"Well maybe, yer not *strong like bull* anymore," she used the movie reference. "But at least yer still built like one!" she flared.

Our eyes met and we both began laughing. "Asshole," we said in unison.

I couldn't see carrying her through the lobby of the Ritz. It just seemed a little more white-trash than we wanted to exude. Not that my next bright idea was much better; Leaning Fitz up against the wall, I went in search of a bellboy with a luggage caddy.

Seeing Fitz, the bellboy's eyes rounded, "Wow Miss, you must really love Halloween!"

Lifting Fitz onto the cart, I told her to hang on to the clothes bar overhead as the bellboy wheeled her outside. Wrapping her woolen trench coat around her and holding her upright against the wind, we waited for our driver.

When our driver pulled up and stepped out of the car, his brow furrowed. "I hate workin' Halloween," said the large black gentleman with a shake of his head.

I picked Fitz up like an oversized Christmas package and leaned her against the town car.

"Hi, I'm Janie and this is Fitz," I told our driver.

The hulk of a man nodded his head, "Edam," he said.

"Uh, this is going to be tricky," I told him, eyeballing the door.

"You don't say," he looked at me with no sign of humor.

"Maybe…we could…lay her down…across the backseat," I fumbled with the idea.

Edam, seeing my wheels turning, said, "I got this." Edam lifted Fitz into a lying position; like she was a poster-board cut-out, and just scooted her in, headfirst. Fitz let out a "*Weee*" as he slid her across the leather seat. Pulling her upper body into an almost, but not fully inclined position, Fitz got enough of her legs in so we could close the door.

"I think I'm going to have to ride up front with you," I winced.

Edam and I stared at each other for a moment before he opened the front passenger door.

As we drove, Fitz chatted away on her phone to Mum about today's events and how Aunt Marble's prediction was correct, but all was well.

The tension between Edam and me was more than uncomfortable as we drove down breathtaking tree-lined streets, hiding the enormous Brownstones behind them.

"Um, I just wanted to say thank you for your help."

Edam nodded and made a deep sound that I couldn't really interpret. It had grunt-like qualities with just a hint of a growl.

"It really goes above and beyond your job description, I'm sure," I offered.

Again Edam made the sound.

"Look I'm really sorry for the inconvenience," I started, getting a little flustered and fidgety from the pissed-off attitude radiating from him.

He shook his head, "Ya know what, I'm sorry. I'm upset and takin' it out on you, and that's not right."

"If you don't mind my asking...what's wrong?" I questioned.

"I was supposed to go trick-or-treating with my girls. I have three babies, 3, 6, and 8. I know they're still young, and I'll have more chances but time flies by so quickly. Missing them being kids, man!" he said and shook his head. "I even requested the night off months ago. But then at the last minute, they said I had to work the 6pm to 2am shift or I'd be fired."

I thought about all the other drivers we had had through this car service. I couldn't help but think they were really threatening to fire the wrong driver. "I'm not going out on a limb at all when I say you must be their best driver."

“I know I am, but I can’t afford to be out of work,” he shrugged.

“I’m sorry to hear that…it’s not right,” I shook my head.

Fitz had joined the conversation, “Not right is damn straight!” she said. “Spending time with yer kids should never be somethin’ ya have to put on the back-burner to protect yer job…it’s bull-shite.”

Edam turned questioning eyes to me, “It’s Irish for bull-shit,” I clarified.

“Yeah, it’s bull-shite,” he agreed with a nod.

As we pulled up in front of Tovah’s, I shook my head.

Fitz was back on the phone but covered the receiver and asked me, “What?” in a hushed voice.

“There’s like twenty stairs, Fitz.”

Fitz arched to try and see through the tinted windows, “Shite!” she said under her breath.

Edam gave us an amused head-shake, “I got you,” he told her.

We stood outside in the cold for a moment while Fitz finished her call. Edam then pulled her out by her legs, stood her upright and carried her up the stairs to the front door of the beautiful Brownstone.

“Funny, it doesn’t look like I’m heavy to him,” Fitz barked over Edam’s shoulder at me.

“You?” Edam asked. “You’re light as a feather!”

Fitz stuck her tongue out at me.

Setting Fitz upright, I started digging for cash to tip him.

“You don’t tip me,” he shook his head.

“I need to thank you properly. I wasn’t kidding when I said you’ve really gone above and beyond for us,” I told him. “Just being delivered here without having thoughts of my mortality has been quite the gift…”

As he continued to shake his head, Fitz said, “Well maybe goin’ home to see yer girls would be a good tip?”

Edam started, “I’d love to, but…”

“But nothin’,” Fitz told him. “I called the service and told them that we needed ya fer the whole night…till 2:30am. They were only too happy to oblige.” Fitz’s smile stretched across her scary face, “Go home…enjoy yer girls.”

“Seriously?” Edam asked her.

Fitz pulled out some cash from in between her boobs and tucked into his enormous palm.

“I can’t take that,” he started to argue.

“Ya can,” Fitz’s face was serious. “I wanna buy those girls of yers some ice-cream…to add to their Halloween candy sugar high.”

Edam gave us each a hug before handing us his personal card, “If you need anything…,” he smiled.

We watched him drive away, “You did a really good thing, Fitz,” I told her.

“Daddy’s are important!” Fitz nodded. “And their babies are only young once,” she added.

I looked at her attire, “There’s some wiggle room for argument in that statement,” I joked.

“Ring the bell…asshole,” she grinned at me.

I rang the doorbell as Fitz stayed propped up against the door frame.

The double door was massive and had black iron scrollwork over leaded glass. When the door opened, I looked up…then up some more.

There stood what I assumed was a butler given his attire; a very tall, thin, elderly man with perfectly styled salt and pepper hair.

Looking from me to Fitz, he said, “We have a candy bowl down the stairs. We appreciate it if the trick-or-treaters help themselves. We also prefer that those who take candy are of,” he cleared his throat, “trick-or-treating age,” he gave Fitz a disapproving look.

Fitz gave him her own displeased once-over, “Excuse me?”

I butted in, “Um, we're here to see Tovah…we're guests of hers.”

He raised an eyebrow, “I'll let the Mrs. know…she'll be so please,” he curled his lip.

“Thanks Jeeves,” Fitz curled her lip back.

His head snapped back when she addressed him this way but all he said was, “Come in, please,” he held the door.

One step was all that separated us from entry and really, there was no classy way to get Fitz inside. Grabbing her around the waist again, I heaved her over the threshold.

The Butler, that Fitz had less than affectionately nick-named Jeeves, gave us a less than approving look.

“I'm sorry, Jeeves,” Fitz said. “Should I have asked you to cradle my curves, instead?”

His eyes rounded as though he had been thoroughly offended by the offer. The look on his face made Fitz's evil-fairy-grin stretch across her frighteningly painted mouth, making the fangs, widen.

Turning his back to us, Jeeves said, “This way…ladies.”

The man although still tall with no visible stoop, shuffled his feet a bit making it look almost as though Fitz was mocking him as she shuffled along behind him. At a slow pace we walked/shuffled down a long hallway. Antiques and amazing art lined the dark wood walls. I couldn't help but be put in mind of the Callaghan manor; high ceilings adorned with crystal chandeliers, the polished wood floors that you could see your reflection in, were wearing Oriental rugs in crimson and gold. Fresh flowers sat in huge crystal vases. Tovah's home boasted *LUSH,* but somehow, without an ounce of pretension.

Maybe it was because I knew her to be such a *wild thing*, that I didn't fidget nearly as much as I expected I would. I knew she loved the finer things. But her value of these things was in the fact that she loved them; not what they cost, were worth, or what other people would think of her based on having them.

Short walk, long; we ended up in a huge library; lush again, the brown leather roll armed couches and armchairs were decorated with crimson and gold striped silk pillows. One whole wall was nothing but shelves of books from floor to almost ceiling. A ladder on rollers was needed to reach anything on the top three shelves. There was a very ornate dark wood desk that seemed to me like it would dwarf Tovah completely. I noticed that the desk chair was raised as high as the seat would go. A small bar sat against the far wall with decanters of liquor wearing their own silver name-baring tags. One said GIN, another, SCOTCH and then there was my favorite, WHISKEY; all engraved in scrolled lettering. The long drapes carried on the gold and crimson stripes of the pillows and hung every six feet across a wall of windows. What looked like Renaissance style artwork covered another wall.

I didn't know any of the artists names. In fact, I had never seen any of these paintings before. Yet, they looked old (but well cared for) and of professional grade. I stood captivated in front of one, just lost in its beauty.

Four women stood around a stone water well, holding light pink silk ties that connected in the middle, making what looked like a wheel. They appeared to be dancing around the well; the smiles on their faces, euphoric, blissful. I wasn't sure why, but for a moment, I could see them moving in my mind's eye; dancing, laughing and singing. A smile pulled across my own face.

"Oh my word, aren't you a frightening beauty!" I heard Tovah say and turned in time to see her and Fitzy embrace. Walking toward me, Tovah asked, "No costume for you, huh kid?"

We hugged before I said, "Someone had to be available to carry Fitz around; down hallway's…up stairs…to the toilet…really looking forward to that one," I nodded. "I find that more easily done when not dressed like a French maid."

Tovah gave me that one sided grin, "Somehow I knew you'd be standing in front of this particular painting."

"Really," I cocked my head.

"Absolutely, I wish I would have had someone here to take odds on it...would of made a fortune."

"It is beautiful," I looked back at the painting. "I've never heard of the artist, though," I admitted.

Tovah's smile stretched further across her face, "Ellie Goldstein, was her name," she reached out to lightly touch the canvas, "she was my great-great-grandmother."

"Wow," I said, somewhat stunned. "She was very talented."

"I believe she was," Tovah gave her head a nod. "But back then, it was hard for a woman to break into..." she hesitated, "well, almost anything. Art, along with most other things, was male dominated."

I tried to think of any female artists of that time, circa the late 1800's, I guessed. I knew the painting by Cecilia Beaux; *Sita and Sarita*, drew some attention in the late 1800's for having a *witch-like quality*, one critic had said. I knew of Florine Stettheimer, Anne Goldthwaite and Elizabeth Shippen Green, all amazing artists who received very little acclaim until the feminist art movement of the 1960's and 70's.

"She's the reason I wanted to own a gallery," Tovah smiled. "I wanted a place where great art would be viewed as great art regardless of who the artist was," she gave me a palms-up.

"Ya could have made your Gallery for women artists only, then," Fitz thought out loud.

"I could have," Tovah nodded, "but I just can't understand how oppressing one sex, one race, one...anybody...could somehow equal, equality," she shook her head. "If segregating was wrong when it was done to someone in the first place, more segregation, bigotry and sexism, isn't going to make things right.

It's simply a form of retaliation at that point…and this will do nothing but separate us even further."

This was yet another reason why I loved Tovah; she accepted the past as a learning experience; a place to move forward and upward from, proudly, without using blame as a crutch. She was powerful and within moments of being in her presence, you knew this, felt it radiate from her. I felt stronger just standing beside her, like a little of her could rub off on me.

"Are these all hers?" Fitz asked, examining the other paintings.

Tovah shook her head, "No. Unfortunately my family couldn't bring much with them when they came to America."

Fitz cocked her head, "Where did your family immigrate from?"

Tovah gave her sardonic smile, "Poland…April of 1939."

My eyes rounded as I considered what 1939 Poland would have meant to her family.

Seeing the look on my face, Tovah grinned, "The last thing my great-great grandmother said before she died was "It's time. You must leave and go to America." She told her girls she loved them then passed away. They left Poland two weeks later with very little. This painting and two more, made it to America. Benny has one, Vah has the one her mother left her when she passed, and I have this," she touched the canvas again.

"They never questioned why they had to leave their home?" Fitz asked.

"They had it on good faith that great-great-grandma always had…a way about her. They never questioned her when it came to…well, anything," Tovah shrugged. "And it was more than a given that she had great insight when it came to her family. The family didn't know for some time just what the move had saved them from."

The horror of this reality hit me hard and my face showed it.

Tovah patted my hand, "It hurts my heart, too," she nodded to me as my eyes began to water.

I felt myself being drawn to another painting, but this one… this one left me with mixed feelings. It was well done…beautiful work really, but something about it turned my stomach.

"How do you feel about this one?" Tovah watched me.

"I…think it's well done. I think the colors, shading, light, are all…great."

"Okay, once again, how do you feel about this painting? Or better yet, how does this painting *make* you feel?"

Biting my lower lip, I hoped a family member of hers hadn't painted this piece. "Well…" I considered my words carefully. "It's not the one I like most."

"You, my dear are practicing the great art of *bullshit and avoidance*."

I winced knowing how transparent I was. Absolutely refusing to lie to her but trying desperately not to offend her.

"If I tell you I won't be offended by whatever your opinion is, will you give your *FULL* honesty?"

I nodded feeling just as conflicted as I had just openly revealed myself to be.

"I will NOT be offended," Tovah laughed at me. "Take it in and tell me what you *FEEL*."

"Okay," I let out a long breath.

I stood and cocked my head. Before me was a painting of four women; on the right stood a young girl, maybe 9 or 10. Her smile was carefree and full of what I saw as joyfulness.

A woman stood next to her with her arm around the child; she bore the look of pure exhaustion, but somehow, still seemed very content. Her smile was small, but her eyes were happy. My immediate feeling, while really looking at her, brought to my mind the old saying; *This, Too, Shall Pass.*

The third woman, who had her arm around the second

woman, was an old woman; her skin was lined, her eyes didn't shine as brightly as the two before her. There was something in those eyes though; she had lived….and lived well. She knew great love…she knew many things. Wisdom and tenderness pushed their way off of the canvas when I looked at her. She was the mother, of the mother of the child. I was sure of it.

But the fourth, she did not touch the other women, her hands clutching something to her chest as she turned her body away from the others. Standing in a slight shadow, she held onto whatever was in her hand, like she would not share. Whatever she was coveting shined like a precious stone or gem. Her eyes were cold, hard and I could almost feel her disdain for the others in the painting. I saw her as greedy, calculating and not to be trusted.

When I finally explained what I thought and felt, Tovah nodded.

"These are the four faces of the Goddess," she told me.

Being completely new to this Goddess stuff, my face wrinkled up, "I really don't know what that means."

"The first," she pointed to the girl, "is the Maiden. She is who we are as we start on this journey of womanhood. She is *innocence* and *wonder*."

I nodded.

"The second, as you may have guessed is the Mother. This stage of life is when you are grown, have blossomed. She is the *bringer of life*, the *protector* and the *teacher*. She is *sacrifice*…that's why she looks so tired," Tovah joked.

A laugh escaped me as I nodded some more.

"The third woman, is *The Wise Woman* or *Death Crone*, as some call her. She holds all the wisdom, secrets and teachings of those who have come before her. She is *magic* at her very finest."

I let out a sigh knowing that if we are truly lucky, truly blessed, we become her.

"The fourth…" Tovah raised one brow to me.

I too, raised my brow. This was the one that bothered me, the one I wanted to know more about.

"The fourth face of the Goddess…is *Darkness*," Tovah shook her head like it was a shame that she existed.

I shook my head, too. I was taught not to be afraid of the dark, but I assumed she had a whole other meaning than *be home by the time the street lights came on.* "So, she's like the Boogy-Man," I joked.

"In a way," Tovah's head cocked. "She is everything dark. She is greed and jealously…envy and resentment. She has a liar's tongue and a soul that offers destruction and condemnation without guilt. Her warped conscience talks to her, much like your overabundant conscience talks to you. But hers tells her that she is never culpable for the suffering she has caused. She is not accidental; she chooses this, just as she chooses to feed the dark side of herself and bring sorrow to those around her."

I was shocked…but not shocked. I had personally known women like this in my life, if I thought about it.

Fitz piped up, "So yer sayin' these women *CHOOSE* to be this way?"

"Absolutely. It comes down to this; The Beast YOU feed…is the one who runs the pack. You feed goodness and love, or in your case," she pointed to me, "fear and worry," she grinned, "that's what *RUNS* your pack!"

I stood there mentally going over my pack. "Son-of-a-bitch!" I said under my breath.

"Exactly!" Tovah exclaimed. "Now, on to your paintings; I want to know more about *The Blue Woman*."

Fitz's eyes rounded as she mouthed *The Blue Woman*, and pointed at me from behind Tovah's back. Fitz covered her mouth with her palm.

My head cocked; when Tovah saw the painting of *The Blue Woman* at my home, she had showed interest in her. At the time, she had asked if I would display the painting in her Gallery. As much as I loved the idea of someone else loving and wanting my work, I couldn't bring myself to put her out there. In all truthfulness *The Blue Woman* wasn't just a painting my mind pulled out of nowhere…it was a self-portrait. The dark blues used, almost black in some areas, showed the confusion surrounding me; the face with its eyes closed tightly, a side view, was turning away from whatever light the painting held. It was done at a time when my life was in turmoil, even if I wouldn't admit it to myself, it was right there for me to see. I even remembered wanting to add bright colors to the painting, to make it have a meaning other than what it was. But in the end, I saw her for what she was; saw me for who I was, everything I was feeling at that time. And even though I struggled with what I knew the painting meant, I talked myself into believing that it was just an emotional day that pulled the swirling midnight blues around me. But somewhere deep inside… I knew the truth.

"What about her?" I asked.

"As you remember, I took pictures of all of your paintings," Tovah said.

I nodded, knowing that she had.

"I can't get that piece out of my head, kid," Tovah's head shook a bit. "If you don't mind my asking, what does she mean to you?"

I stared into those deep eyes of hers for a moment before dropping my own to the ground. "She's a *Reminder*. She reminds me that…things have been worse, no matter what I'm going through." My own head began to shake, "She reminds me that I don't ever have to be there again…not that I won't ever feel that way again…but that I don't have to stay there."

Tovah was nodding, "What else has she taught you?" she asked softly, reaching out to take my hands in hers.

My eyes welled a little, "That I deserve better…especially from myself."

I looked to Fitz and saw her dab the sides of her own eyes.

Tovah smiled and leaned in to kiss both of my cheeks, "Then she's done her job. Maybe…you could let her go, now?"

Biting my lower lip, I thought about it. She was a big part of…me.

"Maybe, you should paint another self portrait…one of who you are now. One of who you've had the courage to become?" Tovah suggested.

Maybe she was right. Maybe seeing who I had allowed myself to be, didn't have as much of a driving effect as seeing who I had made myself into.

A smile pulled across my face and I nodded. "Will I be able to get the painting here in time for the show?"

"You leave that up to me," Tovah said.

My face squished up wondering how she could do that.

But oddly enough, I started to feel lighter in a way, like I was truly letting go of who I once was. It wasn't a feeling I had expected to have, but it was welcome.

Fitz started shuffling toward Tovah and me. She threw her hands up in the air, "I'm so proud of ya, Janie," she said as she inched her way closer, literally. "This is ridiculous," she said, starting to huff.

Laughing, Tovah and I met Fitz the rest of the way and had a group hug.

Tovah and I took a seat on the couch while Fitz tried to lean against its rolled arm.

Tovah had drinks brought in and I was happy to see that a love of great art wasn't the only thing we had in common. As her butler passed each of us a doubles glass with whiskey on the rocks, he gave Fitz another disapproving look. Shaking his head he shuffled back out of the room.

"What's with Jeeves, anyway?" Fitz asked Tovah.

I almost spit whiskey through my nose and shook my head.

Tovah cracked up, "Did you just call him Jeeves?"

"I did," Fitz admitted.

"That's hilarious!" Tovah clapped her hands to a joke Fitz and I didn't get. "You see, he was my husband's butler. He never liked me when we were dating, kind of gave me the cold shoulder and did that lip curl thing at me."

"I got the lip curl, too," Fitz told her.

Tovah laughed harder, "The day we announced our engagement, oh that man was fit to be tied. He gasped, rolled his eyes, I thought his head was gonna blow off his shoulders. Finally, I took him aside and told him, whether you like it or not, I am going to be the woman of this house and you will treat me with some damned respect as such. If you can't do that, you and I are going to have a problem. Do you understand me, Jeeves?"

Fitz and I began to laugh, "Seriously?" I asked.

"Yep. I called him Jeeves for almost two years before he finally told me his name."

"What did yer husband say about yer…battle?" Fitz asked.

"He said, I married you because you are a strong beautiful woman…who takes no shit from anyone," she added with a grin, "I don't ever want you to stop being that woman for anyone."

Fitz nodded, "Alright Mr. Schumer!"

"Absolutely," Tovah nodded. "So eventually I broke Jeeves down and found out his name is Wilson. You must have brought on one hell of a flashback for him," she winked at Fitz.

Fitz's laughed so hard her ass slid off the arm of the couch. Neither Tovah, nor myself were fast enough to catch her as she hit the floor with a thud.

"Dammit," Fitz howled. "I couldn't even shift in this damn thing to move the impact point. I landed straight on my ass-bone," she winced.

"Are you okay?" I leaned over to heft her upright.

"You were right about this damned costume. I'm gettin' ready to strip it off and just wear my coat!" Fitz huffed.

"No need," I said, pulling the witches robe costume out of my purse. "I knew there was no way in hell that you would make it through the night in that get-up."

"Ah Janie, what would I do without ya and yer magic bag?" she kissed my cheek. "Now...I need ya to come with me to the restroom and peel me out of this thing so I don't fall again and break my already cracked ass?"

Tovah pointed the way to the restroom. Trying to peel Fitz from her zombie-mermaid costume reminded me of the *great leather pants* incident in the 10th grade.

They were the great leather pants, because they made my ass look great...to a degree. That time, it had been Fitz and me as well. But that time, I was the one who had become glued inside her pants.

An unexpected heat wave hit Southern California hard causing everyone everywhere to sweat buckets. Fortunately for most, they hadn't worn their brand new ass-shaping leather pants. I can still remember sitting on the toilet seat in a locker room bathroom stall, my legs fully stretched out in front of me, as Fitz pulled and yanked, both of us grunting and cursing.

Trisha Addison thought she would spread the rumor that she saw the two of us indulging in a little *girl-on-girl* action. What she didn't expect was that Marne would be the one to show her another kind of *girl-on-girl* action that she really wasn't going to enjoy.

Trisha, known to the boys as *Trish the Dish*, spent the better part of ten minutes with her head shoved in a toilet until she admitted she had lied and apologized. And it wasn't just any toilet Marne had dunked Trish's face into...it was the boys bathroom toilet, known as the *Devil's Hole*. A large crowd of good Catholic boys cheered Marne on. If I had known then, what I know now, I would have had to wonder whether she was just defending Fitz and me, or if she was also taking a stand for all gay women, everywhere. Either way, she was always the Aramis to our Athos and Porthos (or the Curly to our Larry and Moe). *Trish the Dish* was known as *Trish the Fish*, from that day forward.

As I stood in front of Fitz, the memory was too real to want to relive. Completely out of breath, cheeks turning red, I asked, "Are you *REALLY* attached to that damned costume?"

"I promise I will never pull this damn sausage casing up over my thighs again. Just get me the hell out of this thing!"

Reaching into my magic-bag as Fitz had called it, I found my buck knife. "You're sure about this?" I asked as I clicked the blade open.

"How the hell did ya get that on the plane?" Fitz's face contorted.

Shrugging, "It was in my purse when it went through the detector!"

Fitz's red mane, wild, her eyes set on mine, "Cut it!" she said through a tightened jaw. Beginning at her ankles, I ran the blade upward. Every inch that tore free made Fitz's smile widen.

"How the hell did you breathe in this thing?" I asked as I pulled just enough fabric away from her body to slide the blade underneath as carefully as possible.

"Tiny breaths," Fitz closed her eyes as little round bits of sequins flew.

I shook my head, "What you put yourself through!"

"The struggle is real," she panted. As the last inch of fabric was released, she yelled at the top of her lungs, "*FREEDOM*!"

All down Fitz's legs were tiny indents from what was supposed to be scales. Lifting her off the ground I caught a view of her booty-shorts that read *Enter at Your Own Risk*.

"Why would you wear something that says that?" I pointed to her shorts.

"I was supposed to see Scotty," she answered like this was a stupid question.

"Yeah," I nodded, "but those make it sound like there's something…wrong going on down there."

"It's supposed to mean there is danger ahead…like I'm warnin' him of what I have in store for him."

"No, I get that. Unfortunately, it seems like what you have in…store, will have him going to a free clinic," I laughed.

Fitz looked down and squished up her face, "Huh, I guess that could be taken…wrong."

"Little bit," I told her while wadding the mermaid rag into a ball and putting the torn remnants in my bag. Scooping up all of the sequins that had popped free, I made sure we left the bathroom as we found it…impeccable.

Fitz was busy taking nice deep breaths, "I never thought just breathin' would feel so friggin' fantastic."

"Glad to be of service," I told her.

"Hey, ya know how you and Tovah were talkin' about, The Blue Woman…?"

"Yeah," I nodded.

"Don't ya remember the reading? She said she saw a Blue Woman!"

I just stared at her. It wasn't like the thought hadn't entered my mind. But as soon as I found myself humoring the idea, I had rejected it.

"Ya have to admit, that's a little on the nose," Fitz looked at me sidelong.

"I'll admit it's a strange coincidence," I allowed the thought.

"Yer still unwillin' to believe? Ya know, If God has to work too much harder to convince ya, yer probably not gonna like it much when he finally does," Fitz warned.

I gave her an eye roll, "Let's get back to Tovah. I'm sure she heard your cry of liberation."

12

THE BAT-SHIT-CRAZY-MAN . . . COMETH

Back in the Library we went where we interrupted a call already in progress; Tovah looked as though her last nerve had someone dangling from it.

I pointed back toward the door, silently asking if she'd like privacy for the call. Tovah shook her head *no*.

"Look, we've been over this...I told you I had no room for your work in my Gallery," Tovah said into the receiver.

There was silence while my brow furrowed.

"No...you misunderstood the comment. What I was being too polite to say was that there is no room for art work *such as yours* in my Gallery. Now I don't know how you got my home number, but I suggest you lose it and say goodnight as politely as you can muster."

There was another moment of silence before I saw Tovah's eyes slit, "You sir, and I use the term lightly, have threatened the wrong woman. You don't ask for a favor, and a big favor is exactly what my doing this would be, and then raise your voice to me, lowering your respect for me!"

She didn't raise her voice; she didn't sound threatening in any way, shape or form. But the way she used her words; direct, unflinching and final, let me know she was pissed-off. I bit my bottom lip like I myself need fear her wrath.

The last thing Tovah said before she hung up the phone was, "Bring an army then, son....you're gonna need one!"

Grabbing her rocks glass, she walked over to the whiskey decanter and poured herself a double. "Refresher?" she held up the decanter to offer us a pour. Grabbing our glasses in complete silence, we walked over to her and let her pour us each a double as well. I couldn't help it, I knew her displeasure had nothing to do with me, and still, I cowered a little.

"What's goin' on?" Fitz asked.

"Oh, I have this deranged artist who keeps insisting I promote his work," she took a long pull off her drink.

Now I was a little worried. I saw the exact same look I knew I was wearing, reflected on Fitz's face.

"This guy," Fitz began, "would his name be...John?"

A look of bewilderment flashed across Tovah's face. She looked from me to Fitz to me again, "How do you know his name?"

I covered my eyes with my hands, "Oh shit."

"Is John a cab driver?" Fitz needed to be sure the John in question was the same man that was harassing us. I, on the other hand, had no doubt.

"Oh shit is right," Tovah said. "Has he contacted you personally? What has he done? Has he threatened you?" Tovah may not have ever carried a baby in her womb, but her mommy face and body language, was that of a *scary-assed-mother-bear's.*

"Not exactly," I said. "He picked Fitz and me up one day..."

"Twice," Fitz reminded me.

"Right," I nodded. "The first time, he made mention of having seen a picture of me and my bio on your Gallery's site. He called me by name."

Tovah moved closer to me, "And the second time?" she raised her brow.

"It was weird…he implied that my work was only being shown due to nepotism," I told her. "Then Fitz and I had a late night; we got back to the hotel at around 3-ish, and he was there in the cold…just standing outside at the far end of the building."

"He just stared at us, then when I started to walk toward him, he moved into the darkness and just…disappeared," Fitz shook her head.

I couldn't tell by Tovah's face which emotion was in the forefront of her brain; *worry* was present and accounted for, but the starring-roll was still *pissed.*

"How dare he!" she hissed. Walking over to her huge desk, she rolled out a hidden shelf that held her laptop. Bringing up the Museum's page, she moved to another file she had created; The JOHN file.

As the file unloaded its contents onto the screen, there was a picture of John; walking a New York street while sipping coffee, then another and another and another.

"How did you get these pictures?" I wondered out loud.

"You have to see the emails he's sent me over the past three years to fully understand." Tovah moved to another file and as she pulled up the most recent email, I noticed that it said 1 of 147. "I have them numbered from last to first so I could show the police how the threat has escalated. His first emails were praises of the Gallery: kind words about a few of the showings. I assumed by the pictures he had sent, he was actually in attendance. Nothing about his posts seemed odd or out of place," she shook her head. "Then he started sending me personal information about some of the artists I had presented…really personal; sexual preference, drug use, people who cheated on their spouses, mistresses names."

My brow furrowed, "Why?" I gave her a palms-up.

Tovah shook her head, "After I wiped his posts from the page,

I sent him a personal correspondence, basically just telling him that the artists' personal lives were neither mine, nor his, business. I show their artwork, period. I am not interested in private aspects of their lives that they have chosen not to share with me. I would be remiss if I did not inform you that any further posts will be sent to a SPAM file and you will be blocked; not only from this site, but also banned from my Gallery. If you persist, I will bring action against you, as well as recommend that the artists do the same," she read her email.

"So…what happened?" Fitz shrugged.

"He sent me an email, apologizing, saying that he now realized that his actions were in poor form. I didn't hear from him for months, so I figured he was a whack-job that had backed down after being schooled. That wasn't the case," she shook her gray faux-hawk, again. "A few months went by then I started noticing rude comments under some of the photos of paintings and other artwork on the site. People leave all kinds of remarks about the art; they love it…or *that piece would look great in my office*…that kind of thing, right?"

I nodded, wondering what would be said about my own work.

"Well then there were his replies," she brought up a few of them: *Looks like a three year old painted this with his boogers.*

Fitz's face showed disgust, "That's so wrong."

We read another: *I've seen better art on bathroom stall walls.*

My face squished up, "Did he reply on…all of them?"

"All of them!" Tovah confirmed. "I'm running a Gallery, not a gossip and slander page. So I had to have everything he sent, go straight to a SPAM file. He's not completely without grey matter and changed his email a few times. But as soon as we got something horribly derogatory, we'd block that one, too," Tovah sighed. "Eventually I had to go to the police with everything. Even though he had posed no real physical threat, a good friend of mine cyber-searched him; found out where he lived and then another old friend, a detective, paid him a visit."

"Okay, but he's still..." I couldn't even come up with a word, "harassing you?" What I really wanted to say was harassing you and now terrorizing me.

"He was quiet again for months and then just like the tide, he rose again," Tovah finished her drink. "That's not the worst of it..." Tovah pulled up another file she had affectionately named the *Bat-shit* file.

As Fitz and I watched the screen, both of our faces contorted.

"Is that a squirrel...dressed as a ninja...with a lightsaber?" Fitz asked for confirmation of what exactly her eyes were seeing.

I had seen memes of squirrel ninjas online and they were kind of cute, funny. These on the other hand were not cute or funny in the slightest.

Tovah sighed and nodded, "Yep...and all the blood you see, is from the squirrel's attack on the acorn. See the bleeding crack in it?" she pointed to the screen.

My jaw dropped, "Is this...*HIS* artwork?"

"It is...and he's sent quite a few more of them...all ninja squirrels...all very gruesome," Tovah stood to refill her drink.

"He's a *bloody-nutter*!" Fitz exclaimed still staring at the screen then scrolling down to another disturbing squirrel painting.

"Yep, but now my fear is that he's actually a dangerous *bloody-nutter* instead of just a *pain-in-the-ass bloody-nutter*," Tovah offered us another drink.

Up until now, the drinks seemed like a social thing. But suddenly I wanted another pour to help stop my visible hand shaking. Of all the weirdness I had just found out about John, his painting scared me the most. They were dark...and not Geiger dark; this was a whole different kind of weird. Although, to look at the paintings as an artist, and not just as a woman with a potential stalker; the lines, his use of shadow and light, was pretty well done.

Tovah refilled our glasses and brought up something I hadn't really thought was a threat. "So he knows where you're staying." Her facial expression switched back to the *angry-bear-mom* look.

Fitz's rounded eyes shot to mine, "Ah crap!"

"You'll stay here," Tovah gave us a curt nod of her head.

Her comment wasn't posed as a question, or a suggestion. Tovah had made her decree.

"We don't want to put you out," I told her.

Fitz took a good look around the Grand Library then down at her glass, "Not gonna lie, I kinda do."

Finally something made us all laugh.

"I would have had you stay here in the first place if I wasn't worried about you girls feeling *mommied* by me. Now, I insist. I wouldn't be able to rest at all wondering what that weirdo has in mind."

"But our stuff?" Fitz said.

"Tomorrow, Olaf will take you to get your things. Tonight, I have fresh pajamas and can have a bath of bleach ran for you," she pointed to Fitz.

I laughed, "I'm not sure even bleach would work."

"Seriously," Tovah asked, "did you paint ALL of yourself green?"

"Go big or go home," Fitz winked, taking a drink of her whiskey.

We were torn from our current preoccupation when Jeeves announced visitors were beginning to arrive.

Following Tovah down the hall to her Great Room, I saw a handful of women helping themselves to drink and food that had been catered.

Fitz, who had been too busy prepping for tonight's festivities to eat, made a B-line for the heaping platters. I saw the other women jump and laugh when they caught sight of her; her painted face and dyed body.

Taking a good look at the space, it was only then that I realized that Tovah's Brownstone was actually two Brownstones that had been converted into one. I knew she had another two floors above, but I hadn't realized the home was also twice as wide. I had to wonder what a home such as this would go for in the New York market.

The Great Room, which I'm sure used to be two Great Rooms once upon a time, boasted high ceilings with intricate woodwork in dark mahogany. As you walked in, there was a billiards table to the right lined in rich crimson with claw footed legs. At the far end of the room by the wall of windows, was a black grand piano. Was Tovah a master of both? It wouldn't surprise me in the least, I grinned. The huge brick fireplace that was aglow, popping and crackling had an exact replica on the opposite wall.

Over the mantle of the fireplace closest to me, hung a large gold framed painting of who I assumed was Mr. Schumer. Dressed well in a dark grey pinstriped suit, his dark hair, with just a shock of silver at the temples, was parted at the side and slicked back. I knew the pose was supposed to look regal, dignified, and so it did. But something in the hazel eyes sparkled with mischief. A warm feeling washed over me; this man had really loved his life.

Tovah caught me staring and walked over to where I stood, grinning.

"The great love of my life," she raised her glass to the painting of her late husband.

"He was quite handsome," I said.

"The most gorgeous man in the world…inside and out!" Tovah smiled. "From the first moment I laid eyes on him…I was smitten."

"You were very lucky to have found each other," I offered.

"Lucky my ass," Tovah's head shot back, "He was my *Basherter*!"

Shaking my head, I said, "I don't know what that means."

"It's Yiddish…for *destiny*," she took my hand in hers. "We both believed, from the moment we met, that we were in fact soulmates. That doesn't mean we didn't have to *learn* each other… but oh boy was the *learnin'* fun!" her eyes rolled.

With this I laughed, "I bet," was all I could say. "Do you think…everyone has a soulmate?" I asked.

"I do," Tovah squeezed my hand. "But I don't think all soulmates…are lovers."

I cocked my head, wondering.

"See, I think a soulmate is someone…" Tovah thought carefully about her wording, "is someone whose absence would leave you feeling incomplete…even though you were never incomplete before them," she shook her head like this was a mystery. "It's like…together, a different part of you, of them, was created. You *NEED* that person in your life…in a different way than you need anyone else."

Looking at the ground, I pondered a short list of people and wondered if I had ever felt anything like this. When I looked up, there was Fitz; standing across the room in her witch costume, dyed green from head to toe, her face painted with the nightmarish eyes and mouth of a rabid vampire zombie, and a huge smile pulled my cheeks upward as a laugh escaped my lips.

Tovah's eyes found Fitz and she squeezed my hand again, "It doesn't surprise me in the slightest," she said giving me a wink. "You two should have been born of the same womb, as close as you are."

I thought about our mothers; my mother could never have handled (or broken) Fitz's spirit. Mum, on the other hand, may have instilled more backbone in me, taught me how to be less self-conscious.

Just then Vah walked in. Dressed as Little Red Riding Hood with a faux-hawk, she pulled off her red woolen cape. Handing the garment to Jeeves, she stood on her tippy toes to put a kiss on his cheek causing his face to light up. I couldn't hear what she said to him, but he reached out his palm and placed it against her cheek.

Tovah saw the look of wonder I aimed at the interaction I was witnessing.

"He's always loved her," Tovah whispered. "She was a little girl when she came to live here with Mr. Schumer and me. Both Wilson and Vah had lost their mothers at a very young age, but Wilson had never let go of his anguish until Vah drew it from him. She was just a tiny thing when she worked her magic, used her gift for him. I wouldn't be surprised if she was the only reason he stayed on after Mr. Schumer passed away. They have a truly unique bond."

My heart warmed toward Jeeves, Wilson, whatever. He may have come off as a crotchety old goat (and maybe toward most of us, he was), but he did have a soul and he allowed it to be touched by another.

Vah crossed the room to where Tovah and I stood. Leaning in to kiss her aunt's cheek, she then embraced me. "How are we doing on this glorious night?" she asked.

"I'm kept well," Tovah smiled.

"Ugh, me too," I added.

Vah's eyes slit as she studied me, "Why are you nervous around me?" she asked.

I looked to Tovah, wearing her famous one-sided grin, wondering just how to answer this question. I hadn't even realized that I gave off this feeling. "Ugh, I guess after I watched you...*draw*...and I knew you had also *drawn* from me...I guess I worry that my energy," I thought again, "that my energy was too much. Too negative!" I added.

Vah chuckled a little, "That's what I do, though. I take negative energy from people who are being burdened by its existence in their lives."

"I was just worried mine was...too much...a burden for you,"

I shrugged.

Vah's laughter rang out, "It's a burden to you…that's why I take it. I don't keep it," she shook her head.

I nodded and tried not to fidget. I knew this; had even seen her release it, but I still felt like her feeling the *NEED* to do this for me, was me being a burden to her.

"You worry a lot, don't you…what people feel because of you…how you affect them…how what you say, and do, impacts on their lives?" she turned her body to face mine head-on.

I felt a lesson coming; one that Diane, fellow Lady of the Moon member and psychiatrist, would be proud of. "I do," I sighed, waiting to hear how this was my greatest setback in learning myself. "I'm sorry," I added for no good reason I could think of after it was said.

Vah shook her head, "Don't be."

"I guess I'm more self-conscious than most," I admitted.

"Yeah…that's not what I'm getting from you," she gave me her own Tovah grin.

"No?" I asked perplexed.

"No," she looked at Tovah who was still grinning as well. "You don't care what people *THINK* of you, per-se. You care about what people *FEEL* because of you."

I gave my head a shake…weren't these kind of…the same, I wondered.

"Janie, you're an empath," Vah smiled.

"What?" my brow furrowed.

"Janie, have you ever had to tell anyone off?"

Now I laughed, "Yeah," I gave her a palms-up.

"Does it take you a long time to finally voice your frustrations with others?" she questioned.

Nodding, "Yes."

"Why?" Vah gave me a palms-up. "What keeps you from saying what needs to be said, right away, the first time you feel it?

What makes you let it build up? Do you have trouble understanding how you feel?" she looked at me sidelong.

"No!" I said with absolute certainty. "I'm pretty clear on my feelings most of the time."

"So what keeps you from saying what needs to be said and doing what needs to be done?" she prodded.

"Because..." I stopped.

"Because why?" she pushed a little harder.

"Because I don't want to hurt anyone's feelings!" I blurted out.

Tovah let out a howl and clapped her hands.

"There it is!" Vah nodded. "*Empaths* aren't *AFRAID* of their feelings and they do *KNOW* exactly how they feel. They're not *AFRAID* of confrontation, and when pushed, they WILL PUSH BACK."

Fitz walked up to join the conversation.

"What they ARE afraid of," Vah explained, "is how much damage they will cause another. They can't stand to see someone hurting. They catch their words and look for the least painful way to express how they feel about a situation, that ironically, someone else has expressed without care or concern for how it might make you feel. The reason *empaths* do what they do...is they can *FEEL* how their words...actions... affect someone else."

I bit my bottom lip as Vah continued.

"If they think they've hurt you, they feel that...then they feel guilt for causing someone else to feel that way. Even if they're in the right, even if it had to be said, they feel guilt over even the thought of causing someone mental or emotional pain. And...they apologize all the time just *IN CASE* something they said or did was taken the wrong way."

Having come in on the ass-end of Vah's explanation, Fitz joked, "Jesus, is she talkin' about ya, Janie?"

Slowly I nodded my head.

Fitz looked at me, "Really?"

Vah and Tovah nodded as well.

"Okay then," Fitz turned to Vah, "I'm gonna need ya to start back at the beginnin'."

As Vah laid it all out for Fitz, Fitz began to nod her head faster and faster. Vah said, "It's the reason she could see the energy I was *drawing*. She feels it and sees the physical manifestation of the work being done."

"That's awesome, isn't it Janie? All this time, we just though ya had low self-esteem and were overly self-conscious. Turns out, yer mother didn't damage ya as much as we thought. You were damaged from birth!"

My face squished up.

Vah laughed (at which one of us, I wasn't sure). "That's not quite how I would put it. It *IS* a gift, but you have to learn to control it so you don't completely stifle yourself, while worrying for others and their well-being."

"I don't understand…If this IS what I am, why didn't, or, why haven't I…seen energy before?" I shot confused looks to all three of them.

"I think maybe you needed to see it *drawn out* to actually…see it. It's almost like the energy is hidden behind closed doors when it's in body. But even though you've never seen it before, I *know* you've felt it all along."

The fact that I wanted to apologize right now for no reason I could think of, made me wonder if she was in fact right.

Fitz gave us the pouty lip, "I wish I had a gift."

Vah's smile widened, "Oh, you do," she told Fitz with absolute certainty.

"Okay, would ya happen to know what that might be?" Fitz laughed.

"You don't know?" Vah looked confused.

"Well, there's a few things I'm REALLY good at, but not many have seen that side of me," she joked.

Tovah rolled with laughter and clapped her hands, "I love this, kid!" she grabbed Fitz's cheeks.

With a chuckle Vah said, "Well, I'm speaking of a gift you were born with."

"Yeah, that's the one I want to know about," Fitz giggled.

"You...can read people quite well. You hear the words...*I'm fine*. But you know they're not. You hear *that doesn't bother me...* but you know it does. Someone may say, *I'm not worried*, but you KNOW they are. You're able to do this with not only people you're close to, but complete strangers."

Fitz looked like she was considering all the times this had happened.

"The truth is...it's very hard for you to be deceived. Words, for you, take a backseat to what you are actually picking-up on. And when someone's actions don't match their words, you go in search of the truth. As much as you would like to take people at face value, you know that face value is sometimes nothing more than a mask."

Now I was confused. "If I feel what others feel," I pointed to myself, "and Fitz can read people...doesn't that make her an empath as well, and me...well, not a good one?"

Vah and Tovah both laughed. "You have two different gifts. You feel what affects people," she told me. "And Fitz," Vah turned to her, "she may not feel what they feel but she is a human bullshit detector. She picks up on unspoken truths...she knows for the most part when someone is trying to deceive her...and others," Vah shrugged. "You both have wonderful gifts...but like anything else, you need to practice them to become good with them."

So...do I feel everything...but deception? I wondered. Or do I just refuse it?

I couldn't help but remember how Fitz got a little *bat-shit-crazy* in Ireland. Her boyfriend, Scotty, had told her repeatedly how everything was fine, but she didn't buy it and went in search for the truth. Granted he had been unable to perform (making any woman question), but still Fitz knew there was a truth being hidden from her. Not to mention *KNOWING* something was amiss with a few of my significant others despite how mushy in love they appeared to be to everyone else…including me. But had I actually *FELT* their love…or pretended I did…because that's what I wanted to feel? I mentally went over just a handful of the times I felt like something was wrong with a relationship and had pushed the thought away as either my own fears or insecurity.

"And all this time I thought I was just a good judge of character," Fitz pondered aloud, dragging me away from my thoughts.

"You are," Vah emitted, "and that's why. This is your gift…and your gift has helped not only you, but the people you're the closest to." Vah's eyes shot to mine as she gave me a nod of her head.

I knew I was included in the list of people she had helped with her gift. I may have actually topped the list. But, if I was understanding Vah correctly; Fitz knew all the things I felt but wouldn't dare say for fear of hurting someone. Fitz knew…she was my safe place to say and do and be…me. She *read* me. In return, I responded, all the times that I could feel Fitz's energy. I knew when someone hurt her, pleased her. I let her be scared, happy or sad, and responded without her ever having to say these things out loud. I *felt* her.

Fitz looked very pleased with her gift; she read people well and this served her well. I, on the other hand was stifled by my gift. And if this was my gift, I had to take even more blame off of my mother and put it on me. The thought that she hadn't created this in me (although she may have fed it raw meat from time to time) made me wonder how ALWAYS worrying about others to the point of driving myself *bat-shit-crazy* at times, was a gift? But if I went over several previous interactions in my head, it was all there. I was too worried about Mona's feelings to rip her a new one, instead letting her torture me for years. I wasn't afraid of her, her wrath or confronting her. I was worried about all the people I could hurt or put in a bad situation by doing this. My mother; I was always so afraid of her hurting, causing her tears, that I spent years and years refusing to stand up for myself. Had I been any more worried about her feelings, I'd be dating a red-headed, bug collecting cousin who was arrested for stealing fecal matter from the lab where he worked. I did a quick full body shudder. Yeah, that was a line I wouldn't have crossed even for my mother's happiness. Even John, the airport dumper, had gotten off easy. There were so many things I could have, and maybe even should have said to him. Is this the crap Vah had removed from me; the build-up of all the crap I had never expressed?

Tovah was busy asking Vah if we had everything we needed.

"Yer makin' the face again," Fitz whispered.

"What face?" I whispered back.

"The *lost in thoughts that aren't healthy fer ya* face."

Tovah finished her conversation with Vah, "Come," Tovah said, "meet the other women."

Ripped from my inner dialog of self-shaming, I walked with Tovah, Vah and Fitz to where the other women had gathered. The three huge brown leather couches made a squared U shape that surrounded the far fireplace. I wasn't sure what to expect as I took a seat between Fitz and Vah. I didn't recognize anyone from our Ladies of the Moon night, but since they had all been hooded, and there had been so many of them, I wasn't sure I would have.

Jeeves entered the room pushing a large silver serving cart. I had already decided that I had had enough whiskey for the evening during our great revelation of *John the Cab Driver's Bat-Shit Crazy File.*

But as Jeeves rolled the trolley in front of the fireplace and removed the domed silver lid I was a bit more confused. For some reason I was looking at a stack of dried corn cobs. Fitz shot me a questioning glance.

Tovah stood and addressed the gathered women;

"Good evening and welcome to the sixth anniversary of *THE BURNING,"* she announced.

The crowd began to clap with Fitz and me joining in a few seconds behind.

"Now we do have a few new faces tonight and I'd like everyone to make our new guests feel welcome. So if you would please stand, ladies," Tovah extended her hand.

Fitz and I stood while another woman directly across from us, also rose from her seat.

"I would like to introduce Fitz, who doesn't normally look like something that should be guarding the gates of hell," Tovah grinned. "Standing next to her is Janie, a featured artist at my Gallery for the upcoming show. And over here, we have Marie, a kindergarten teacher from Brooklyn."

As the other women applauded I forced a smile. I hated to be the center of attention. Fitz on the other hand, nodded her head and blew Tovah a kiss. I had to laugh; I loved Fitz in her normal state. And in her abnormal state the kiss was hilarious, like she was choosing which one of us to eat.

"So, many of you ladies have done this before, so I'm sure the background on this ritual will bore the hell out of you, but please bear with me as I explain to the others."

All the other women nodded and smiled.

"On this night we not only honor those who have passed, we honor our own past; the revelations of the last year...blessings and joys...goals and accomplishments," Tovah looked at each of us individually. "What you have learned this past year, I guarantee, is unlike any year before. I want to take you through an exercise..."

Vah passed around small notebooks and pens to each of us.

"Some of you have done this before, so if you choose not to participate, that's okay with me," Tovah grinned. "I'm going to give everyone a list of words. Please number them from 1 to 6. First, is *moon*."

I wrote a 1 and put the word moon next to it.

"Number 2, is the word *sun*," Tovah continued. "Number 3 is clouds. Number 4 is *lake*. Number 5, I want you to pick an organ."

Fitz's hand went in the air, "Like a bodily organ?" she asked.

"Yes," Tovah grinned.

"Any bodily organ?"

"Whichever one you like," Tovah blew her a kiss. "Last, number 6, I'd like you to pick an animal."

Next, we're going to start back at number 1. In one word, what does *moon* mean to you? What do you think of it or how does it make *YOU* feel?"

How does the *moon* make me feel? I thought and tapped my chin with my pen. I wasn't sure exactly. But the moon is beautiful to me. *Beautiful* I wrote.

"Next," Tovah began, "the *sun*...what does it mean to you or how does it make you feel?"

This one was a little harder. I wasn't a sun lover. I mean I liked having a tan and all, but the sunshine was overbearing to me for the most part. So I wrote *overbearing*.

"Okay, continue going down your list," Tovah said.

Clouds, I thought to myself. What do clouds mean to me? I closed my eyes and pictured all the different clouds I loved. *Happy* was what I came up with.

Number 4 *lake*, immediately hit me as fear. I tried to think of something brighter that I felt about it, but in the end, I went with *scared*. Not only was I afraid of the water and water creatures, the word lake, had taken me back to Friday the 13th marathons I had watched with Fitz when we were young. I made a mental note back then; no summer camp, no lakes, no drugs, drinking or sex. I amended a couple of those rules.

Number 5…an *organ*? To be honest, the thought of organs… kind of grossed me out on the whole. I leaned a bit over to spy Fitzy's list.

Pulling the paper pad against her chest, she said, "Eyes on yer own page!"

I took a deep breath and thought some more. The heart…I loved the heart. Maybe not the anatomically correct version, but I used to spend hours drawing and cutting out hearts made of crepe paper as a kid. They hung from my ceiling and were taped to my walls during those early teenage years of angst. So I wrote *heart*.

The last was an animal. My brow furrowed. I was sure whatever animal I picked was supposed to represent me. My first thought was kitten. But if I wanted to be seen as strong, would I pick a miniature cute little furry thing that was splattered all over the internet for being adorable? For some reason I was fidgeting again. Lioness, I though, then remembered they were part of a pride. I had reluctantly been part of a pride (albeit a small one…I think) and I was no fan. Panther, I thought. Panthers don't run in packs. I practically sprung to write it down on my list.

When I looked up, I realized that I had been the last one writing. Everyone sat patiently while I finished my list.

Grinning Tovah said, Number 1, the *moon*, this is how you see the world around you."

I looked down at my word; *beautiful*. That was pretty good, I thought.

"What did ya write?" Fitz whispered. Showing her my list, she said, "I wrote *bright*," and smiled.

"Number 2, *sun*, this is how you see the people around you," Tovah explained.

Oh, that's not good I thought, looking down at my word; *Overbearing*. I hoped Fitz wouldn't want to exchange answers on this one. She started to say something but Tovah cut her off so I brought the *hush* finger to my lips.

"Number 3, *Clouds*, this is what you secretly wish for."

I looked down to see *Happy*. Okay, I agreed with this one. I did wish happiness; for others as well as for myself.

Fitz's hand raised, I got *fluffy*…ya know, what I think about clouds. I don't know how I wish for *fluffy*!"

Tovah grinned, "What does the word fluffy mean to you?"

Fitz thought then a smile pulled across her face, "Warm…content."

Tovah smiled back as she nodded her head, "Not too bad to wish for warm and content."

"Not bad at all," Fitz beamed.

Tovah continued, "Lake is next…this is how others see you," she looked around the room.

Fitz leaned over to me, "I wrote *Beautiful*." What did ya write?"

My face scrunched up as I stared at the word, "*Scared*," I said under my breath.

"An organ, this is what guides you, or your superpower, if you will," Tovah gave us a palms-up.

People started revealing their words almost immediately. One lady said, "I got *brain.*" Another piped up with *heart*, just like me. "I got *stomach*," one of the women announced happily.

Strange looks were sent her way.

"I'm a chef," she gave us all a palms-up as we all began to "*Oh*" and *nod*.

Fitz was biting her bottom lip staring at her word.

"What? What was your word?" I asked.

"Well, ya know, I figured everyone would go with *brain* or *heart*..."

I nodded, "I was *heart*."

"I went the other way...like south of the heart."

I shook my head, "Like how south?" I asked her.

"Like south of the belly button but north of the thighs," her eyes slit and she winced.

I had to laugh, "Ruled by yer V?" I asked quietly.

"Apparently so," Fitz whispered. "It's my superpower," she giggled.

"The last one; you were supposed to pick an animal. This animal represents the struggles you still have to overcome," Tovah told us.

My jaw dropped...I was going to write kitten...my first thought was kitten! I was so sure that the last one, the *animal*; would be directly connected to how strong or powerful you were, not the struggles one still had to overcome!

"What did ya put fer that one?" Fitz leaned in and read *Panther*, "Oh," Fitz looked worried for me.

"It's just such a big, big, kitty," I worried out loud. "You?" I asked.

"A *mouse*," she said.

A whimper emitted from a woman on the far couch drawing our attention, "Oh my God, I wrote *Sperm Whale*...it was the first thing I thought of!" A look of hopelessness transformed her face.

I searched for something comforting to say, but then the woman blurted out, "I'm pregnant...again...and just today...they called and said they thought they heard a second heartbeat."

This thought would devastate me, but for most women this was a blessing. I was gonna go with that, when the woman piped up again, "This is number 6...or possibly 7..." she trailed off.

As my eyes rounded, Fitz leaned over to me, "I'm guessing her kitty is bigger than yers."

The poor extremely fertile woman, Melody, stood and sniffled as Vah escorted her to a restroom to blow her nose. I felt bad for her, I did. But I had some problems of my own. Did people see me as scared? Is that the way I came off? Technically, picturing a lake did bring to mind *scared.* Just like oceans, boats, sharks, heights and flying. Huh. And turning a *kitten* into a *panther* because I thought it was a representation of my strength? I was so worried about seeing myself as strong, now I had to add that to my panther sized burden list! Shit.

"Okay, even though that exercise may not have made everyone feel…rosy and warm, the next will make us all very warm, indeed," Tovah said. "I want everyone to write down three regrets you've had this year…something you wish you could change or something that you're holding onto that is unnecessary in your life."

And this is where my mind started really going…

I had somehow thought that only going back one year would keep the list short, but as I thought about this last year, my face scrunched up, I bit my lip.

The first thing I thought of when I thought of something that I wish I could change; was John. Not cabby John; ex John. I wish I would have paid more attention to that inner voice that was practically screaming *DANGER, DANGER*! I also wish I had had as much moxie as Miss Yolanda; the security guard from the airport who came to check on me while I hid my breakdown in the bathroom. I also kind of wished I would have kicked him in the junk like she said I should have. If I was seriously still mad about John, obviously he HAD to be on the list on things I needed to let go of.

Next…was Barry. Without even trying to, he popped into my mind.

Fitz put down her pad and pen then scooted back against the couch.

"You're done?" my shoulders dropped.

"Yeah," she said without hesitation. Grabbing her list, she showed it to me.

1. Punch John in the junk.

"Oh," I said and gave her a heartfelt smile.

1. Not wish Miss Elanor a run-in with an angry but horny wolverine.

Reading number 2, I grimaced.

"I know, I know, it was a difficult time fer me. It's one of the things I wish I could change…like the ball breaker, thing," she pointed back to number 1.

"You only have two, here?" I pointed out.

"I know…I couldn't think of a third. Plus I think the first one is a twofer because I wish I could have changed *not punchin'* John, *to punchin' him* and I haven't been able to let go of the opportunity I let pass," she gave me a palms-up.

I looked back at my list; Barry was #2. Beating up the girl in the bar who attacked Pauly (Although knowing what I know now…I think I would have let her connect at least ONE first) she was number #3. Thinking Betty was a cradle-robber, should probably be on there (I still felt guilty for that one.) Mona definitely belonged on the list of crap I needed to let go of. Then there was mom…I needed to let go of her opinions and stop taking them to heart. I had run over everyone else I could think of, when Cecil popped into my mind. All of the sudden I was both smiling and sad. I missed him. He wasn't something or someone I wanted to let go of...he was a *regret.* I regretted leaving him in Ireland.

I don't know why I had never thought of this before. I wasn't just sad that I left and we were apart for weeks on end...I regretted boarding that plane and coming home. My heart began to pound the way it does when you finally realize that you really messed up. Panic! I was starting to do my panic breathing. Here I had been petrified that he would ask me to marry him, and now? Now I was scared to death that he was happy with the way things were and eventually we would grow apart...all of that *out of sight out of mind* shit.

"What are ya doin'? Fitz asked out of the side of her mouth.

"What, why?" I asked quickly through shortened breaths.

"Yer doin' yer weird breathin' thing, again. What's wrong with ya?"

"Nothing," I grabbed her hand and squeezed.

"Okay ladies," Tovah addressed everyone as Melody and Vah re-entered the room, "fold your papers like so."

We all folder our papers lengthwise.

"Now come up front and each of you grab a corncob," Tovah instructed.

As I watched the first woman, I got the gist of what we were doing. Around the cob she wrapped her note then when Tovah told her to, she said, "I release what does not serve me in my highest good...and I am prepared to change the things I can for my highest good." Into the fire she threw the dried corncob.

I couldn't help but wonder if the corncob held its own significance. I didn't know much about rituals in general. But I was aware that different races, religions, hell, even self-help groups all had their own versions of ritual. Was this a Ladies of the Moon thing?

After I threw my corncob into the flames, I stood watching the fire quickly begin to eat it away.

"You were supposed to say somethin'," Fitzy blurted out.

"I ugh, um," I stammered trying to remember the words, "I do this for my higher good."

"Good enough," Tovah's voice rang out.

Fitz offered her lines verbatim and added a "Yeah I do," to the end before walking back to her seat.

As the fire blazed on, Jeeves brought treats: chocolate brownies and maple fudge, peanut butter and coconut balls, individual pumpkin, lemon and raspberry cakes with cream cheese frosting and homemade chocolate chip cookies. For a moment I thought I died and went to The Chocolate Factory, which for me could have been a substitute for heaven.

"Hell, if I had known all these goodies were goin' to be served I wouldn't have filled up on the tiny sandwiches," Fitz looked dreamily at the cart.

I couldn't help but notice that Melody had filled an entree plate with all the sweets it would hold. Was she eating for three, or drowning herself in comfort food?

As the small crowd began to talk amongst themselves, Fitz leaned over to me. "I was kind of hopin' tonight would be a little more...I don't know...veil-thinnin'."

"We're you hoping for a séance or graveyard tour?" Both of which she had dragged me on in the past.

"Just somthin' a little more spooky, ya know?"

"Have you looked at yourself in the mirror? You've got all kinds of spooky goin' on," I laughed. "Plus...I'm not sure Jewish people even celebrate Halloween. And for the record, not all people who *DO* celebrate...celebrate like you."

"Oh you loved that séance," she barked.

"Six people in a room sitting at a round table all jumping and saying repeatedly; *DID YOU HEAR THAT*?"

"Well, I DID hear somethin'!" Fitz nodded.

"Yeah me too…It's called a car alarm, Fitz," I gave her the airplane attendant smile.

"Yer getting good at that," she pointed out. "But yer still an asshole," she smiled back the same way.

As the night drew to a close we were shown to our rooms. The walk up the staircase led by Jeeves was an excruciatingly long one. Traditional wedding marches were done much the same way; right foot…pause…left foot…pause…and so on until you finally reached your destination.

13

A NOT-SO-FUNNY-THING, HAPPENED

Looking through the open doorway into my bedroom for the evening, I was again reminded of Callaghan manor. It seemed that Tovah's home, too, had a gothic suite. The rain that began falling an hour ago, added to the room's medieval quality.

The huge four poster bed made of rich dark wood, wore a canopy of white flowing chiffon. The fireplace in the corner had been lit, and I noticed its fuel was more corncobs. My brow furrowed; I really did need to ask if there was any significance to them. A bed gown had been laid out for me complete with a matching ankle length robe, both made of soft cotton. Comfort at its finest, to me.

Fitz and I shared a Jack-and-Jill bathroom. I heard the faucet turn on and knew that she would be hunkered down for a while in the tub while she soaked off the green dye. All of the sudden I heard Fitz begin to sing *Tiny Bubbles.* I had to laugh; even when she wasn't trying to, she amused the hell out of me.

As lightening crashed overhead, the view outside my window illuminated. I was half undressed and it made me realize that the lights should be off. Clicking the switch off, I pulled the gown over my head and moved to roast my backside in front of the fireplace.

Fitz called my name from the bathroom, "Janie, would ya come see if I got all of this crap off my back?"

Fitz was in a claw footed tub surrounded by green bubbles. Immediately I began to laugh, she looked like she was being cooked in a witch's brew.

"What's so funny?" she asked with make-up streaking lines down her face.

"Nothing," I shook my head. "How did you dye your back in the first place?"

"One of those sponges on a stick."

"Ah," I looked at her back, "you missed a spot of green in the middle."

"Of course I did, I don't have my sponge on a stick," she handed me the washcloth. "What had ya so worked up earlier?"

"What do you mean?"

"Ya know damn well what I mean. What threw ya into yer panic breathin'?"

Letting out a deep sigh, I told her, "You know how guilty I always feel."

"Boy, do I. Even yer personal thoughts, stuff ya never even said out loud, stay with ya. Is it somthin' said or unsaid that's messin' with ya?"

I thought about the Betty thing. "Both!" I knew if I told Fitz about the Betty thing, she'd laugh…at me for counting it among my list of things I'd like to change.

"Okay…what's got ya goin' the most…the big one?"

"Cecil," I admitted.

"What…about yer fight in Ireland?" Fitz searched for the only thing she could bring to mind. "I'm guessin' he's forgiven ya fer that…a few times, if I'm not mistakin."

"No, it wasn't that. I…I regret leaving Ireland."

Fitz spun around to face me. "Ya wish ya would have stayed in Ireland?" she looked baffled.

"Well, not exactly."

"Well what exactly?"

"I wish…I would have stayed with him. I wish I wouldn't have left him," I clarified.

Fitz pondered her next question for a moment before asking, "And if he did propose…and ya said yes…would ya move to Ireland?"

"Well," I huffed a little, "if he DID propose and I DID say yes…then yeah, I guess I'd move to Ireland."

Letting out the thinnest of laughs, Fitz said, "But yer JOB is here!"

"No…Cecil's job is there. My job is…wherever I do it. I've proven that with the two paintings I did in Ireland for the Callaghan family," I added.

"But ya know I can't go. Scotty's job is here! I'd be nothin' more than a *lonely* third wheel there!"

I knew what she was saying and should have told her how flattered I was that she didn't want us to be apart. Instead I went full asshole. "Do I really need to point out the fact that that's exactly what *I* am, here?"

"Hey, we always try to include ya in everything we do…except *that*!" her eyes rounded.

"That's my point, though! That's what a third wheel is! And I HAVE been the third wheel here! One, I may remind you, who doesn't get any of *THAT* ever!" I pointed out.

Just then, a roll of thunder crashed overhead and lightning cracked a second behind. Out went the lights.

"Crap!" Fitz growled. "How will I know if I got all the green off, now?"

I walked out into the bedroom, the fireplace my only light.

"Where the hell did ya go?" Fitz barked.

Through a tightened jaw I barked back, "I'm looking for a candle!"

On the bedside table I found what looked like a soot stained mason jar. Opening the lid, I could make out what was left of the candle. Walking over to the fireplace I hoped and prayed for one of those long matches that were used to light a fireplace. Lighting the candle, I started back toward the bathroom when something seen out of the corner of my eye stopped me in my tracks. Looking out the window into the backyard, I saw what looked like a flash of light. One second it was there, then it wasn't...then it was there, then it was gone again.

Trying to rub the moisture the warmed room left on the window, I still couldn't see much but a flash of light. Right before I turned to take the candle back to Fitz, the thunder boomed again. And this time when the lightning flashed, I saw a man...I think it was a man, standing under the tree.

"Fitz!" I hurried into the bathroom, "there's someone outside...under the tree in the backyard."

"What are ya on about?" she grabbed her towel and followed me to the window. "I don't see a damn thing," she shook her head.

"Wait for it," I told her.

"What was that?" she asked when there was a small flash from under the tree.

When the lightning struck this time, there was definitely a man, and it looked as though a body was hanging from the tree, "Oh my God," I yelled. "Oh my God, where are Tovah and Vah?" I headed for the door with bathtub Barbie in tow.

As the door opened, first I, and then Fitz let out a scream. There stood Jeeves or Wilson, whatever.

"The Mrs. asked me to bring you a candle," he looked unamused by our wild eyes.

"Where is the Mrs., Vah?" I blurted out.

"I have bid them good evening. They are in their rooms."

"Look, Jeeves, there's someone in the backyard!" Fitz said.

He looked less than concerned about what had to be a Halloween prank pulled on him by an adult woman wearing a towel. One who had previously dressed herself as a mermaid for a child's holiday. Looking Fitz up and down, he rolled his eyes.

"It's true," I confirmed.

Still Jeeves stood there, unruffled by our agitation.

"Ya know what? Fine! Just go check on Tovah and Vah. We'll take care of it," Fitz blew past him pulling me along behind her.

"We're gonna do what?" I asked as we hit the stairs.

"We're gonna keep Tovah and Vah safe…if it isn't already too late."

"Um, not to point out the obvious," I huffed as we ran down to the library. "But who's going to keep us safe? You saw the look on Jeeves' face…he's not even going to look in on Tovah and Vah. It could be morning when they find our dead bodies! AND…" I pulled her to a stop, "you are in a towel!"

"Yer right I can't go out there…" Fitz looked down at her attire. "Yer gonna have to!"

"Um, *NO,*" I shook my head.

"What if the body hangin' from the tree is…?"

She couldn't even finish her thought as my eyes rounded in horror. "Oh God," I covered my mouth with my hand. Nodding, I swallowed hard and pulled the door open. "Go check on Vah and Tovah and call the police!"

The wind had picked up and whipped my hair ruthlessly across my face. Bone-chilling cold attacked me from my ears to my bare toes. As my teeth began to chatter, I saw him…I think. Wearing a huge dark colored parka with the hood pulled over his head, I couldn't be sure it was John. As the lightning flashed, I finally saw his face looking directly at mine. My eyes were quickly drawn to the hanged body. From this distance…the size, the faux-hawk, it looked like Tovah.

I felt my gut lurch with twisting agony. Adrenaline hit me like I had taken a shot of it directly to my heart. The scream that escaped me was later described as primal as I rushed at John the cab driver like a bull seeing red. He stood frozen; fear contorted his face as the lightning flashed again.

Over the thunder I heard a loud and familiar sound but it didn't really register with my brain at the time; I was in pursuit. John snapped-to with a squeak and a pivot, making his hasty retreat. Knees high, he raced across the backyard. Scaling the seven foot wall like Spiderman, I heard his body *thud* as he fell down the other side. He emitted a moan before I heard a dog let out one very deep and very loud *WOOF.*

The next thing I heard was a whimper and pleading sent to God. As his high pitched screams trailed off, I dropped to the ground and began to sob. I couldn't turn around. I couldn't bring myself to see her that way. Tovah was a mentor, a teacher and beloved friend. Tears ran warm down my frozen face as I sat there willing myself to breath.

All of the sudden I heard a voice yelling, "Janie! Kid, get your ass in here before you freeze!"

I spun quickly to see Tovah standing at the backdoor holding a shotgun. In her powder-blue nightdress and robe, she held the gun across her body; one hand holding the stock and the other cradling the barrel. I had never seen such a demure version of *RAMBO.*

Standing, I began to laugh as I ran to her. She handed the shotgun to Jeeves, taking me in an embrace.

"What the hell were you doin', Kid? That guy could have hurt you," she put her palms to my cheeks and stared into my eyes. "If Fitz hadn't come to get me…" But I was still smiling and crying so hard, she just pulled me back into a life affirming hug.

Fitz stood close and rubbed my back while my sobs melted away into gratefulness.

"You're going to want to see this," Vah said, looking up at the body swinging from the tree branch.

Already wet and cold, Fitz, Tovah and I walked over to stare at a makeshift body. A clay mask of what I thought was supposed to be a face was formed, painted and attached to a mannequin's body. But closer up, I realized the face looked more like a Michael Meyers mask with lipstick, horribly painted eyelashes, electric blue eye-shadow and a skinny brow-line with a rounded arch to make it look frightened…or surprised depending on the angle you saw it from. On top of its head was glued a broom head that I guess was supposed to be the faux-hawk. The mannequin wore a purple cape just like all of the women had worn at The Ladies of the Moon meeting. That little realization let us know, either he had followed Fitzy and me to the LOTM meeting and waited for everyone to exit, or…he had been following Tovah for quite some time. Neither thought left any of us with a warm fuzzy feeling.

Fitz's eyes shot to mine as she began to shake her head slowly, "Wow…that thing is…" Fitz shook her head harder. "I give up, what the hell is that supposed to be?"

When my eyes set on Tovah, I expected to see fear. I was wrong. From her expression, she was almost amused. "Kid, did you think this was me?"

"I ugh…I was more focused on John. The hairstyle…and cape…" my voice trailed off as I gave her a palms-up.

"That nutter thinks I look like Tammy Faye Bakker and Michael Meyers had a baby?" Tovah's nose squished up.

"Ah yeah, I see it now," clapped Fitz.

All of us shot questioning eyes at her.

"No, No, I mean the Tammy Faye Bakker, thing," Fitz explained.

Jeeves had just walked up with a knife to cut the mock-body

from the Oak, when he saw the painted face, his brow furrowed. "I'll never understand this new art," he shook his head.

"I guess it's time for me to phone an old friend," Tovah sighed.

Back in the library, Tovah wrapped a heavy throw around my shoulders and sat me in front of the fire. Fitz brought me a double whiskey, no rocks.

"You were gonna attack him," Fitz rubbed my free hand in hers warming it as best she could.

I nodded, "I'm pretty sure that was my plan. Thank you for checking on Tovah and Vah. I really think the sound of the shotgun being racked scared John more than I could have."

"Well, thank God she didn't have to try to shoot the damned thing to get her point across."

"I'm sure she could have handled it if it had come to that," I shivered.

"Oh I'm sure she could have, too…if she had had time to load it before we ran downstairs."

My eyes went wide, "It's not loaded?"

Fitz shook her head. "I asked her what she would do if he rushed her."

"And?"

"She said she'd beat him to a bloody friggin' pulp with the butt of the gun and shove the barrel clean up his arse."

I turned to see Tovah across the room, talking on the phone. "I think she probably would have," I nodded.

"No doubt," Fitz agreed. "I love that woman."

"Me too," I took another sip of my fire-water. "Remember when we thought being mugged and arrested was the low point of our time in New York?"

Fitz raised her glass, "Good times!"

"Well they AREN'T NOW! Did the veil *thin* enough for you?" I asked sarcastically.

"Hey, I wanted spirits and premonition, not a psychopath huntin' us!"

"I wish Cecil was here," I said.

"Aye, I wish Scotty was here, too," Fitz stared off, biting her lower lip.

"I meant for safety purposes," I corrected.

"Oh...well yeah...me too," Fitz gave me an embarrassed smile.

"Should we tell them...what's going on?"

Fitz thought about it and shook her head, "No."

"You're not gonna tell Scotty?"

Fitz shook her head again, "It'll just make him worry. He'll blow off work and rush to New York...to do what? Sit with me? Hunt down the deranged little *squirrel man*?" she gave me a shrug.

"You don't think he'll be pissed when he finds out and you didn't tell him?"

"I'll explain it. Every cop in New York has their eyes peeled fer the psycho. Two officers are parked out front and some Olaf guy will be stayin' here in the house with us. It's like we're on lockdown."

I let out a sigh, "That it is. I think John the cabby was attacked by the neighbor's dog."

"I heard that thing bark. We may not need to worry about John the cabby, anymore," Fitz grinned.

Jeeves walked in with the mannequin and presented it to Tovah. Fitz and I moved to inspect the creepy effigy. The bottom of the cloak had char marks.

"I guess that was the flash I kept seeing from the window. He was trying to get it to catch fire," I bit my lower lip.

"In the rain and whippin' wind? That boy isn't the sharpest tack, is he?" Fitz questioned.

"No, he's not. But that could make him more dangerous," Tovah's brows rose. "Why don't you girls try to get some sleep?"

Fitz and I raised our eyebrows to her.

"Fat chance of that happinin'," Fitz told her.

"Well at the very least why don't you finish soaking off the green dye? I'm not sure if that kid ran from her," she pointed to me, "the sound of the shotgun racking, or if he got a look at ya and thought we were surrounded by banshees."

"You do still have some makeup on your face," I pointed out. "And truthfully, it's even scarier, now."

Walking back up to the second floor, I felt every ounce of exhaustion hit me. It had been a long day and I was happy to wish All Hallows Eve, goodbye. Surprisingly, I did kind of miss our Fitzpatrick traditions: Bobbin-for-Beers, the costume contest, and the family. Since I was a little girl, Fitzpatrick's has been a Halloween tradition. What started out as cream ale, cider, and playing snap apple, turned into the back patio bonfire and Bobbing-for-Beers. (Pretty much the only time we drank our Guinness from a bottle.) Mum and Aunt Marble always dressed as witches, which now made me grin. And…there were no psychos lurking about. Well, not any that wouldn't have been quickly handled by the Fitzpatrick's brood. Polite and understanding, or swift and painful, it was really *psycho's choice.*

As Fitzy ran another hot bath and soaked, I lay on the bed and thumbed through my phone. It was 3am here…I could call Cecil. Without so much as a blink, I hit his name in my speed dial.

"Well good morning, luv," he answered.

"Good morning to you," I smiled from ear to ear just hearing his voice.

"So are ya late to bed, or really early to rise?"

I bit into my lower lip. Part of me didn't want to keep all of this John madness from him. But the bigger part of me didn't want him to worry. "We stayed at Tovah's, so we're late to bed," I laughed.

"Am I gonna see ya on the news?" Cecil laughed.

"That's a weird thing to say," I said almost defensively. "Why would you ask that?"

"Ugh, I meant because Tovah is such a wild child?"

"Oh, right," I bit my lip again. "No we stayed at the house. It was pretty…" look for and adjective, I yelled at my brain, "interesting."

"Is that a good thing, or a bad thing?" he chuckled.

I chuckled back trying to totally dismiss the question, "How are you?"

"I'm good. I miss ya like crazy…but despite this, I'm good."

I melted a bit. "I miss you, too. I miss being there with you." Right after I said it, I mentally smacked my own forehead. Why did I say *there?* I miss you was clearly enough.

"You do? Bein' here?" He asked for confirmation, "Do ya mean…ya miss me...or do ya miss bein' HERE with me?"

The sound of concern in his voice about how I had phrased the comment didn't make me feel secure. "I just…I just miss you."

"Oh," he laughed. "I'll be there tomorrow night, luv. I can't wait to wrap my arms around ya. Truthfully, I can't wait to do a lot of things to ya."

I smiled from ear to ear, "Me too!"

"So is the Gallery all set, then? Have ya seen yer paintin's hung?"

"I have," I giggled with pure delight. "The Gallery is amazing! I can't wait for you to see it."

"So which paintin's did ya decide on fer the show?"

I told him about the ones I had sent.

"Not the The Blue Woman?" he asked, confused.

Cocking my head, I said, "It's funny you mention her?"

"Why?"

"Well, I didn't want to part with her, but Tovah convinced me that…it was time to let her go. I don't think she'll make it here in time for the sale, but Tovah is looking for a buyer on her Gallery page."

"Are ya ready?" he asked seriously.

"I really think I am. Tovah even convinced me to paint another self-portrait...one of who I am now."

"Well I hope she won't be the woman I see when I close my eyes," he said.

"Why not?" I was almost worried.

"Because she's not wearin' any clothes...and I'd rather keep that vision all to myself."

I had to laugh "Well I can guarantee that's just an *all for you* thing."

"Ah, just the way I like ya...mine. Well my sweet, it's that time again. I have to get on about my day. I love ya, Janie girl."

"I love you, too."

One more day I told myself as I hung up the phone.

I had no expectation of sleep finding me, so you can imagine how surprised I was when my eyes opened. Less surprising was the fact that I was not alone. A cleanly washed and exfoliated Fitz was curled up next to me. All the green was gone and the hellish fangs and black socket eyes were back to Fitzy status.

As I stood to go to the restroom, Fitz broke into a stretch. "What time is it?" she yawned.

Her contagious yawn was returned by me, "It's noon," I said looking at my phone.

"Oh my God, I'm so tired," Fitz whined and pulled the covers back over her head.

"I know. But I think hunger is going to kick sleep's ass. I need to eat something."

"Ya know what this room needs...?" Fitz asked.

"A coffee maker," I suggested.

"And that's why yer my friggin' soulmate," she said from under the blanket.

I couldn't help but smile. Tovah was right. Soulmates don't have to be actual mates. Sometimes, they can be people who have bypassed friendship and even sisterhood to end up somewhere that makes the soul feel more complete in their presence.

As I walked out of the bathroom, Fitz was wearing the witch's robe.

"Why are you putting that back on?"

"The empress has no clothes," she reminded me.

I could almost imagine the walk of shame; the two of us, in last night's clothes for me, and last night's costume for Fitz, returning to the Ritz.

All of the sudden, Fitz let out a howl, "Oh my God!" she turned to me, eyes wide with fear.

"What?" I asked excitedly.

"I don't have any makeup!" Fitz threw herself back down on the bed.

I had to grin, "And? You look better completely natural than most women can boast with a made-up face."

"Well, now that more and more people are recognizin' me, I hate to be seen undone."

I looked down at myself, "I really wish I could feel sorry for you, Fitz. But my ass, standing next to your size two ass all these years," I shook my head, "I just can't do it."

"I'll have you know my size two, is winter-gain."

I blank stared at her before saying, "Come on…I need coffee," and headed for the door.

14

OH, FOR THE LOVE OF . . .

As we hit the stairs, we could see Jeeves dusting the banister below.

"Ladies," he said as we approached, "the women are waiting for you in the sunroom." Giving Fitz's witch robe a look of total exasperation, he pointed the way.

"Boy that guy really doesn't like us," Fitz shook her head.

"Not the first and won't be the last."

"Well that's pessimistic of ya," Fitz told me.

"No…it's realistic of me," I corrected her.

"Oh here we go, yer not a pessimist, yer a realist," she mocked.

"A realist sees everything for what it is. Sometimes there are good things, sometimes bad. It's not optimism or pessimism."

We heard voices coming from the sunroom that made us turn and look at each other.

"Is that Mum?" Fitz's eyes rounded, excitedly.

We listened harder and then our jaws dropped.

"Is that YER mom?" Fitz asked in a hushed tone.

Slowly I began to nod.

"Huh, so…how ya likin' yer realism, now?" she grinned at me.

"Asshole," I said under my breath.

As we walked into the sunroom, I had the biggest, fakest smile you could imagine, plastered to my face.

"Oh my God," I said, throwing my hands up in the air. "How…did this happen?"

Fitz leaned over, "Ya really are getting' fantastic at that attendant's smile."

"Shut it," I said without moving my lips.

"Oh, my baby," Aunt Marble rushed to take me in an embrace.

I saw my mother's face contort, "Excuse me?" she said.

"Ugh, it's a long story…" I began.

"She's my spirit daughter," Aunt Marble beamed. "I hope ya don't mind sharin' her!"

"Not at all," my mother did the same smile I had painted on.

"Holy crap, yer mom can do the smile, too!" Fitz said quietly.

As hugs were exchanged, I got the lowdown from Betty.

"Well sugar," Betty began, "Yer mama, Mum," she pointed to Fitz, "she came over to Janie's house to pick up the paintin'. But Janie's mom and I were doin' some work on the house…."

"I'm sorry, what?" I asked.

"Well that bathroom of yers was just beggin' fer a make-over, so I decided; no time, like the present," Betty grinned.

"Ah," I forced my smile wider. "Great."

"Well, we had also changed the door locks…"

My brow furrowed but no one seemed to notice.

"So when Mum showed up, she couldn't get in with Fitz's key. Then I heard someone messin' with the door so I grabbed my gun…" Betty said matter of factly.

My eyes shot from Mum to Betty, both of whom were cracking up at the memory.

"Needless to say, when I realized who Mum was, she said she was comin' to the show! Well then I called this wonderful Tovah lady," Betty and Tovah joined hands and gave each other's hand a little squeeze and smiled. "and asked if she still had any tickets available. I didn't know how this worked," Betty admitted. "And when SHE found out that I was gonna bring yer mom, she invited us both here. Isn't that a hoot?" Betty smiled from ear to ear.

My cheeks began to ache from fake smiling, "That is…WOW," I said and looked around the table. "Wow," I repeated.

As conversations turned to what everyone would be wearing for the show, I noticed my mother mad-dogging Aunt Marble. I made my way almost to the coffee maker before my mother started in on me.

"Janie, you look so disheveled, did you sleep in that outfit?" she gave me a look of horror.

I let out a long sigh, "No mother, I didn't," I poured my coffee.

"You didn't MEAN to look that way, though, did you?"

With my back to her, I chuckled and started counting to ten, "No mother, I didn't."

"Oh, that's my fault," Tovah came to my rescue. "I made the girls stay the night here. They didn't have any of their things with them."

"Did you get a little too…" mom made the sign of throwing back some drinks.

"Oh. It was nothing like that," Tovah told her. "After the psycho guy, John, started stalking the girls, I wouldn't let them leave."

Fitz and my eyes rounded as my mother's head threatened to blow clean off her shoulders. "The what…the who?"

"The stalker…John," Tovah annunciated slowly. "He's a nut job who's been trying for years to get me to show his work. Now he's taken a fancy to trying to terrorize your daughter."

I shook my head at Tovah. She had no idea what size can of worms she had just opened. Then I saw Tovah grin and wondered if maybe she knew exactly what she was doing.

"I'm not sure I want you here if there's some crazy man hunting you!" mom blurted out in true mom fashion.

"Believe me, she's safer here," Tovah tried to assure her.

"How? How is she safe here?" mom shook like she was getting ready to explode.

"Olaf…would you please come introduce yourself to my friends and family!" Tovah called out.

I could almost feel the ground shaking as something… someone, started walking toward the sunroom. As I looked around the table at all of the concerned faces, I knew I wasn't the only one.

Olaf stood 6'8; his arms were as big around as my thighs; (and not down by the knees, but up by the hip). His chest looked like we could view a movie off the damn thing. There was no discernable neck, per se; it kind of went from ears, into deltoids. His bald head bore a long scar that made me wonder…"what did the other guy look like?" As he extended his arm to introduce himself, I noticed that his hand was big enough to palm my skull like a basketball. He did have beautiful hazel eyes, though, that shined as he said in very broken English, "I Olaf, I protect."

All I could do was nod as I watched my own hand completely disappear in his.

"Olaf, this is Janie's mother. Will you let her know that her little girl is safe?" Tovah asked him.

Olaf turned to mom, her eyes bulging, "I protect," he slammed his hand over his heart. "Promise," he said.

Mom stammered, "Oh…oh, oh…I believe you. Thank you," she swallowed hard.

Tovah introduced Olaf to everyone else in the room. I couldn't help but notice how Betty looked at him, "That is one tall, no, huge glass of water," she said when he left the room. "Do ya feel better, now?" Betty asked my mother.

"Well…it's not like he's bullet proof," mom shook her head.

"Honey, I think you may be mistakin'," Betty laughed.

Changing the subject, I said, "So you brought The Blue Woman?"

"We did," Mum nodded.

"Well, where is she?" I looked around the table. No one was saying anything, though. "Anyone?" I did a palms-up.

Tovah looked at the women and then piped up, "Honey, I've already found her a buyer."

The shock showed on my face, "Already?" I was confused. "I only agreed to sell her…like less than 24 hours ago."

"I know," Tovah gave her head a nod. "An offer was made. You can still reject it if you want to, but…it's pretty impressive."

"By yer standards?" Fitz posed the question. All eyes shot to her. "What? Tovah's Gallery has sold some really expensive pieces!"

"Well, it's not a Van Gogh offer but it's impressive for a new artist, no matter the Gallery," Tovah explained.

All eyes shot to me then back to Tovah. Tovah grabbed a piece of paper and a pen. Writing down the number, she folded the paper and handed it to me. Unfolding the paper, my eyes rounded, I went silent. I wasn't even sure I was breathing until Fitz spoke.

"Janie…ya okay?" she asked me.

I began blinking repeatedly and nodded.

Fitz came to my side, "Can I see?"

I nodded some more as I handed her the paper piece.

"Holy shit!" Fitz roared.

"What…what?" everyone asked as I spied Tovah's grin.

"Can I tell them?" Fitz asked me.

All I could do was continue to nod.

"A hundred and fifty!" Fitz announced.

Mum made the *Oh* face. Aunt Marble covered her mouth with her hands. Betty said, "Holy Crap!"

"One hundred and fifty dollars…that sounds fair," my mother said.

Tovah and I shot my mother a look.

"No," Fitz's head swiveled back and forth. "One hundred and fifty THOUSAND dollars, Mrs. O."

Hoots, hollers and congrats were thrown to me from every direction…except one.

My mother sat with this dumfounded look as all of the other women stood and circled to hug me.

"Isn't that great?" Tovah nudged my mother.

"For that painting?" Mom finally said like she just couldn't believe that anyone would pay that kind of money for my work.

All of the women around the table fell silent.

Mum looked like she was biting her tongue.

My eyes fell closed as I wondered how I was going to act like her reaction didn't annihilate me. I let out a held breath and began to laugh hysterically. "Why…in God's name, did I expect you to be proud? Seriously, at some point, I'm going to have to stop giving you the benefit of the doubt and just EXPECT you to be disappointed somehow."

"Oh Janie," mom huffed, "I didn't mean…"

"Yes, you did. Just once, I would like you to be on my side. I'm not asking you to cheer for me…just not putting me down, would be plenty." I walked out of the room with Fitz in tow.

"Janie," Fitz called to me.

As I turned to face her, I said, "Fitz, if you're going to tell me I overreacted or that I have to be proud of the strides my mother has made…"

"No," she shook her head. "You were in the right…and I'm so sorry…" her eyes welled up as she fell silent.

Wrapping her arms around me, I let a tear fall. "Why did she even come?"

"I'm gonna go give 'er a piece of my mind!" Fitz tried to pull away.

"No. Don't bother."

"She needs to know that she hurt ya," Fitz said angrily.

"Do you really think she doesn't know?" I asked her honestly. "I'm going up to the room."

"Janie, come on. You said yerself that you needed to eat. Come back to the sunroom."

"I've lost my appetite," I said as I walked up the stairs.

Thirty minutes later, Fitz knocked on the door. "Janie, can I come in?"

"Yeah, come in."

Brandishing a plate with cheeses, salami and crackers, she was even more welcome. "I brought ya a nibble, just in case ya found yer appetite."

I gave her a weak smile, "Thanks."

"Ya know, I hate to bring up everything, but I think ya should talk to yer mom."

A thin laugh emitted from me, "Why?"

"Well, when I went back into the sunroom, Betty was havin' a go at yer mom."

"Well, as much as I appreciate it, she doesn't have to. Mom is who she is. Period."

"That's what I'm gettin' at…"

"What do you mean?" I sat up.

"I think ya should hear why yer mom felt that way, that's all."

"Ya know what, why not? I can take the abuse, right?"

Fitz moved to the door and told my mother to enter.

"That was sarcasm, Fitz," I huffed.

"Just…hear her out," Fitz backed out of the room and closed the door behind her.

"This is a nice room," mom said like she was trying to find something to say.

I let out a sigh, "Yep, it is."

"Look, I need to explain," mom sat on the edge of the bed. "I have a problem with that painting."

"Yeah I think I got that," I told her as I stood and began to pace.

"But you have to understand why," Mom pleaded.

"Okay…explain it," I crossed my arms over my chest and waited.

"You know I studied art?"

So was this the part where she was going to tell me that it wasn't up to standard; that the light was wrong or the shadowing?

"I know mom. So what in your opinion is the problem? Is it just not good enough? Is that it?"

"No," she shook her head.

"Then what?" I gave her a palms-up. "You're opinionated enough not to like it, but you can't say why?"

"It's the context," she blurted out.

"Oh my God, my shoulders are bare, I'm NOT NAKED!"

"No, it's not that!" she started shaking.

"What then damn it, what?" I shook my hands to the heavens.

"I don't like it because it's a self-portrait of you…at your lowest," her eyes were tearing up.

"What do you mean?"

"I know what the painting means…I've always known. And I've always hated the damn thing because I knew how much pain you were in and I didn't know how to fix it."

My eyes rounded; my mother said *damn*?

"I didn't know how to help you out of it, what you were going through. That painting shows more than your pain…it shows the pain of a woman who was also cursed with a totally inept mother."

She patted the spot next to her so I sat down.

"I *love* your work," mom said. "I think you are so talented… and brave. I was never brave enough to even try," she shook her head. "And I was good, too. But what mattered most…what I was never good at…was knowing how to be the kind mother you needed."

With this, my eyes threatened to water.

"I tried. I really did. But my not trusting others around you came off like I didn't trust you. Me wanting you to get A's made it seem like I wasn't proud of your B's. Me knowing that you look great in dresses made it seem like I didn't like the way you looked in jeans."

I laughed a little at that one.

"I just always see so much in you. And I always harp because I know who the real you is, inside! I know your potential, even if I haven't done the best job showing you. Right now I should really be telling you how I feel about you, for you, Janie. Just so you know, ALWAYS, I am so proud of you; who you are, how you treat people, all the amazing things you do!" Mom wrapped her arms around me and hugged tightly.

I cried and hugged her back.

"I can't believe someone wants to see you at your lowest..., knowing it existed, you went through this and I didn't know how to help you, it kills me. And despite my parenting flaws and in spite of my flaws you became such an amazing woman."

This broke me and I sobbed.

"I don't know how to say the right things, the right way...I never have...and I am so sorry, baby." She faced me and cupped my cheeks in her hands, "I am so proud...and I love you so much."

"I love you, too, mom," I said through my hiccup cries.

"I love ya both," we heard Fitz cry from outside the closed door.

As I began to laugh, all of the women barreled through the door and took mom and me in a group hug.

"I knew ya weren't the Devil, Mrs. O," Fitz told mom as she hugged her tightly.

I waited for mom to stiffen up, but instead she laughed and squeezed Fitz back, "Right back at ya," mom told her.

We decided it was time to retrieve our things from the Ritz. Tovah called a limo and we piled inside; Fitz, Mum, Mom and me. Olaf rode in the front seat with the driver. As Mum, Mom and I, jumped out of the car, Fitz told us she wasn't going up.

"What do ya mean?" Mum asked her daughter. "Am I to be yer valet?"

"Ah, come on, Mum. I don't have any makeup on and I'm wearin' a witch's robe!"

Mum huffed, "Fine."

Olaf took up the rear as we headed to the rooms.

In my room, there wasn't much to be packed. I really hadn't unpacked much.

Mom asked, "What can I do?"

"Um, you can go help Mum. Fitz always has so much more stuff than me. Oh, don't forget to check the drawers. Fitz always puts things in drawers and forgets something."

I was in the bathroom grabbing my toothbrush and deodorant when I heard my mother scream. My head snapped up as I considered what would make my mother scream. "Oh shit."

I met mom in the hall. She looked embarrassed; she couldn't look me in the eye.

"You okay, mom?" I asked.

Mom nodded. "I thought it was a makeup brush holder."

I winced.

"It wasn't," she shook her head at the silver box in her hand.

Olaf, who was standing in the hallway, also blushed. Apparently when he heard my mother scream, he flew through the door and got his own view of what had scared the scream out of her.

When Mum and I carried Fitz's last bags to the luggage trolley, Mum said, "I know what I'm *not* gettin' yer mother for Christmas this year."

I threw an arm around her, "Yeah, really not something she needs."

"No?" Mum's brows rose.

"I'll explain later," I laughed, "after a few drinks...and then a few more."

Back at Tovah's, a *girl's night* was just beginning.

"What do you like on your pizza, Kid?" she asked me.

"Everything but anchovies," I grinned.

Mum and Aunt Marble were making their famous Bloody Marys with bacon, olives and asparagus. Betty was the official taster and no matter what Mum poured, Betty would say, "Mmm that is perfect!"

I looked around the room and smiled from ear to ear; almost all of my favorite ladies, all in one room. Except for Nance, my old boss and Fitz of course, who had decided that she wouldn't go another step without a shower and mascara. This was my support group and I felt blessed to have them here. The truth was, the showing was tomorrow night and I was a bit nervous. But these ladies, they kept me, well...level might be going a bit far, if I really thought about it. But I knew they loved me, supported me, and in Fitz's case, would beat someone's *gonna-be sorry* ass for me if need be.

I was also still in shock every time I thought about the sale of The Blue Lady. It was more than I had ever even hoped of, much less allowed myself to dream about. Things were changing in my life and I hoped I was ready. The thought that I could actually make a living, doing what I lived to do, was amazing and mind-blowing in the best way.

Heading upstairs to check on Fitz, I heard Olaf coming up behind me. Turning, I said, "I'm okay Olaf. You can relax."

"I protect," he bowed his head. His giant stature almost seemed childlike in a gentle giant kind of way.

"I'll be right back down," I assured him.

Almost sullen, he turned from the staircase and lumbered away.

"Fitz," I called walking up to the closed bathroom door. "They're ordering pizza and making Bloody Marys. You almost done?"

"UMMMHHMMMM," is what I heard.

"Fitz?" I repeated.

"UMMHHMMMMMM!"

Opening the bedroom door, my eyes rounded. "Oh my God," I rushed to her.

In her fluffy bathrobe, Fitz had a net over her head that went down to her knees. Duct tape had then been wrapped around her body, holding her arms pinned-down to her sides. Another strip of tape was stretched across her mouth. Trying to pull gently, I removed the silver adhesive.

"It's on, I'm gonna go full *Irish* on that boy's ass!"

"What the hell happened?" I panicked while trying to break her free from the mile of duct tape it took to secure her arms.

"That crazy son-of-a-bitch came at me from behind when I walked out the bathroom door. He threw one of those netted laundry bags over my head. I had my arms down at my sides trying to find the bottom of the damned thing, so I could pull it off and he had a yard of duct tape ready. He went around me, like twice!"

I couldn't help but think there was no way that would have worked on me. My boobs would have prevented the netting from ever passing them, I thought to myself.

"I got in a few shots; a few good head-butts to his nose and I know he's hobblin', wherever he is, from my foot ringin' his jolly bells."

"Oh my God…he may still be in the house! I have to warn everyone!" I tore off for the door.

"Um, Janie, I'd like to be freed if ya don't mind!" Fitz's eyes practically popped out of her skull.

I had trouble deciding what I should do first as I looked from Fitz to the door to Fitz, again.

"Seriously Janie? Me first!" she yelled.

Cautiously, I looked into my room before entering. No John. Grabbing my purse, I found my buck knife and ran back to the bathroom to free Fitzy.

Luckily, the tape stuck more to itself and the netting than anything else.

"Come on, we have to warn everyone and tell Olaf!" I ran for the door with Fitz in tow.

Before I ever reached bottom of the stairs, I just started yelling, "He's here! He's in the house!"

As the women ran toward my shouting, we met at the bottom of the stairs.

"You saw him?" Tovah asked me.

"I didn't, but he had Fitz bound and gagged in her bedroom!"

"He had my baby bound and gagged?" Mum's green eyes flashed with just a hint of homicidal maniac.

"I did get a few in after he bound my arms. He came at me with the net and the duct tape the second I opened the door and ran the damn tape around me as I tried to fight 'em. But he got a rackin', three head-butts and few good skull dings from my right foot before I lost my balance and fell on my arse."

"That's my baby," Mum said.

"Ya see," Betty said to my mother, "this is why every house should have a gun!"

"I'd have to agree," Tovah said and motioned to Betty to follow her up the stairs.

Before Tovah and Betty made it to the landing, we all heard a loud bang and a curse coming from the library.

Fitz was the first to charge, but as she went to pass Olaf, he picked her up and put her back on her feet behind him, "I protect," he said and headed toward the library with all of us pulling up the rear.

Once Olaf's huge frame moved enough for us to see into the room, we saw John just about to make his escape out the library door into the backyard. He was definitely hobbling and when he turned his surprised/frightened eyes to Olaf advancing, we saw that he had bloody tissues shoved up both nostrils and the beginning discoloration of two black eyes.

"I did that," Fitz nodded and high-fived Aunt Marble.

John's mouth opened but no sound came out. It was like he was scared stiff and mute. Then I heard the most high-pitched-girlish scream I had ever heard emitted from a man in all of my life. I expected the crystal liquor decanters to shatter into a million pieces. I'm not sure why, but my mother screamed back at him, like they were speaking in dolphin. John leapt into action; hobbling away as quickly as his injured sack, gimping leg and what I had to assume from his shifty eyes was double vision from his freshly broken nose.

Olaf took off in not so hot pursuit. Speed wasn't something he boasted; it was more like the determined *stomping of the bull* rather than the running of them. But the look on his face; that Neolithic brow protruded even further with the angry crunching of his face. As he walked at John, only his legs moved. His arms stayed bowed at his sides, causing the trunk of his body to swivel…right, left, right.

As I watched John trying to pick up his pace; small squeaks, almost whimpers were present with every breath he emitted. In that instance, I felt sorry for him. It was like watching a small animal who knows death is imminent.

Once Olaf exited the back door, all of us women ran to the doorway to watch the show.

John had just made it to the back wall. Even as slowly as Olaf approached, John knew he was between a rock and a hard spot. (Or in this case; stuck between a man who looked like he could draw and quarter someone with his bare hands…and the huge dog he had already had the misfortune to meet.)

The dog on the other side of the wall let out one deep *woof.*

John looked from Olaf to the wall, back to Olaf and began to cry. Just then, Tovah and Betty stepped out onto the porch, each of them with a firearm by their side. John's eyes screamed panic as he tried to climb the wall. Still Olaf swiveled toward him, his arms rising from his sides. John made a choking sound and the bloody tissues shot out of his nose. Summoning all of his strength, he climbed. As he made it to the top of the wall, legs hanging, one on each side, you could see the dilemma on his face; arms ripped off by Olaf and possibly shot by the gun wielding women, or another run-in with the hound from hell.

As John considered his options, he peed himself. Olaf's hands were almost there, reaching for him. John dropped down the other side of the wall. There was a blood curdling scream that again trailed off, as all of us women winced.

Olaf turned to us; his mouth turned downward in a frown, his shoulders slumped. As he walked slowly back toward us, Tovah met him halfway. Standing beside him, Tovah only came up to his ribcage. Comforting him like a mother, she rubbed Olaf's back and told him, "You'll get him next time."

"Next time?" my mother shrieked like she couldn't handle the thought. As she stood there shaking her head, Mum suggested a stiff belt off a whiskey bottle.

"I'm sure it will all be over soon," Tovah told mom. "He's just trying to scare Janie and pissing me off in the process."

Right now, looking at Tovah's expression, I would have put her up against Olaf.

"Are ya okay, kid?" Tovah asked Fitz when we all calmed down a bit.

"I'm…" Fitz searched for a word.

"Fit to be taped?" Aunt Marble asked.

All eyes shot her way as Mum started to shake her head at her sister.

"Too soon?" Marble asked.

"Too soon, Marble," her sister told her.

Back in the house the doorbell rang, but Olaf wouldn't let us answer the door. I wish I could have seen the look on the pizza boy's face when he saw the hulking man asking him for more parmesan and red pepper packets.

Sitting at the round dining table, all of us ladies and Olaf ate heartily. Vah had showed up after all of the action. She was introduced to everyone then filled in on the day's events. Tovah and Betty had bonded, and were discussing the benefits of revolvers over semi-automatics.

Mom just kept shaking her head until Betty said, "Keep shakin' your head like that and I'm gonna drag your behind to the range, too."

"Oh I'd love to go to a firing range," Aunt Marble said.

Everyone's eyes rounded, even Olaf's, but no one had the balls to point out the fact that handing her a gun was no different than handing a lethal weapon to Mr. Magoo.

Fitz politely changed the subject, "Ya think the dog got him again?" she asked me.

"It did sound that way," I answered. "He was kind of dragging his leg to begin with. I don't know if that was from his first run-in with Cujo or if that was you."

"I didn't touch his legs. I know that I flat-footed his crotch, but nothin' to the legs. Ya know, ya almost sound as if ya feel sorry for the freak," Fitz pointed out.

"Well…" I began, crinkling up my nose.

"Ya've got to be kiddin' me!" she blurted out. "That screwball bound me with nettin' and duct tape! Feelin' sorry fer the underdog is one thing, Janie. Feeling sorry fer a guy who's stalkin' ya?"

"Are you gonna tell Sizell about this?" Mom asked.

The whole table corrected her, "Cecil!"

"Really mom," I clapped my hands over my eyes, "you're going to have to learn his name. I can't have you calling him pretzel or some nonsense when you meet him. And, no! Truthfully, Fitz made me realize why I shouldn't," I shook my head.

"Yeah, well that was before he laid hands on me!" Fitz grabbed another piece of pepperoni pizza. "Now…I'm gonna tell Scotty and he better hope Scotty gets to 'em first!" Fitz's eyes slit.

Vah sat listening intently to everything and smiling that one-sided grin from time to time. Even in her silence, I could see her wheels turning. Maybe it was her silence that made me more aware.

As Olaf stood to go make his rounds, the topic changed to the showing and I admitted my nervousness.

"Everyone feels that way when they have a showing," Tovah patted my shoulder. "And anyone who says they don't is full of malarkey."

"It's too bad ya don't have Cecil here…for a little stress relief," Fitz grinned.

Everyone laughed, but my mother. "Oh, she doesn't need that," she shook her head.

"Says the woman who has never been without it," Fitz shot mom a look.

Mum looked at me, recalling our conversation at the hotel. Her head cocked and her eyes went wide, as I began to nod.

Betty piped in when my mom made the *Who…me,* face. "I hear that."

"What does that mean?" Mom asked Betty.

"It means, I can't speak for Mum, Marble or Tovah, but as for me, Fitz and your daughter, you've had more sex than all three of us combined! And I mean just this year, for God sakes," Betty eyes widened.

"Oh…that's not true!" mom huffed.

Fitz's and my face scrunched up as we began to nod.

"Oh, you're just saying that to make me feel bad!" mom added.

"Honey, exactly how would us saying that, make ya feel bad? The way I'm seein' it, we should be the ones feelin' bad," Betty explained and pointed to the rest of us sexless creatures.

"We have a normal amount of sex," my mother shook her head.

"Fine, honey, whatever you say!" Betty patted my mother's hand.

"Um, just for the record…what is normal, to ya?" Mum asked my mother.

Mom looked embarrassed and I hoped this would end the conversation before…

"Usually once a day…or every other day," mom said. "Used to be more, but we're slowing down, like we all do!" she made the sad face.

Oh the looks; Tovah's head shot to my mother, a blank stare. Mum's eyes slit, like she was trying to be sure what she heard was what was said. Betty leaned back and folded her arms across her chest, just like Fitzy did. I sat with my eyes closed…trying not to picture…anything. But when Aunt Marble piped up, all eyes shot to her; "That sounds about right," she said.

We all stared at Aunt Marble in silence until Mum said, "What?"

"Well we do that tantric thing…so," Aunt Marble gave a palms-up.

"Oh, we tried that once," my mother waved her hand like the idea was overrated. "But we're good with the hour, hour and a half of you know…regular sex…and then just finishing."

All heads swung back to my mother. Mum's jaw dropped a little.

At this point, I just covered my eyes like the darkness could make the conversation end, or stop time.

"And the two of ya," Mum pointed from my mother to Aunt Marble, "think this is normal…at our ages…and as long as you've been married?" she asked my mother.

Mom and Aunt Marble thought about it then reluctantly nodded.

Mum's wheels were spinning. "Ok, I know that you couldn't have kids," she said to Aunt Marble and gave her hand a squeeze. "But you," she looked at my mother, "How did ya not have a truck load of children?"

Hearing this said, I began to ponder; we're Catholic. Why didn't I have a shit-ton of siblings? For as…*active* as my parents are, how was I the only little O'Connelly? I stared at my mother questioningly, and waited for her response.

Now everyone stared as mom shrugged, "You know, I really don't know."

Out of the corner of my eye, I saw one side of Fitz's mouth pull into a grin. We looked sidelong at each other. I knew exactly what she was thinking as her head began to nod slightly.

"You couldn't have children?" my mother asked Aunt Marble with a visible note of sadness.

Aunt Marble's eyes welled up.

It was heartbreaking for me to think that after all these years, Marble being of a certain age, and all, that it still hurt her so deeply; left a hole in her.

Marble shook her head, no.

Mom's eyes turned to me. The look on her face; it looked like she was contemplating what her life would have been like if she had never been a mother.

When Tovah's detective friend showed up, he explained that

John had slipped away. They had posted unmarked officers out front of his apartment, but he hadn't returned home.

"Well, that explains the smell," Fitz surmised.

"What smell would that be?" the detective asked.

"Putrid," Fitz said, "with a healthy splash of urine."

"Well I interviewed your neighbors and met King," Detective Ryan said to Tovah.

My mother piped up, "King?"

"Yes ma'am, that's the large Mastiff who apparently is quite the…*lover*." Detective Ryan really punched the word making all of us squint then say, *"Ah."*

Mom was a moment behind the rest of us, but when she got it, her eyes rounded, "Oh my, Beastiality?" she grabbed at her chest like the thought would cause a heart attack.

"Almost. I guess King assumed that this man, John, was going to be his mate. Before the neighbors knew what was happening, why this man was in their backyard, they had to save him from becoming a human sex toy," Detective Ryan told Tovah with a little grin. "John bolted as fast as he could the first time. The second time, well, the dog's owners weren't home. I guess they assumed that John wouldn't be heading into their backyard again, anytime soon."

Betty howled with laughter and began clapping her hands, "Oh my word, can ya picture it in your heads, cause I can!" The rest of the women thought for a moment then joined her in laughter.

"But the fact that this guy came back, and went again over the back wall knowing exactly what the outcome could be? I gotta say, he either has an unnatural fetish," Detective Ryan cocked his head, "or he had to be scared shitless. And after your friend Olaf met me at the door, I'm pretty sure John just picked the lesser of two pains. But either way, the guy has to be nuts, so you need to be on guard."

"He was limpin' pretty badly, even before I got to 'em," Fitz told the detective.

"Yeah, like I said, I don't think King was trying to hurt him," the Detective chucked, "but 140 pound Mastiff who is looking for love from a reluctant partner…could do some damage if rejected."

I don't know why, but I felt a little bad for the psycho stalker. I now understood that this was my gift/curse. But I couldn't help but understand how it would feel to think that your passion, how you express yourself, what you pour all of your heart and soul into, no one wanted to see. Wouldn't…couldn't this make you feel… horribly invisible? I wondered. Not everyone had a Fitzy in their life much less a whole table of friends who thought you did something amazing; that *you* were amazing.

"Ya better not be feelin' bad fer that psycho-squirrel guy again, so help me Lord, Janie!" Fitz said when she caught me looking off into space.

Vah was staring at me, but I couldn't really read her expression. She still had her one sided grin, but her eyes…seemed warmer, like maybe she could understand why I felt sorry for John.

15

NERVES, PILLS AND CHILLS

This was it, my big night. Well the first of many I hoped. I guess I had already had a big night as far as my career went, but I was laid up on my couch for that one, nursing a concussion.

Tovah left earlier to see to all of the last minute details that went into a successful showing: making sure the servers knew what was expected, that the art friendly food was art friendly, champagne had been chilled along with white wines and the reds were breathing properly.

I sat on the edge of the claw-footed tub, wringing my hands. I had only been this nervous once before that I could remember; when Cecil brought me home from the hospital and said he was staying with me until I was well. I remembered thinking that I was like a wounded wildebeest and he was definitely a predator. At that time, I barely knew him and my first impression of him was somewhat mixed. On the one hand, he had spent our whole first night together acting like a pompous, arrogant, philandering ass. Turns out he was really only one of those things; a man-whore in recovery. The next day, though, Cecil came to my rescue against my ex, another John, who wrongly decided that the caveman approach of winning me back would be effective. I wasn't conscious for the ass beating John had received. But I hear it was an epic display of brains and brawn vs. too stupid not to be hit. Then, I wanted to keep Cecil at bay. And now, I waited as patiently as I could for his arrival. Somehow, I was sure he would be able to keep me calm. I felt safer with him than I did even with Olaf.

"Are ya gettin' in the bath, or not?" I heard Fitz yell through the door.

I let out a breath I didn't even realize I was holding, "Yeah, I'm going."

Dropping down into the hot bubbled water, Fitz opened the door a bit, "Can I come in?"

"Come in," I said.

"Ya okay?" Fitz sent me worried eyes.

I sighed, "I think so. It's just a bit nerve wracking."

"I know, but I really don't think ya have to worry about Cab Driver John. I mean, Cecil and Scotty will be here, there's police and security everywhere and *Olaf*," her eyes widened. "I wonder where the hell Tovah found him?"

"It's not just that."

"What then? Talk to me," she sat on the floor with her back against the tub.

"I'm worried about the showing…I'm worried about the squirrel guy, yes…but I'm most worried about Cecil," I admitted.

Fitz turned a confused look my way, "Why would ya worry about Cecil. Are ya still scared he'll propose? Look, I said some things that weren't fair to ya. I know that now. I was bein' really selfish and…"

"It's not that," I shook my head.

"Well what then?"

"No matter what happens, he's going back to Ireland," I

shrugged. "I'll have him for a few days..." I shook my head, "then I'll put him back on a plane for...for God knows how long." My eyes started to tear, "I just spend so much time missing him."

Fitz reached out to pat my arm, "I am sorry, Janie." Standing she got me some tissue. "Just fer the record, if he does propose..."

My eyes shot to hers.

"and ya do say yes...I'll be so happy fer ya, Janie...even if ya move across the ocean."

With this I started to cry.

"What the hell did I say that yer cryin'?" Fitz gave me a palms-up. "That was supposed to make ya happy, fer Pete's sake!"

"What if he doesn't propose?" I asked, biting into my bottom lip to try and keep my jaw from quivering.

Fitz's face dropped like she had never really considered the possibility that this wouldn't happen. Sitting down on the floor behind me, she wrapped her arms around my neck as I sobbed.

"Shhh, shhh, shhh, it's okay. Everything's goin' to be okay," she soothed.

After I cried myself out, blew my nose through half a box of Kleenex and the water went cold, I emerged feeling emotionally dehydrated.

"Will ya let me do yer makeup and hair?" Fitz asked.

"I kind of wanted to look like me," I said.

Fitz nodded, "I can do that."

After my makeup was done, Fitz put my hair into a pomped ponytail. Showing me a beautiful round silver clasp that fit over the hair band, I said, "That's lovely. Where did you find it?"

"I got it fer ya at a little store in Manhattan Beach. I knew you'd wanna wear a damn ponytail," she laughed, "so I got this so ya could dress it up a bit."

I almost started crying again and had to throw my head back to keep tears from running.

"Ya ruin yer mascara, I'm not doin' it again," she scolded like a mama.

When she was all done, and I had on my black floor length halter dress, I was finally allowed to look at myself. My smile was huge. Fitz had made me-up as just a slightly more done-up version…of who I really was.

"I like this dress better than the one ya originally picked. It's more…you," Fitz smiled. "Ya look amazin', by the way."

"Thank you," I hugged her tightly.

From the top of the stairs I could see all the women gathered below: Mom, Mum, Aunt Marble, Betty and Vah stood waiting, all dressed to the nines. As I started down, with Fitz by my side, all the women began to clap. Again my eyes welled.

"I swear, I'm gonna lose it if she smudges!" Fitz warned, dabbing her own eyes.

From out of the kitchen came Olaf. Dressed in a tuxedo, he looked like a giant sized Telly Savalas. Curving his arm to me, I smiled and looped my arm through his. "I protect," he said softly and smiled back.

The limo was parked out front and as we approached, Olaf took my hand in his and brought it to his lips for a quick kiss. Releasing my hand, he lumbered over to the driver's side and pulled the man from behind the wheel by his jacket lapels.

My eyes rounded as Edam, not a small man himself, shouted out, "Man, what the hell are you doin'?"

From behind me, Fitz came running, "No Olaf, he's okay. We know him," she pointed to me then herself.

As Olaf released him, Edam looked to us and asked again, "WHAT THE HELL?"

Fitz quickly ran down the whole story after which Edam looked Olaf up and down, "Well, I hardly think you'll need my help with the Abominable *whoa man*, here," he pointed to Olaf, who still stood on guard. "But if you do, I got your back."

"Thank you," I said.

Olaf rode up front with Edam as the rest of us piled in the back seat.

On the ride to the Gallery, I began to fidget again. Fitz reached out her hand to mine and squeezed it. Mom watched me start to calm almost immediately and she smiled at the two of us.

I kept waiting for a crazy cab driver to pull up next to us, run us off the road, something. But as we sailed along, on the smoothest ride we had experienced since we landed in New York, I chose to be grateful instead of fearful.

Pulling up out in front of the Schumer Gallery, women in gowns and men in tuxedos, I still couldn't believe I belonged here.

Aunt Marble piped up as I let out a deep breath, "You've got this, Clematis."

Mom's questioning eyes shot to Aunt Marble.

"Let 'em see ya shine, Babygirl," Mum said, beaming with pride.

"You hold that head high, Puddin'. You deserve this!" Betty leaned in, pressing her check against mine. "I'd kiss yer cheek, Sugar, but I'm all *Hooker Red* here," she pointed to her painted lips.

Mom sat curiously quiet, watching and listening.

As we all started out of the car mom said, "Wait."

We all stopped scooting our asses across the leather seats and looked at her.

"I need to thank you ladies," mom said. "I had no idea…how much of a support system my daughter has."

Mum, Marble, Betty and Fitz began to smile.

"I mean, I knew she had friends…that she loves with all her heart. But until now…I don't think it dawned on me…just how much all of you…love her, too." Turning to Mum, mom said, "I owe you a debt of gratitude…and an apology."

Mum looked confused.

"You...you're the kind of mother...I thought one couldn't be and still raise a wonderful daughter."

Mum's eyes slit as she tried to figure out if she was offended or not.

"What I mean is," Mom tried to correct the possible damage. "What I mean is, you've never tried to act like a saint, or be seen as perfect, or hide who you really were from your kids...and you've raised an amazing daughter."

A smile began to pull at Mum's cheek.

"And you, Fitz, all those years...I treated you...so badly," Mom's eyes closed and she shook her head. "You've been there for my daughter...like a best friend, no, a sister, no..." she couldn't think of a word to describe just how much Fitz meant to me.

"A soulmate," Fitz finished her thought as I grinned from ear to ear.

Mom's eyes welled, "Yes, her soulmate."

"Betty you haven't been in her life as long, but you've been so good to her. Whether it be advice, or a safe place, or even keeping an eye on me for her, you've been there for her, whatever she needed."

"And you Marble..." Mom shifted and took Aunt Marbles hand, "I was uncomfortable with you referring to Janie as your daughter..."

Aunt Marble dropped her head.

"But now, I'd be honored to share that honor...with you!"

Aunt Marble's huge magnified eyes shot up to Mom, then to me, then back to my mother before she yelled, "Oh," and embraced my other mother.

As Mom and my *Spirit Mother* hugged and cried, my eyes started watering, too.

"Ugh, you," Mom pointed to Vah, "I'm sorry, I'm not sure what for, but I need to thank you for something, too, I'm sure."

Vah smiled and nodded.

"Okay, enough of this!" mom rubbed her tears with the back of her hand. "Let's go watch my baby, our baby," she smiled at Aunt Marble, "take New York by storm! Come on Climax!" she yelled.

All of us women gave her a shocked look then broke out laughing.

"Clematis," Aunt Marble told her. "Although, now that you say it…that could be an unfortunate name," she wondered out loud.

As we scooted, Mum said quietly to me, "And you were worried about her callin' Cecil pickle or sizzle…I think yer gettin' the worst of this one."

"Yeah, thank God his name doesn't sound like a sex act or a body part…"

"Or an STD," Mum gave me the sad eyes and patted my hand. "I really did try to change her mind, darlin'."

I kissed Mum's cheek, "I know you did. Come on, I'm gonna go full Clematis on this place!" I announced and began scooting to the door.

"I'm not sure what that means, but I'm with ya come hell or high water," Mum said.

Olaf stood next to the door and waited for me to emerge. Taking my arm again, he led the way to the front door.

16

THE SCHUMER GALLERY

The Schumer Gallery was so impressive during the light of day, I couldn't imagine it would be more so at night, but it was. The trees that lined the sidewalk out front wore soft cream colored twinkle lights on every bough. Through the wall of windows, in the warm glow of the room, I could see a few people looking at the first collection. From where I stood, all I could think was what a beautiful piece this would make. I asked Olaf to give me a moment, to take in this view and commit it to memory. Before we ever made it to the wide open double glass doors, we stepped onto a red carpet. Taking a deep breath, pushing my shoulders back and setting my jaw, Olaf looked down at me and smiled, "We go, now?"

Smiling back, I nodded, "We go now."

Walking in, I felt an amazing sense of pride mixed evenly with my nervousness. But I didn't fidget. A cute waitress wearing a dress shirt and paisley bowtie presented us with champagne. Olaf declined, but grabbed a glass for me. Fitz stood close, champagne in hand, she raised it to me.

"So proud of you," she beamed.

Mom, Mum, Aunt Marble, Betty and Vah also raised their glasses.

I wasn't sure how to respond. Was I supposed to make a toast, say a few words? "Thank you all for being here…not just tonight…always," I raised my glass to them.

Looking at the first collection, my mind was blown; a painting of Central Park from above. The lines, the lighting…it was perfect. I looked as closely as acceptable at the reflections in glass, car windows and puddles left by the rain. Someone saw this, this way. The artist's eyes didn't miss the small details, the shadows and change of light with direction and movement.

As I stood in awe, I caught something out of the corner of my eye. Turning my head, I spied Scotty. When he saw me, he put the one-fingered *hush* sigh to his lips. Fitz had her back turned as he sneaked up on her.

Just as Scotty was going to reach out to his beloved, he was snatched off his feet and put in a Full Nelson. My eyes rounded, "No, no Olaf! It's okay…this is Fitz's fiancé."

Fitz turned quickly to see her man dangling like a wooden marionette two feet off the ground. Covering her mouth she stifled a laugh.

"Would someone like to tell me why I'm being restrained by this huge gentleman?" Scotty asked.

Olaf slowly set Scotty back down on his feet and released him.

"Olaf," Olaf patted his chest with his huge palm.

"Right," Scotty nodded and held out his hand to greet Olaf correctly.

"Ya shouldn't have been sneakin' up," Fitz moved into Scotty's arms.

"Indeed I shouldn't have," Scotty's eyes rounded. "What's with the bodyguard? I haven't been to a lot of art shows, but I don't remember the artists bein' surrounded by this kind of security," he looked around at the other security dressed as patrons but wearing earpieces.

I had to admit, I hadn't been paying enough attention to the other people to notice.

As Scotty said his hellos to the rest of the family and was introduced to my mother and Vah, Fitz explained the situation.

The look on Scotty's face was a mix of concerned and upset.

"Why didn't ya tell me what was goin' on?" he pulled his soon-to-be bride closer. "I would have come right away!" he told her.

"That's why I said nothin'. You had work to do, and I was in good hands, I assure ya," she gave a head nod to where Olaf stood on guard, watching everyone who approached.

Scotty nodded, "That I do believe," he said before giving Fitz a deep kiss. "Still, next time, if there is one, a situation, you tell me," he lifted her chin to look her in the eyes. "Nothin' in this world is more important to me than you are."

All of the women shot Scotty a dreamy look, like he was the dashing hero in a great love story, which of course he was in my estimation.

"I love this boy," Mum said, pulling Scotty down so she could kiss his cheek.

"I don't mean to sound like I don't miss you or I'm not happy to see you, but…" I said to Scotty.

"He's about thirty minutes behind me. He had to land at the private airstrip," Scotty smiled at me as my face went into a *perma-grin.*

I swear I wasn't trying to babysit my mom, but I couldn't help but notice when she picked up glass number three of champagne. I also noticed Betty quietly telling her something and mom giving her the hand-wave. Suddenly I was worried mom might go full sexy, grinding up one of the statues on display.

As we walked further on to another collection, there was an

amazing sculpture of a woman with a full womb. Her hands were cradling her blooming stomach, and her face was pure joy.

Aunt Marble stood admiring it and said to my mother, "Is that how ya felt when you were pregnant?"

Mom kind of giggled...I knew that giggle. "No," Mom said, "but if they have one of a woman holding her stomach with one hand and cradling a toilet bowl with the other, that one's me."

My eyes rounded; Mom was drunk.

Marble gave Mom a bewildered look and said, "Oh, okay."

I watched Betty quickly grab the glass from Mom's hand and replace it with a small bottle of water.

I had to laugh. I agreed with Mom. As much as I loved the captured moments of a woman loving her growing tummy, the beauty of motherhood, I had been around enough pregnant women to know the truth; it was no cake-walk and was no joy-ride for most. The best you can do, is try to capture the beautiful moments when your head isn't in a toilet.

On I went to another collection. As all of us stood silent in front of a huge painting, I noticed we all wore the same expression; WTF? I knew what I was looking at. Never being a huge fan of the abstract, I kind of wished this one was a little more so. It reminded me of my time spent at *The Prick Collection.* I was trying to decide just how long of a look was proper. I mean, was it offensive to the other artist to just move away?

Fitz had her lips pursed as she and Scotty exchanged looks. Aunt Marble squinted at the painting, but I wasn't sure if she was examining it, or just couldn't make it out with her horrible vision. Mum looked like she was remembering... *something.* She wore a little grin like she had just been told a dirty joke. Betty looked like she was trying to measure it in *real size.*

Then there was mom. "I don't know why...but this painting speaks to me, ya know?"

All of us turned heads to my mother and watched her nodding.

Fitz was the first to bust up laughing, quickly followed by all of us, except Marble. Now I was sure, she hadn't actually *seen* the painting or she'd be laughing, too.

"What?" my Mom asked honestly confused.

"Put on yer damn glasses," Betty suggested.

Pulling her glasses from her purse and looking again, Mom's hand shot to her mouth as she stared. The rest of us waited; would she be embarrassed, offended? Suddenly, Mom began to crack up.

"Oh my word," she tried to catch her breath. "Well, it still speaks to me," Mom giggled and walked to the next painting.

"I know it does," Fitz patted me on the shoulder as we turned to follow my mother.

"What does that mean?" Scotty asked.

"It means ya have a new limit to reach," Fitz joked.

Scotty looked back at the piece of the giant penis, "Uh?"

"Not that!" Fitz laughed. "I'll explain it later."

As we moved on, we stood in front of my collection. I took a deep breath. The first was *The Mod Girl*. I didn't know if it was the lighting, or if I wasn't being as critical as I usually am of my own work, but the piece looked even better on the wall now than it had when I first saw it. I was overwhelmed with emotion as I let out a breath filled with joy.

"You know, baby..." Mom wrapped one arm around me and the other around Fitz, "this one is almost as good as the pin-up painting you did of Fitz." She kissed both of our checks then wandered away.

My eyes shot to Fitz, "She has a favorite of my work!"

"And it's of me!" Fitz added with a huge smile.

I wanted to go in line; the first, then the second and so on, but, something on the wall; a little further down caught my eye and I went to it; *The Blue Lady*. I stood staring at her, confused. I thought she had sold, was no longer…*mine.*

"Are you surprised to see her, Kid?" I heard Tovah's voice behind me.

Turning to her I said, "Very. I thought she sold?"

"Oh, she has," Tovah took my hand. "But the owner said that he wanted to see it hung in a Gallery before it became part of his private collection."

I stared back at my self-portrait.

"I hope I didn't overstep?" Tovah's head cocked.

It took a moment to figure out how I felt. I was there, bared for all to see; my misery, pain, loneliness, confusion, open to all…like my soul had been slit and every thought and emotion poured out on the canvas. All the other artists in the room were migrating toward her, *The Blue Woman*. Or were they migrating toward Tovah?

Fighting back tears of…I wasn't sure what, I shook my head. "No, you didn't overstep…it's okay," I took in a deep breath and let it go with a smile.

Vah's stare caught my attention. When she winked and raised her glass to me all I could do was give her a nod of my head.

As other artists approached, I realized Vah was right; I really didn't care what *EVERYONE* thought of me, or my work, or my life for that matter. A small group of people in this world meant the world to me, so why would I care what the rest of the world thought of me?

As the other artists critiqued the painting, not knowing the artist was standing behind them, I heard different takes on what the painting meant.

"It's brave," said one. "Bold," said another. "Tragic," said a woman standing in front of me.

My eyes shot to Tovah as people made their comments. We held each other's gaze and then someone asked Tovah for the price.

"I'm afraid this piece has already sold," Tovah said.

The man leaned in, "I'll make a great offer," he raised his brows to her.

"I've already accepted a great offer," Tovah assured him.

Just then, a voice rang out over a megaphone, "Janie O'Connelly," reverberated off the walls. "Come on down!"

Confused looks shot all around as security tried to pinpoint where the voice had come from.

I could tell by the look on Tovah's face that she also knew whose voice we were hearing.

My eyes were drawn up to the catwalk of the cordoned-off second floor. There he was, John the Cabby.

Looking a might bit more deranged than our first meeting; his hair sticking out all over his head, what looked like big chunks of pink hubba bubba clumped in his wild mane. The same clothes I had last seen him in, but dirty and ripped. His jeans bore grass colored stains around the holes in the knees, like he had crawled across both pavement and lawn. Two black eyes tried to look straight through his taped broken glasses with one completely scratched lens. The flannel shirt, that I'm sure was once a discernable color had the elbows torn out and a tear down the front. Every body part that peeked out from ripped clothing was road-rashed with dried blood.

His eyes darted around the crowd like he was trying to find something, someone. I couldn't tell if he was drunk or if the scratched and broken glasses just weren't capable of doing their job anymore.

Finally he picked me out of the family crowded around me and pointed his finger. "Ah there you are…the golden child," he yelled through the mega-phone, causing horrible feedback. Everyone in the gallery covered their ears.

Security was heading for the stairs when he yelled, "Stop, or

I'll blow us all to smithereens!" he warned them producing what looked like a remote of some kind.

Hired security and officers alike, backed down not sure what threat the crazed man may really pose to all the innocent people gathered below.

"Ah Janie," John said, moving to the staircase, "how'd you sleep last night? Were you scared? Yes?" he questioned. "No?" he gave his head a shake. "Move!" he yelled to the officers below, again showing the remote in his hand. As the officers moved away from the first floor landing, John made it down the first stair then stopped, turning his attention back to me. "Me, you ask? Well, I slept in a garbage bin…just me…my new friend, Homeless Al…and a rat that he thinks is God." He moved down another step with visible effort. "But I didn't mind, because I knew…today…I was coming for you!"

Watching him; *step by step*, wasn't quite the way he was approaching. It was step, squeak, wince, pause, step, squeak, wince, pause. You could see his pain with every slowed, lumbered movement. I swallowed hard, having no idea what to think.

My eyes darted to Fitz, whose jaw was so tight, I could see the muscles in her neck, protrude. She wanted him so bad; it was like seeing a starving Rottweiler with fresh meat dangling over head.

Scotty looked like he was about to do something, but I hoped like hell he wouldn't.

Another squeak emitted from John as he hit the halfway point on the stairs. "Come to me Janie," he slowly raised his arm; it looked like this small feat was excruciatingly painful for him. Finally, his fingers waved me forward as the one eye I could see, began to twitch.

"She's not goin' anywhere!" Fitz yelled, lunging as Scotty tried to hold her back.

"Go ahead," John smirked (I think). "I'll blow us all skyyy high," he laughed.

I couldn't help but notice his speech was a little slurred.

"I'm on enough pain killers not to give a damn!" he announced.

The crowd seemed even more alarmed now. A psycho was one thing, but a drugged out psycho, was a whole different ball of bat-shit. But from his obvious pain I wondered how well they were actually working.

"Come on, Janie. Be a good *girrrrl*, and no one gets hurt!" he laughed at his own crazy, I imagine.

Olaf took a step in front of me and stared at John like he would block the blast with his own body if need be.

I patted Olaf and he turned to look down at me, "It's okay. I'll go," I told him.

"I protect," Olaf said softly and touched my cheek.

Pulling him down, I gave him a kiss on the cheek, "It'll be okay. Protect them," I pointed to my loved ones. "Don't let them do anything stupid," I requested in a whisper.

As I started to walk, Mom slurred, "Oh no you don't, buddy! You want her…you're gonna have to go through me!" Mom started toward John, but Betty caught her by the arm.

"I'm not sure you should try and play savior considerin' your wobblin' almost as bad as that guy," she gave a head nod to John. "I got this," Betty started rolling up her sleeves. "And for the record," she told Mom, "If ya woulda let me bring my damn gun, this woulda' been over, already."

John rounded his eyes at Betty.

"That's right, Sugar, I would have given you a Southern Circumcision," Betty nodded.

You could see the moment John figured out what she meant; horror flashed across his face.

"Well, I'm NOT standin' idly by while he hurts my baby, either," Marble started rolling up her sleeves as well.

Olaf put one giant hand on each Betty's and Marble's shoulders.

"Please" my eyes shot to the people I loved, "please, just do as he says."

Poor drugged, beaten and crazed, John, had lost his sense of humor and screamed, trying to jump up and down, "That's right! Do as I say! I'm not kidding and I'm not bartering! Either she gets her big ol' booty over here right now or…"

My head shot backward, "*Big 'ol booty*?" I asked, wondering; exactly what did my ass look like in this dress?

"Yeah, I like 'em thin, ya know," John said squishing up his face like we were just getting to know each other. "Like the boney chick," he pointed to Fitz and attempted a wink that came off looking more like a facial tick.

"Boney?" Fitz hissed venomously as her eyes bulged from her head. "I shoulda rang yer jingle bells!"

"Liking them thin is fine…" I cut off Fitz's train of offense, "but that's no reason to say derogatory things to me, or to Fitz. I mean…what the hell?"

John nodded, "You're right…that was unnecessary." Then he yelled, "Could you please get your not *boney* but not *big ol booty*, over here, now!"

"Seriously," a man standing nearby holding a frightened woman in his arms said to me, "Your friends need to shut up, lady, and you need to get your ass over there. I'm not dying for you!" his head shook.

Fitz's eyes narrowed, "Ah, ya only think that!" Fitz tried to lunge at the man, but Scotty held her tighter.

"You better keep your woman in check," the guy pointed at Scotty.

"Fair warnin'," Scotty smiled, "if I let 'er go, there won't be much left of ya. And the scraps she leaves…shredded and bleedin' on the floor…those are mine," he winked and blew the man a kiss.

"*HELLO*," John yelled, waving the remote above his head, "guy with the fucking *bye-bye* switch would like *ALL of YOU* to *SHUT UP*! You!" he pointed at me, "Now!"

As I started to walk, Tovah joined me at my side. I shook my head at her, but the look on her face wasn't one of compromise.

"Hey," John yelled at her, his jaw starting to quiver, "I said *HER*," he pointed at me.

"You mean I'm not the one you want? Even though you come to MY home, you call ME, you harass ME, you show up here, at MY Gallery!" she cocked her head.

"Ya know what, you're right, both of you, over here, now!" John attempted a nod that looked stiff and painful.

"Please Tovah, I don't want anything to happen to the people I love…you're included on that list," tears began to fall as I tried to sound braver than I felt.

Tovah patted my hand, "Kid, we're always stronger in numbers."

"I'm not sure that applies right now," I furrowed my brow.

"Me either," she admitted.

I looked over my shoulder to where Olaf had Mum, Marble, Mom and Betty in his huge arms. Scotty was holding tight to Fitz as she shook with fear and rage. "I love you," I mouthed to them.

Turning back to John, Tovah took my hand and we started walking toward him.

The guy that had piped up before, said, "It's about time."

Fitz growled at him, baring her teeth like a rabid dog.

"To shreds," Scotty repeated. "She's gonna rip ya to fuckin' shreds," he said.

So this was the part where the snipers were supposed to take him out, right? With each step I wondered, *where the hell were the snipers?*

John inched his way to the front door waiting for Tovah and

me. Not gonna lie, my ass was baby-stepping like Fitz in her mermaid costume.

"Hurry up!" John was so enraged his face had flushed almost purple. One side of his broken glasses, hung down off of his face, leaving his blackened eye without sight.

I tightened my grip on Tovah's hand and began to shake inside.

"Everything's gonna be okay," Tovah squeezed my hand in return.

"Would you happen to know how?" I asked her.

"No idea, Kid," she confirmed my worst fears.

Just then, my eyes were drawn to a blur moving quickly at the glass doors behind John. It happened so fast, I wasn't even sure what had happened for a moment.

Cecil came running through the door, flowers in one hand and a manila envelope in the other. His eyes set on me, he didn't even notice the beat-up psycho holding us all hostage as he barreled straight into John. Both tumbled to the floor with Cecil on top, pinning John beneath him. Officers rushed in from every direction with guns drawn.

Cecil, having had a run-in with the law in his younger years, put his palms straight out to his sides as he lay on top of the man who was half in and half out of consciousness.

"Get off me," the man below him moaned as the police moved in to try and retrieve the remote from John's hand.

"Yeah, sorry buddy, as long as they have guns aimed at me, I'm not movin' an inch until they say I can," Cecil told him.

"Get up, get up, get up!" the officers yelled at Cecil. One of them grabbed Cecil under the arm, pulling him up and yanking him away from the beaten, bruised and flattened man below him.

Just then John gave a weak smile. Holding up the remote, he pushed the button.

A loud *POP* was heard, like the confetti poppers you hear on

New Year's Eve. As everyone drew in a deep breath, squeezed their eyes shut and went ridged as boards, we waited for a huge boom...a fire…something. Waiting and waiting, we all started to look around, but there was…nothing? Nothing happened that we could automatically see.

Someone pointed to *The Blue Woman* as a small plume of white smoke rose from behind the frame and then blew away leaving a slight sulfur smell tingeing the air.

"No!" John yelled when he realized his homemade explosive that was meant to destroy my work, had failed.

Turning back to Cecil, I ran to him and jumped into his arms. Kissing every square inch of his face, he asked me, "What the hell is happenin'?" But I was too busy making sure I kissed him for every day I hadn't been able to, to explain.

"Is that Cecil?" I heard my mother yell in her tipsy slurred voice.

I saw everyone shoot their eyes to her.

"Better late than never, honey," Betty patted her arm as all the women rushed to us.

Scotty let go of Fitzy. She was barreling toward me when she did a complete 180. Running, full Fitzy speed at the guy who had been so verbal about his willingness to sacrifice me; his eyes just had time to round, before she threw a Right Cross and knocked him out cold.

Scotty looked at the man's bewildered date and grinned, "When he wakes, tell him I'll be back."

I ran down the gist of what happened as the girls began to surround us.

"That guy?" Cecil pointed to John and then gently moved me aside as he marched over to where the police had finally pulled John off the floor.

Without thinking, Cecil cocked back and prepared to give the poor, beat up psycho, a whipping, police or no police.

"No," I heard a familiar voice ring out, sweet, but radiating off of every wall. Walking through the crowd…came Vah. People moved out of her way as she approached. Cecil dropped his clenched fist and stepped aside with a furrowed brow.

John looked like a half-blind animal in a trap, wild and frightened.

Vah stared at him, her gaze; soft, like the way a loving mother looks at her child when they are scared. As she reached her palm out to his cheek, he flinched a little.

"This won't hurt a bit," she smiled at him. "I'm going to take the hurt away, okay?"

After a moment, he was mesmerized by her. He slowly began to nod as the police stood there wondering what the hell they were supposed to do.

Tovah gave a curt nod to the officers.

Vah brought her palms out to her side. Letting her head fall back, a sound began to emerge from her. At first it was low and quiet.

I watched, still in awe.

As her voice rang louder, everyone in the room cocked their head. I'm sure many were confused but, a handful…knew what they were witnessing. Even some who didn't KNOW for sure what was happening, looked absolutely captivated.

Even being held by officers, when John's legs went limp from Vah's drawing, they almost dropped him.

I saw the darkness being pulled in big billowing clouds of smoke. Entering Vah, I saw her mouth open wide. One last long note was pushed from her lungs as the black swirls released from her and rose above until they disappeared. Now she turned her palms toward John as the golden light began to leave her in slow waves. When the waves hit him, it was like his soul pulled them inside. A glow took over his whole body as the tears began to stream down his face. There, barely able to stand on his own, he wept.

When Vah went to touch his face this time, he pressed his check against her palm and whispered, "Thank you."

"You'll be fine," Vah nodded as the officers took him away.

There was silence for a moment before Cecil finally asked, "No really, what the hell is goin' on?"

I wasn't exactly sure what had me in tears: was it Cecil, was it knowing everyone I loved was safe…or did Vah's *draw* pull from me, too. Maybe it was everything.

As the bomb squad rushed in, we were all asked to leave the building. When the police pulled the man Fitz had dropped, off the floor, he started yelling about pressing charges against her. Waving his hands like a lunatic, he threatened legal action, not only against Fitz, but against the P.D. if they didn't take her into custody. All of the women: Mom, Mum, Betty and Aunt Marble started to get their Irish up. But in the end, it was Olaf who was most convincing. He simply placed a giant hand on the man's shoulder. When the man turned, ready to throw another fit for having hands laid on him, his eyes rounded and a sound I couldn't fully understand, like a gulping, rendered him mute for a moment. In the end, the gentleman left without his date and simply walked out, choosing to keep all of his body parts intact.

Mom and Aunt Marble had me in a bear hug as Cecil gave his account of what happened to the officers.

Marne and Jen showed up as the huge crowd thankfully walked away from the Schumer.

"What happened here?" Marne asked. "What? Was there a bomb scare?" she laughed.

All of us stood there, nodding our heads.

Marne's jaw dropped and I told her, "I'll tell you all about it…later."

"Oh my God, is that little Marne?" my mother finally realized who was standing in front of her.

"It is," I smiled. "And this is Jen…her fiancé," I added, wondering how Mom would react to this news.

Mom's eyes filled with wonder before she grabbed Marne's arm and said, "I have some questions." Mom led Marne and Jen away and started with, "You two probably don't fight over the remote, do you?"

All I could do was shake my head and laugh.

When everything calmed down and Mom sobered up a bit, I *FINALLY* got to introduce Mom and Cecil properly. I couldn't help but notice how she looked at him; she blushed when he kissed her hand.

"Oh my," she said, batting her eyes like a star-struck girl. "You're a big one, aren't you?'

Laughing, I squeezed him tighter.

"I do have a question, though…?" Mom still teetered a bit.

Not knowing what to expect, I held my breath and braced myself for anything that may come out of her mouth.

"What was all that swirling smoke, stuff?" Mom questioned. "Was it like a magic trick?" her head bobbled on her slightly drunk shoulders.

Tovah's head spun in our direction and both of our jaws dropped. Vah stood close, grinning from ear to ear.

"Sir, sir," an officer walked up to Cecil. "You dropped these!" Handing Cecil the flowers and the big manila envelope, Cecil thanked him.

"Of course, the flowers are for you," he handed them to me. "And where's Fitzy?" he looked behind him. "Yer gonna wanna see these!"

Opening the envelope, he produced the proofs from her shoot. As per usual, she looked fantastic.

"Oh I love these," Mum gushed and kissed her daughter's cheek.

"Well, there's somethin' to go along with the prints," Cecil looked at her sidelong.

Fitz raised her brow, "Yeah?"

"An offer...one of Dad's friends would like ya to come back to Ireland for another shoot," Scotty told her.

"There is a catch though," Cecil said, "You'll be in Ireland fer Christmas."

Fitz gave a long sigh then looked at her Mum. Fitz shook her head, "I can't be away from Mum durin' the holiday."

"Of course ya can, dear," Mum patted Fitz's cheek, but Fitz just kept shaking her head no.

"I understand," Cecil nodded. "But...I was invitin' the whole family."

Everyone spoke at once, "What, huh, really?"

"Yes, yer all invited...as many of ya as ya wish. We have the room and Dad and Elanor think it's important for the Families to meet before the weddin'."

Everyone hooted and hollered.

"Am I invited?" I asked Cecil with a grin.

"I guess that depends on the next two minutes," he kissed my cheek and pulled a ring box out of his pocket.

"Oh my God!" my mother clutched at her heart.

Betty covered Mom's mouth, "Quiet, I wanna hear this!"

Mum and Marble, too, put their hand across their mouths.

As Cecil opened the ring box, I guess I assumed he would go traditional; get down on one knee, but he didn't. Instead he pulled the ring from its box and turned to me.

"Janie, I know we haven't known each other long...but I'd like to spend the rest of my life...learnin' ya and lovin' ya, and wantin' ya...more and more each day of our lives."

Picking up my right hand, I stood there a little confused. Wrong hand; I thought, but stayed silent.

"This…is a promise ring," Cecil said. "My father gave it to my mother…when he promised her his heart, mind, body and soul. Now I ask that you'll accept this ring with the same promise," I saw him swallow like he was worried about my answer.

Looking down at the white gold Claddagh ring with a diamond for the heart, my eyes welled. Nodding, I said, "Yes…I promise…heart, mind, body and soul."

Throwing my arms around his neck he lifted me up and placed the kiss I had missed so terribly, on my lips as everyone else began to applaud. Fitz whistled so loud, my mother jumped.

"I don't understand…was that a proposal?" Marble asked Mum.

"It's the beginnin'," Mum beamed and dabbed at her sparkling eyes with a tissue.

Tovah had decided that Cecil and I, as well as Fitz and Scotty, needed our alone time. With it safe to be on the city streets again, she made us reservations at the Ritz.

"The Ladies," Tovah looked back at Mom, Mum, Marble and Betty, "are comin' with me," she said from the open back window of the limo.

"My stuff," I said looking down at my dress.

"I don't think you're gonna need it, kid," she winked at Cecil.

"Breakfast, my house, 10am," Tovah smiled.

As the car began to slowly roll, I heard, Tovah yell, "Now pop those bottles, ladies!" to which all the women howled.

This made me a little nervous; for all the other ladies or just my mother, I wasn't sure. But as they hit traffic, I started to laugh, "Have fun, Mom," I whispered a prayer above.

Back at the Ritz I was exhausted. Walking around in my bra and panties, Cecil patted the spot next to him on the bed.

My face squished up.

"What is that face fer?" Cecil asked, worried.

"I just wish I had my toothbrush."

"You can use mine," he laughed.

In the bathroom I went to brush my teeth then I heard Cecil ask, "Did ya get any good pictures while ya were here? Any of you in a dominatrix outfit?" he asked hopefully.

I walked out of the bathroom, toothbrush in mouth and nodded, "Look in my phone," I garbled through a full mouth of paste.

A minute later, mouthwash sprayed everywhere when I heard Cecil ask loudly, "What the hell is the *Interactive Prick Tour*?"

Laughing, I ran in the bedroom and jumped on the bed, "Let me show you!" I leaned in.

"Oh," Cecil nodded. "I may want to take the tour twice."

"I'm counting on it."

17

TOVAH'S SURPRISE

Pulling up in front of Tovah's, not quite well rested, but oh feeling so good, we made our way to the front door.

Entering, Jeeves turned to Fitz, "Madame," he bowed his head to her.

Fitz looked even more confused than I did.

"The ladies are in the yard," Jeeves said.

As we stepped out into the yard, the women raised their champagne glasses.

"Oh God," I whispered to Fitz. "You don't think they've been drinking all night?"

Fitz shrugged, "Who cares…they're the flight attendants problem now," she gave me the exaggerated smile.

Cecil and Scotty made the rounds, kissing cheeks. I noticed my mother fanning herself as the Callaghan brother's each planted one on her cheek.

"So what are we celebrating?" Cecil pulled a seat out for me to sit before taking the one on my right.

"Well, the showing was a success," Tovah beamed.

My brow furrowed wondering if she had somehow forgotten how badly last night had turned out.

"What I mean is, two of your paintings, besides *The Blue Woman*, sold."

"Really?" I was flabbergasted. "I just assumed that no one would have been in a very art-buying-mood after all the…craziness."

"Never assume that. Not only are some artists crazy, so are some of their fan club," Tovah explained.

This could have been taken a few different ways, but I decided to take it the way that made me feel good about the *crazy*.

I'd like to keep the third, *The Mod Girl*, on display…if you don't mind. I still think she has a buyer," Tovah nodded.

I gave her a palms-up, "Sure, that would be great."

"I'll send you a check for the others."

I noticed that we didn't discuss price this time and I was surprised that I was actually looking forward to a surprise.

"Also, I talked to the buyer of *The Blue Woman* and explained everything that happened last night. There is some slight frame damage…to the back of the frame, but he said it didn't matter, so it's being shipped today," Tovah waited for me to comment.

I nodded to her and let out a deep breath, "Ship it!" I said raising my glass.

"Now," Tovah addressed all of us, "we only have an hour until we get all you ladies to the airport, so let's get cracking!"

All of the women stood, leaving Fitz and I to wonder what was happening now. As the ladies walked to the lawn and joined hands, Mum yelled to us, "Well come on darlin's, get your tushies over here and complete the circle!"

Cecil and Scotty looked on as we formed the circle.

Tovah, Mum, Aunt Marble, Betty, Fitz and I joined hands. Where was my mother, I wondered. For that matter, where had Vah gotten off to?

Out of the back door they came, both wearing flowing dresses of white. They looked like two of the four goddesses I had seen in the painting hung in Tovah's library; *The Maiden and The Mother*.

Mom, holding onto Vah's hand as she slipped off her shoes, beamed with both excitement and nervousness as her feet touched the grass. I looked at her sidelong, what was going on, I thought I knew. But how, WHO, had talked my mother into a drawing?

As Mom and Vah approached the circle, Tovah opened it with a swish of her hand so they could enter. Holding hands Mom and Vah stepped into the middle. Facing each other, the way they stared into each other's eyes and smiled, put me in mind of a marriage ceremony.

None of us knew the chant, or so I thought. Mum and Marble, also being Ladies of the Moon began to vocalize. I guess this really shouldn't have surprised me. I was, however, very shocked when Betty joined in. My eyes shot to her and she gave me a quick nod.

As Vah's head dropped back once more, I saw Mom's eyes widen, she looked scared and a little worried. Her eyes darted to mine and I smiled and mouthed, "It's okay…I promise."

Smiling from ear to ear now, Mom nodded and let Vah do her thing.

From the first sound, a low moan that escaped Vah's lips, Mom's eyes fell closed.

I smiled as I watched the plums of dark smoke rise out of her and push their way toward Vah. She let go of my mother's hands and absorbed the darkness. Howling louder, she offered it to the sky where it was pulled to the heavens. Just as in awe as I was the first time I saw this done, I watched my favorite part; the gold… the golden waves of light rolling their way to my mother; her body absorbing it like a dry flower during a hard rain. Tears ran down Mom's face as her head fell back. I knew that feeling; reborn, clean...weightless. Laughing and crying at the same time, she was glowing.

My own eyes ran freely and I began to sob. Seeing her like this, made my heart so grateful.

When it was over, all of us women rushed in to embrace my mother as she wept. We just held her, Mom's new support system.

When we turned back to where the men sat waiting for us ladies to finish whatever we were doing, Scotty and Cecil sat silently with dropped jaws. Jeeves who stood nearby said, "It's quite the show," before bowing to Vah and walking back inside.

When I sat back down next to Cecil, he quietly asked me, "What the hell did I just watch?"

I turned my face to his and inspected his expression. "A better question is...what did you see?"

He looked away like he was thinking it over; what he should say. "Later?" he asked.

I smiled and nodded, "Later."

18

GOODBYE'S

I had always hated goodbyes and I wasn't good at them, either. But I knew now that these women would be in my life forever and that made it seem more like, *Until We Meet Again*.

I hugged Tovah and thanked her for all of her help, both with my career and privately.

"Did you want to know what the other two paintings sold for?" she asked quietly.

I thought and then shook my head, "No, I'll let it be a surprise."

Tovah's eyebrows rose, "As you wish, Kid. You do know I love you, right?" she cocked her head.

"I love you, too," I told her as we hugged for the tenth time.

I took a deep breath before saying goodbye to Vah. "I don't even know how to thank you," my head shook.

"The pleasure was all mine…Clematis," she added with that little one sided grin I had loved on Tovah and now on her, as well.

I had to laugh as I hugged her.

"I do have something else for you," Vah said with a twinkle in her eye.

Leaning in to whisper in my ear, she gave me a little not so well known knowledge.

"Really?" I asked.

Vah nodded and hugged me again, "Everything will be okay, Janie."

We also said goodbye to all the other women, Fitz and Scotty since Cecil and I were taking the private plane back.

As Cecil and I boarded the private plane, I said hello to the pilot and co-pilot. Cecil immediately poured me a shot of Callaghan's whiskey and cuddled up next to me on the couch where I sat staring at my ring.

"You do like it, right? I mean I could give ya another ring if this isn't your likin'."

"I love it, and I love you," I kissed him.

"So, is it okay if I bunk at your house for a few days?" he asked like he was some lounge-about who I barely knew. I laughed because I remembered when he was this to me.

Curling in closer I said, "Hmm, I guess so," I played back.

"Are ya worried about flyin', luv?"

I thought and then shook my head, "Not so much anymore."

"Hmm," he sounded almost upset to hear that I wasn't scared out of my mind like I was during our first flight together.

"What's the *Hmm* all about?" I asked.

"Well ya know…the last time we flew together on this plane, ya had a great dream, If I'm not mistakin'."

"I did?" I asked as innocently as I could.

"Oh yeah!"

"And how do you know that?" I asked remembering full well how he knew this. I tried not to visibly blush.

"Oh, cause I had the best seat in the house to watch it from," he nodded.

"So, are you trying to get me to…go to sleep in hopes that you may see a repeat of me having a great dream?"

"Actually, I wanted ya to tell me about yer dream and maybe we could…act it out," he leaned in and put a warm kiss on my neck.

"Well," I pretended to ponder the idea, "that does sound amazing."

"Yeah," he kissed some more.

"Oh yeah," I agreed, "but…"

"But what," he whispered, his motor already running.

"But…where are we going to find a monkey?" I grinned.

His eyes shot to mine, "What?"

THE END

THANK YOU

To all the people who believe in me and enjoy whatever my little mind comes up with…I thank you from the bottom of my bat-shit-crazy heart.

Edith Scheffer

Don't miss WINGED
Available Now

After being reincarnated three times, Arianna has no desire to ever return to Earth, even though that means she will remain a wingless angel. But when Ari is requested to go on a very special mission, she cannot refuse.

Her mother from Life #3—the only life in which she ever felt truly loved—was none other than God's favorite creation, Eve. Now, tasked with saving her mom's trapped immortal soul, Ari will have to fight pure evil with the help of the most unlikely of souls, the Fallen Angel himself—Lucifer.

Turn the page for an excerpt from *Winged.*

1

WINGED

He did say, "You'll know her when you see her." He was right about that. Without a single doubt in my mind, this was her. This frizzy, red headed bitch was the one who ruined my life. Well, one of my lives, I surmised. I can, however, blame her for this life sucking, as well. Seeing as how I would never had to be reborn, if it weren't for her. One part of me, the part that was human, wanted to scratch her eyes out! The other part of me…the part that wasn't human exactly, wanted to slit her throat with my wings.

My name is Ari, short for Arianna, and this is how and why I was born into this world…again.

IN THE BEGINNING…

Just kidding, I love that shit though. Anyway, I was called into His office. Who is, 'His' you may ask? Well, 'He', is the Big Guy, the Head Cheese, the Commander and Chief. No, not the president…GOD! Yeah, you heard me, God. Yes, I call him God. No that doesn't make any of my past religions correct, either. He is called by many names, and do you know what all of those names have in common? They all mean 'God' or 'The Divine' or 'One-True-Something-Something'. So your first misconception will be revealed right now, HE DOESN'T CARE WHAT BY WHAT NAME YOU CALL HIM! Anywho, he calls me into his office, points to a chair and asks me to have a seat.

"Ari," he begins, (he always calls me Ari) "I would like you to go on a Mission of Wings."

He would call you by whatever name you wished, and Ari was my soul name. No matter how many spirits I had had or how many bodies I had occupied, Ari was what, or who, I always came back to, and that was fine by me. I felt like an Ari. Mary Magdalene went through a phase in the 80's (the 1980's), where she wanted to be called BIG MAMA M. And of course, that is exactly what we, and God called her.

Back to it, misconception number two: Some humans are under the impression that when you die, you follow a white light to Heaven then Saint Peter looks you up on a roster, like you're in line at a night club. You are led through the red ropes, and then given your wings. They are wrong.

You don't get your Wings until you have gone on, and successfully completed, a Mission of Wings (M.O.W. for short). In truth, most souls in Heaven didn't have their Wings yet. The Winged, as we call them, sometimes acted superior to those of us Un-winged. But never in front of God if they know what's good for them. Truth is, he loves us all equally, and has a 'No Bullying' policy that must be strictly adhered to, or the person is schooled.

I watched once as he un-winged and re-birthed an Angel who got a little too big for said wings. In his outdoor voice, which we so seldom heard, he said: "Wings shall not be retained by one who is so clearly unworthy of wearing them." We all winced as he made his decree. The man was to be reborn... in Africa... as an Albino. Like I said though, schooled!

God pointed to a dish sitting on his desk, "Nut?" he asked.

I shook my head, "No, thank you." He did love his nuts, I thought.

"I would like you to go on a Mission of Wings," (but of course, you've already heard this part) "How well do you remember your mother, Ari?"

I had only been in three bodies since the beginning of my soul's creation. It doesn't sound like many, I know. But they had been more than enough, as far as I was concerned.

My first life had been in China around 200 and something, B.C. I was a Priestess at The Temple of the Moon. In saying that, I was considered a child of the gods and was fostered in the 'house of the gods', from the moment I was born. No human could claim me as theirs, so I never had an Earthly mother. As a child of the gods, I was trained to know every plant, herb, berry and tree, for protecting, healing and killing. Taught to battle with swords, axes, stones, sticks and daggers, I was educated in what would now be known as, 'The Way of the Assassin'. In short, I was a badass.

One beautiful starry night, I was at the Pool of Enlightenment when marauders broke through the gates of our mountain top retreat. My sisters were under attack as the men were set on raping and slaying my fellow priestesses. I remember calling my breath to calm itself, as I pulled my sword over my head and took my stance. Within moments I left a slew of dead men at my feet. But I could see more were coming. I had no doubt in my mind, that I was not long for this life. No matter, I would not let my sacred virginity be taken. As a large group of bandits ran toward me, I put the tip of my own sword to my stomach and yelled in my ancient tongue, "Only in death may you take this body." I ran the blade through, crumpling to the ground. It was all very dramatic. But, the joke was on me. Turns out, rapists don't seem to care so much if you have a pulse or not. And that one guy, who did that thing to my corpse? Well, I asked God if I could haunt his sick ass and he had agreed that what had been done to me was a hauntable offense. And as a virgin, I did die.

Next life…'A Vestal Virgin': Are you noticing a theme yet? I was made a Vestal Virgin in the year 25BC, at the ripe age of six. Usually, in order to become a Vestal, both of your parents must be living, but my mother had died birthing me. My father was a high born, very rich, muckety-muck, who had me placed as a Vestal despite the rules. I was never to know my mother, or him, for that matter. I was raised in the House of Vestals, educated and untouched.

Our job as Vestals: Keep the Sacred Fire (a tribute to the Goddess Vesta), burning at all times, care for sacred artifacts, collect water from the sacred spring and keep 'the wills' and 'testaments' of the rich and powerful of the time. After 30 years of service as a Vestal, your life suddenly becomes your own. You're given a pension and allowed to marry or own land, whatever you choose.

36 years old, made me a little long in the tooth for those days, but still attractive enough (still had all of my teeth). What I was looking forward to more than anything else was losing my sacred flower. I had heard women speak of it like it was a mind altering drug. I had no desire to marry, even though I would be highly placed. I had 'belonged' to 'someone else' long enough. My plan was to walk down to the local watering hole, find an attractive man and ride him like I was trying to break a stallion. Yep, that was the plan.

The day of my long awaited freedom dawned, and I was ready to be my own woman. The other Vestals, who were like sisters to me, had been given leave to throw me a goodbye party of sorts. I had a little too much wine at said party, but still began my journey down the road to the ale house. I stumbled and staggered, but was set on my goal. I covered one eye with my hand to stop the alcohol induced double vision. But I'm afraid I was more focused on my goal than the road as I fell into a deep hole being dug for a privy. My last word was, "Shhhiiiiiittt!" and as a virgin, I did die.

So, I guessed the Big Guy was referring to life number three.

I had asked him before about my mother, to which he had said, "In time, child." When he said things like this, you knew not to push. But she had occupied my mind on more than one occasion, and I didn't understand why I never saw her in Heaven, or whatever name you call it by.

So today! I thought. Today I find out what became of my mother.

"So Ari, how well do you remember her?"

It was like asking if I remembered the smell of rain or the most beautiful sunrise I had ever seen. I remembered the scent of her hair as I lay curled up in the nook of her shoulder, regaling me with stories of long ago. I remembered skin whiter than fresh snow and hair as black as a raven's wing. She would dance and twirl with me in her arms. When she sang the Angels themselves made no sweeter sound. And I was loved.

"I remember everything about her," I replied.

God nodded at me with a knowing look. "Well Ari," he began, "Do you know what immortals are?"

I furrowed my brow. "Immortals?" I questioned with a grin. Was he messing with me? Sometimes he did that. I knew what the word meant, of course. And, I knew that humans suspected, and even fantasized about the possibility of Immortals. But no one in Heaven believed in their existence.

"In the beginning...,"God started.

There it is, I thought.

"I created two souls. You would know them better as Adam and Eve."

My jaw dropped. I took a moment to let the thought sink in. Finally I blurted out, "You mean Adam and Eve were real?"

God nodded at me, "Very much so."

"And the Garden of Eden? Was that real, too?"

Again God nodded. "But…not the way people believe."

I just stared at him and waited for him to elaborate.

"I hadn't made any other humans," he said, doing a palms-up. "By the time I did, Adam and Eve had been alone on the Earth for thousands of years. They seemed to be unhappy, even exhausted with each other. I figured they needed something new, so finally… I gave them genitals."

I avoided eye contact at this point. It was an unfortunate truth that I was somewhat obsessed with the thought of intercourse, even more so after talking to Cleopatra.

"Well, they woke up one morning and each had their very own, completely separate parts that were totally compatible when joined," he told me.

"So, at first you made humans without, umm, reproductive organs?" I asked.

"Well truthfully, when I first gave them genitals, it was without the ability to reproduce. Sensation only, but then Adam and Eve never stopped...you know."

I nodded, very sure of what he meant, and a little jealous.

"Then, I decided to make more people so Adam and Eve would have others to talk to. Maybe keep them from, well, you know, all the time. I wanted humans to be able to reproduce without me having to spend so much time overseeing their creation. That's how sex organs became reproductive organs. I had an exact blue print of how I wanted them to be made, and even appointed an Angel to oversee creation. I know you've heard of him," God's bushy grey brows lifted.

I raised an eyebrow back. I couldn't even imagine.

"Lucifer," said God.

I had in fact heard of Lucifer. I had also heard all the Christian stories about he, and God's falling out. How he had once been an Angel, cast down for wanting God's power, and so on. Turns out, it was nowhere near the truth. It was one of those, 'Not quite', things.

"When I left him with the blue print, there were specific steps that needed to be followed. Several thousands were made according to the plans I had given Lucifer. Each was to be made, given reproductive organs, and a soul. All would be made from souls I had already created and were in Heaven. They would be born as humans."

I nodded, believing that all humans were made from pre-existing souls.

"A few hundred years or so passed, with the blueprint being followed to a tee. When I checked in, all was running smoothly. I was busy making new plants, oceans, animals, trees, and ridding the Earth of one of my earlier creations that wasn't quite working out. I didn't want to just annihilate these creatures, so I let most of them live out their lives and simply took away their ability to reproduce. It wasn't long before all of those souls were back in Heaven."

"So at some point, souls in Heaven were used for animals, and such?"

"Still are, in some cases."

"Huh," I nodded at this new piece of info. "So what happened? With the humans and Lucifer, I mean."

"Well, Lucifer became bored with his job. And rather than talk to me about it, he got sloppy. See, the whole point of giving the humans a soul, was that Heaven would always pull the souls back when they became increasingly homesick, got very old in their bodies, and so on. Lucifer became so sloppy in fact, that several thousand humans were born without souls, but with reproductive organs. Now here's the kicker, people born without souls, would find each other, like a magnet, and reproduce. And when two people without souls reproduce, guess what they breed?"

I thought I was following well enough to answer, but God cut me off.

"More humans without souls," he answered.

I was really glad I didn't reply. That wasn't my answer.

"So," he continued, "It became a cluster. I asked to see the roster and was shocked. Half of the people created, had no souls. I had set it up that people would be created through intercourse. Following would be a long incubation period, after which the female, who I had given the hole to, or slot B in the diagram, would birth a miniature human."

He saw the look on my face and told me it was okay to ask, so I did. "Why did you make birth painful? Not that I would know but I have been told that it is by far the worst pain ever, almost unbearable. And I was around during the time of human disembowelment, not to mention…being hung and set on fire," I said, raising one eyebrow.

"You really need to let that go, Ari," he said. "The reason I made it painful, was so women would love their children."

I stared at him in confused silence.

"You see, Ari, I made women and men polar opposites. If a man goes through hell, he must kill whatever threatens to kill him, he is a conqueror. If a woman goes through hell, she gives ultimate love to anything that is designed to destroy her, but cannot. She is a survivor."

"Okay," I said, trying not to call BS on God.

God broke out laughing, "I knew you wouldn't buy that one, Ari. The look on your face is priceless." He laughed so hard, he snorted. After he calmed down a bit, he said, "Cut and dry, I gave women a higher pain tolerance. Men, with the pain tolerance I gave them in the original blueprint, well, they would die. Therefore, only a woman's pain threshold was strong enough. I did tinker with some 'A sexual' animals…but it just seemed…lonely," he shook his head. "Anyway, men see this pain that a woman goes through, then he, and the child love her more. He would see her, the weaker sex," he grinned, "as *equals*. Or at least that's what was supposed to happen. The truth is childbirth is the ultimate sacrifice of women."

Great in theory, I thought, remembering how horrible women were treated in my days and ages: Raped, second class citizens, was not what God had planned.

"Anyway," he said, "So the whole human species was all messed up. Humans were being born at a miraculous rate, more humans than I had souls. This posed two problems. One, Soulless people were creating more Soulless people. And two, humans born without souls had no memory of Heaven, or how these souls had known, respected, and loved each other throughout time. All of the souls were connected to each other, bonded. These new Soulless humans had no bond to anything or anyone. This leads us to the biggest problem with the Soulless…no conscience."

Was God saying that my mother was a Soulless human? He could read my thoughts, so a question not asked was still answered.

"No Ari, your mother was not 'Soulless'. When I called out Lucifer on his incompetence, he explained that he had tried to send souls to the Soulless. But as I already stated, more humans than souls was the start of the problem. He then tried various methods of wiping out large groups of people at a time, but only succeeded in wiping out Souled, and Soulless, alike. No doubt you've heard of the Helike earthquake in 373 B.C. and the Minoan Eruption in 1645 B.C. I was horrified. My precious souls had been subjected to horrors. And then, of course, the rumor was started that I was an angry, vengeful God. That I not only let these things happen, I made them happen because I was, I don't know, petty?" He threw his hands up in the air.

I was still confused and I knew it showed.

"Sorry, back to your mom. So, Lucifer, realizing that this

wasn't working the way he had hoped, found Adam and Eve and used the power I had given him, not meant for such things, I might add, to make Adam and Eve immortal. This wasn't his intention exactly. He thought he was duplicating their souls, since I had given him the ability to create life. He then, would put them into the Soulless. If he did that, then he could use them to create more souls and I would never know about the whole soulless fiasco he had put in motion."

I still looked confused, I'm sure.

"See," said God, "I gave every soul a gift. Some can sing or have musical abilities. Others can communicate with animals or understand universal secrets. Still others are peace bringers, have healing hands or are muses for things like love, music and art. Everyone was given some form of magic. But Eve, she was my first female creation."

He smiled when he spoke of her, I noted.

"To her, I gave every talent, every ability, every blessing, and every gift. Lucifer knew this, and thought if he took one blessing, for every soul he tried to create, she would be nothing more, or less, than a normal being. No harm, no foul, so to speak. He was wrong. No one else can take away a blessing or gift I have bestowed."

I nodded, wondering what gift I would be reborn with.

"So, I had given Lucifer the power to create humans, along with a few other gifts." I nodded, in understanding. God continued, "Without understanding what he was doing, he magnified her gifts, until she became immortal."

My eyes grew wide.

I wondered how God could not have known such a thing, especially with the whole 'mind reading' thing.

"I didn't feel the need to read minds until then," he answered again without being asked. "And now, it's just a time saver."

I nodded again. I could see how a slip such as this, would change the way God dealt with things.

"So now, Adam and Eve were immortal. I had to have a talk with them about what this meant. We met at a little outdoor cafe in Sumeria: great food but way too many flies. I still wonder why I created them. Have you ever looked at one close up, Ari? Really, they are magnificent considering the scale in which I was working, but I digress. Anyway, I told them the situation and gave them two choices. I could take them back home and never would they touch Earth again. Or they could stay on Earth through generation after generation and live immortal lives. If they chose to stay, they could not die or suffer any bodily injury until they willed their souls back to Heaven. It was part of this whole 'free will' thing I had started."

I had heard of it.

"Well Adam, after thousands of years, had had enough of the world and had no desire to stay. And truthfully, he seemed a little 'Off' after thousands of years without going home. But Eve, she was adventurous and wanted to see everything Earth and life had to offer. So she had walked the Earth since before time was being kept. In fact, she was alive and well during your first two lives. Weird, huh?"

"Actually, yes, all of this is..." I had no words.

"Mind blowing!" said God, doing the palm motion of a magician revealing a trick.

"At least," I replied. "So what happened to Lucifer? I mean, the Pre-Christians say he rules Hell, but I have always been under the impression that Hell doesn't exist."

"It doesn't. At least not the way they say it does."

I stared at him, just not getting it.

"Ari, Earth is Hell."

"ARE YOU KIDDING ME??? Why would you create Hell?" I asked, forgetting who I was talking to.

"It wasn't Hell when I created it. Once Lucifer did what he did, it became Hell."

"So why don't you just fix it?"

God smiled, "How?"

I stared at him, "I don't know, but can't you...do something?"

"I do, Ari. But short of killing hundreds of thousands of people, I have no recourse. Literally hundreds and hundreds of thousands of Soulless people are walking the world."

My jaw dropped, "That many?"

"I haven't told you the worst part. Over the years, the Soulless learned to better fit into society. And now, they are breeding with the Souled. Their children we're trying to 'Soul' in utero. I have many angels on this particular project."

"How, in the name of...well, your name, did that happen?" I asked.

"They know they're different. Some embrace their disconnection to the world and people around them, becoming serial killers, politicians, and dictators. Others don't want people to know how dysfunctional they are. They become sociopaths, convincing others that they are everything they have ever needed or wanted. Truth is, the Soulless have developed a deep need to be with the Souled. They find their inner light irresistible. Then, before the Souled human knows they are with a sociopath, or a Soulless one, they have reproduced once again."

"And you want to send me back there because...?" I rolled my wrist.

"Your mother's soul is trapped there," God said solemnly.

"My mother…is stuck? On Earth? How?" I asked.

God leaned in towards me and took my hand. "Ari, your mother is Eve."

I was trying as best I could to wrap my head around this. How could that be?

He explained in some detail about things that happened before my time, and were not idle gossip in Heaven. Mostly about the, 'Watchers' and why humans had it so backward. It was a scary history lesson. He told me how Lucifer had given humans great gifts, fire for example. I mean, come on, fire was a big deal back then. Then he gave them the sacred knowledge of herbs and plants and all means necessary to call the forces of nature. God saw this and began to wonder about the intentions in which they were given. Lucifer then turned his attentions to giving humans weapons and the knowledge of how to make weapons.

When brought before the Council of Angels to account for why he had given them means of destruction, and war, Lucifer said that several men (Soulless) had become greedy and tried to harm, and take from others. He simply wanted people to be able to defend themselves from the Soulless (that he admitted to being the cause of). But the Council said that he had overstepped his bounds, and had put more people in danger, both the Souled, and Soulless. The Council concluded that Lucifer had tried to mass a great war against God and the Angels, using the Soulless humans as soldiers in his army. Even though Lucifer denied the plot, his explanations went unheard. The Council was furious and called for his soul to be extinguished. But God, a merciful God he is, refused. He did condemn Lucifer to Earth for all time, and did take away his ability to create new life, but left him with all of his other 'Angel Gifts'.

A great punishment indeed, I assessed. I myself had no desire to walk the Earth again, and it had been a few hundred years since my last visit, give or take.

God broke the silence around me, "Ari, will you do this for me?"

"I still have one question?"

He answered before I could ask. "Your mother wasn't given reproductive organs until much later. And not by me," he added. "Immortals were not meant to be, much less procreate."

He then went on to tell me of my mother's death, as well as my own. What he revealed to me that day would have made my blood boil, if I had any.

Afterward, I nodded my head, and before I knew it, I was in class learning about what had happened on Earth since my last life.

ABOUT THE AUTHOR

Edith Scheffer is a SoCal native, now blissfully transplanted to the Pacific Northwest. A gypsy at heart with the soul of a witch, Edith has wandered but never been lost. She loves sleeping under the stars and moon, walking in her bare feet, dancing to an eclectic playlist of favorite songs, and proudly parenting her exceptionally fierce and fabulous daughter, Brenna. Edith can mix the perfect drink (bartender by trade), massage your aches away (licensed massage therapist), and entertain you with her many novels (yes, she writes, too!). Her works include The Janie Chronicles, *Winged*, and *Fallen Gracefully*. You can discover more at edithscheffer.net.

facebook.com/AuthorEdithScheffer

goodreads.com/edithscheffer

www.ingramcontent.com/pod-product-compliance
Lightning Source LLC
Chambersburg PA
CBHW061617190726
48288CB00007B/2365

* 9 7 8 1 9 5 4 1 7 4 0 7 8 *